From
THIS DAY
FORWARD

❖ *A Novel* ❖

From THIS DAY FORWARD

❖ *A Novel* ❖

MARGARET DALEY

summerside
PRESS™

Summerside Press™
Minneapolis 55337
www.summersidepress.com
From This Day Forward

© 2011 by Margaret Daley

ISBN 978-1-60936-093

Scripture references are from The Holy Bible, King James Version (KJV).

All characters are fictional. Any resemblances to actual people are purely coincidental.

Cover design by Lookout Design | www.lookoutdesign.com
Cover photo of woman by Ricardo Demurez, Trevillion Images
Cover background photo by Terrance Klassen, Fotostock/Photolibrary
Interior design by Müllerhaus Publishing Group | www.mullerhaus.net

Summerside Press™ is an inspirational publisher offering fresh,
irresistible books to uplift the heart and engage the mind.

Printed in USA.

Dedication

To Vickie McDonough for all your
support, guidance, and friendship

One

March 1816

"We are going to die!" Rachel Gordon's young maid cried out.

Rachel looked up at the clouds rolling in. Dark, ominous ones. She shivered and pulled her shawl tighter about her as the breeze picked up. A storm brewed, and she still had several miles to go until she reached her new home in South Carolina. "God willing, we will make it, Maddy."

Fear deepened the lines on Maddy's plain face. "'Tis like the squall on the boat."

Lightning flashed, momentarily brightening the shadows of the forest. A clap of thunder rumbled the ground. Maddy screamed. The old gelding that pulled the cart—all Rachel's meager coins could afford—increased its speed, weaving from side to side. Out of control.

Determined to be there before nightfall and in one piece, Rachel gripped the reins and fought to slow the maddening pace of the horse. Finally it resumed its plodding step. The weather-beaten cart she had bought near the dock in Charleston hit a bump in the road, jostling her into Maddy. Her maid clutched the seat with one hand and held onto Rachel with the other.

Steadying herself, Rachel rested her wrists on her rounded stomach. She had more than herself and Maddy to worry about now. Her life had changed so much since she left her ancestral home in England. She had married, conceived a child, and was now a widow, all in the space of a year. And worse, she was going to a place she had never seen because she had nowhere else to go. Her husband had used most of their money to purchase this plantation she was traveling to. It was her future, whether she wanted it to be or not.

The warmth of a spring day quickly faded as the sky grew blacker. Rachel stared at the menacing clouds through the treetops and realized she would not make it to her new home before the storm broke. She scanned the area for a place to seek shelter.

Sinister shadows lurked just beyond the road. Again she shivered, her imagination conjuring images of wild animals staring at her from the depths of the forest. She'd heard stories about the bears. Huge. Fierce. Sharp teeth and claws. Shifting on the seat, she darted a glance from side to side, feeling as though she were some beast's next meal. She could not stop, even if it poured down rain.

Oh, how she missed England, with its gently rolling hills and refined beauty—not this raw wilderness. Like a fish floundering on land, she did not belong here. Nothing in her life had prepared her for this strange environment.

Drops of water spattered her. The wind picked up.

"That man on the boat told me about a big cat. They are out there." Maddy whimpered, draping her shawl over her head and hunching her shoulders. "Lord, have mercy on us."

Rachel forced herself to keep her gaze fixed on the road ahead. Once they were at the plantation Maddy would settle down. The squall two days out of Charleston had nearly sunk the ship they had traveled in. Surely this storm would not be as bad.

Taking deep breaths, Rachel calmed her racing thoughts and heartbeat. Pain spread through her lower back. She gripped the reins, the leather digging into her palms. The pain dulled to an ache. Another deep inhalation and the panic nibbling at her composure abated. Soon she would be at her new home and could sit in front of a warm fire, put her legs up, and rest. Hopefully the letter her husband had sent ahead would alert any staff to her arrival. Her glance strayed to the tall pine trees, swaying in the gust. Everything would be all right when she arrived at Dalton Plantation.

But even with Maddy next to her on the seat, the feeling she was the only person in the world overwhelmed her.

The wind picked up, whipping strands of her long brown hair that had escaped its coiffure about her face and threatening to whisk away her bonnet. Lightning zigzagged across the sky, followed by thunder. Maddy jumped in her seat. The gelding's ears flattened.

A chill embedded itself deep in Rachel. She arched her back to ease the pang still plaguing her. Suddenly lightning struck a tree nearby, its flash a beacon in the growing darkness. A crack as the pine split into two pieces echoed through the forest. Immediately afterward, a boom of thunder cleaved the air. Maddy shrieked. The horse increased its pace while a few more splotches of water splashed Rachel. Then all at once rain fell in gray sheets.

The gelding lurched forward even faster. Rachel grasped the reins, trying to maintain control. She pulled on the leather straps to slow the horse. Nothing. He kept galloping down the road, oblivious to his surroundings, as though the hounds of hell were nipping at his hooves.

Rachel glanced from one side to the other but saw little except a wall of gray and green. Another peal of thunder spurred her horse into a dead run. The jostling motion bounced her around, nearly throwing her off the seat. A scream from Maddy competed with the din of the storm.

The cart hit another rut in the road. Rachel flew from the seat, the reins wrenched from her hands. The impact with the ground jarred her, knocking the breath from her lungs. Rain pelted her face as she sucked in oxygen-rich air. Stunned, Rachel closed her eyes against the continual downpour. Everything seemed to come to a standstill, as though her body went numb.

Then pain, as she had never felt before, ripped through her lower torso. She clutched her stomach, gritting her teeth to hold back the scream. She rolled to the side.

Need to get up.

Through the dim grayness, she glimpsed the horse's straps snapping free. The gelding broke away and bolted, clamoring down the road and disappearing from view. The cart careened toward a ditch, plunged into it, and tipped over.

"Help!" Maddy's cries sounded above the rumble of the storm.

She's in trouble.

When the pang subsided, Rachel pushed to her hands and knees, the cold mud oozing between her fingers. Her body protested every move she made, the dull ache in her back intensifying. She had no choice. Peering around, she saw no one else to help. No sign of civilization. Her head pounded like the rain hammering down on her. Her world spun a wave of dizziness making her stomach reel.

"Help. I'm trapped," Maddy shouted.

I can do this.

Rachel forced herself back on her heels, dragging in the cool, damp air. Another deep, fortifying breath and she struggled to her feet, her wet clothing siphoning her energy. She swayed. The trees swirled and danced before her eyes. She closed them and willed the dizziness away. No time for it.

She took a step toward the overturned cart, twenty or so feet away. Then another. The trees stopped spinning. She would make it. She could help Maddy.

Almost to her destination, she stumbled over a broken piece of a crate and staggered forward. Another stab of pain knifed through her stomach, its power taking her to her knees into the mud. Agony, like white-hot lightning, cut through her lower back and shoved her over the edge into a black void.

* * * * *

Nathan Stuart yanked the collar of his great coat up around his neck and pulled his beaver felt hat lower on his brow. But still the rain drove into him, drenching him as he rode toward his cabin. Thoughts of a warm fire kept the chill at bay. He concentrated on controlling his horse while thunder sounded around him and lightning lit the road, the only illumination in the darkening surroundings.

Nathan squinted, trying to see better in the gloom of the late spring afternoon. Another flash of lightning smote the sky, and he thought he saw a cart turned over up ahead. He spurred his mare faster, hoping that he only imagined it.

Again a bolt of brightness zipped through the grayness and cast an eerie glow over the landscape. Yes, it was a cart in the ditch at the side of the road. No horse.

Nathan reached the spot and leaped to the ground. He raced toward the wreck. Another lightning streak illumined his way, or he might have stumbled over the woman. She lay a few feet from the cart among some broken crates. The first thing he noticed, she was large with child. Then he saw she was unconscious—or dead. He gently turned her onto her back. The rain washed some of the mud from her face, revealing a pallor beneath her skin. A calmness descended as he knelt next to her and checked to see if she was still alive. A pulse beat below his fingertips.

"Help," a faint voice behind him called.

He swiveled on his heels and searched the overturned wagon. "Where are you?"

"Under the cart. Too heavy."

Divided over whom to help first, he ran his gaze down the length of the lady on the ground in front of him. Cuts, but no deep bleeding wounds that he could see. Her chest rose and fell. He jumped to his feet and hurried to the wagon, examining the debris to find the woman with the faint, high-pitched squeak.

A hand stuck out from beneath the cart. "Here."

He gripped the edge of the wagon and heaved it up until a petite woman scrambled from under it. On all fours, wet and covered in mud, she glanced up.

"Thank you. Where's Mrs. Gordon?" She stretched her body forward and looked around him. "Ma'am? She's hurt." She struggled to her feet and trudged toward the other lady. "You cannot die."

The woman on the ground stirred, moaning.

Nathan stooped on the other side of Mrs. Gordon. "Where's her husband?"

The woman who had been trapped said, "Mr. Gordon is gone."

Gone? Dead? Taken? Nathan peered toward the forest near the overturned cart.

He started to question the young woman when a frown lashed across Mrs. Gordon's ashen features, riveting his full attention. Her eyes—their color like a brown bear in the woods around his cabin—opened, and for a moment as the rain fell, she stared into his gaze, blinking the water away. Suddenly she clasped her stomach and moaned again. The plea in her look tore at him.

"Is the baby coming?"

"I don't know," she said in a harsh whisper. "It hurts."

"I'm a physician. I need to take you to my cabin not far from here. Out of this rain."

The tension in her expression lessened but only slightly. She lifted her head a few inches and scanned the area. "Your cabin?"

The young woman grasped Mrs. Gordon's hand. "Ma'am, he helped me. He can help you."

The expectant mother collapsed back on the muddy road, shivering. Her teeth chattered.

"This is no place to have a child, Mrs. Gordon." Nathan peered over at the cart to see if he could right it and use it to carry the woman to his place. He noticed one of its two wheels was broken. "I will have to carry you."

She nodded, her lips compressed into a thin line. Rain splattered her face, which was as white as his lawn shirt. He strove to remain calm.

"I will be with you, ma'am."

Mrs. Gordon glanced toward the young woman. "Are you all right, Maddy?" Her voice matched the quivering in her body.

"Yes, ma'am. I'm right fine, thanks to this gentleman."

Nathan tucked his arms under Mrs. Gordon and lifted her. Her wet clothes weighed her down, but he managed to nestle her against his chest as she locked her hands behind his neck. While he trudged toward his cabin, up an incline and through a grove of pine trees, his mare followed behind him, along with Maddy. As he neared his home, the rain subsided to a gentle shower, a rumble of thunder sounding in the distance.

A hundred feet from his cabin, the woman relaxed in his arms and laid her head on his shoulder. A mental picture of him carrying a wounded soldier back behind the lines nudged him. He tried to shake it away, but it invaded his mind, as did so many remembrances of the war. When he had reached safety and put the man on the ground, the soldier had been dead. His frustrated outcry still rang in his memories. That was when he knew the Lord didn't care about the men on the battlefield. God had turned away from him, and he was turning away from God.

I have already lost too many people. Not this lady or her baby.

Through the dismal gray, he spotted his home, and his pace quickened. She tightened in his arms, and a look of pain streaked across her face. A contraction. They were coming close together.

He mounted the steps. "How many months along are you?"

"Eight."

He shouldered his door open and let Maddy close it when they were all inside. In the dim light of the interior he made his way into his bedchamber, where he placed her on his bed then lit a candle.

The young woman trailed behind him into the room. "I don't know anything about babies." Hysteria edged her voice.

"I do," he said, hovering over the woman in the bed, her face contorted in pain. Her need underscored everything he wanted to forget—the reason he lived outside of town, secluded.

* * * * *

Another shaft of pain drilled into Rachel, sending her straight up in bed. Her hands gripped the blanket. Her teeth dug into her lower lip, drawing blood, its metallic taste coating her tongue. Sweat mingled with the raindrops on her face and ran down her cheeks.

The large man started to turn away. Remembering he had said he was a physician, Rachel clasped his hand to still his action. Fear seized her as tight as the constriction had a moment ago. "Please stay," she whispered, fighting the last pangs as they faded in intensity.

"I'm going to get clean rags and water. I will be right back."

His smile reassured her that she would not be left alone to have this baby. Her mother, Lady Ashton, would never speak of such delicate things to Rachel. She had no idea what to do, and from the panic on Maddy's face, her maid did not know either.

As another contraction clinched her abdomen, she clamped her teeth together, trying not to scream. She rode the wave of pain, twisting the blanket beneath her hands. She felt like the blanket, contorted, her stomach coiled into a huge, tight knot that was fighting to push its way out of her.

When the pain lessened to an ache, she relaxed back on the bed, closing her eyes and dragging in deep breaths, hoping that would fortify her for the next round. A cool, wet cloth touched her perspiration-covered face. She looked up into the kind eyes of the stranger. Their deep blue color mesmerized her. She wanted to lose herself in them and forget she was alone in this world, about to give birth, with only a frightened eighteen-year-old girl as a companion.

"I was not gone long." He continued to wipe her brow, a gentle smile touching his lips and touching her damaged heart.

The refreshing feel of the cloth moving over her skin made her forget for a moment where she was and why. She responded to his smile with a quickening in her pulse. A sense of security and peace enveloped her until another contraction sliced through her middle. She stiffened.

The kind physician clasped her hand. "Focus on me. Think of a meadow full of flowers in the springtime. The breeze is soft, cooling."

Tightening her hold, she concentrated on the cobalt blue of his eyes, the soft gruffness of his voice. She squeezed his fingers harder as the pain crested. Then ebbed. She sagged against the feather-stuffed mattress, her breath shallow, her throat dry.

"What's your name?" she whispered through parched lips.

"Nathan Stuart."

"Rachel. Rachel Gordon. Thank you for helping us." Her gaze slipped away from him and latched onto Maddy, hovering at the end of the bed, her brow wrinkled with worry, her arms crisscrossed over her chest. "This is Maddy Johnson, my maid."

"'Tis my pleasure."

She half believed it was, by the fervent way he spoke those words of reassurance. The raspy touch of his deep, rich voice, as though he didn't talk much, reinforced his words. "How many babies have you delivered?"

He glanced away and rinsed out his muddy cloth in a basin of water on a nearby table. "Not many."

"Do you know what you are doing?" *Because I don't. I'm scared.*

He grinned, a dimple appearing in his right check. His blue eyes twinkled. "I will be able to manage, unless you would rather do it by yourself. I can understand if you do. Or your companion can help."

"Oh no. Not me. I told you I know nothing about babies." Shaking her head, Maddy backed away from the bed, saying, "I shall get more water." Then she whirled around and hurried out of the room.

Leaving her alone with a stranger. Leaving her to have her baby.

"I will not stay if you want me to go."

A knifing pain cleaved Rachel, bringing her up off the bed. A scream ripped from her throat. "Stay," she managed to say between lulls in the wave of contractions.

"Then I am here for you."

She clung to those words as she became racked with agony as though a hot poker stabbed her stomach. Over and over.

Minutes evolved into hours.

When her body demanded she push her child out, one overriding thought clamped down in her mind, heightening her fear. She was the only person her child had to depend on. She was alone completely, no husband, no family. No family now except her child.

* * * * *

Something is wrong. The baby isn't coming out. Sweat beaded on Nathan's forehead. The child was turned wrong—like Eliza's was. No, he couldn't deliver this baby. He had let Eliza down. He—

The woman's groans permeated every corner of his mind as she tried to push and nothing happened. He had to do something. He did not bring her here to die.

His gut knotted into a lump of regrets.

"I cannot do this…anymore." Mrs. Gordon sagged back against the young woman, her hair damp from perspiration, her face pasty white.

"She cannot die," Maddy said, her gaze latching onto him. "Do something. You are a doctor."

For a moment he recalled that same expression and demand from the wounded soldiers he tried to save. Nathan surged to his feet and hurried from the room. He grabbed the bag with his medical instruments. His hand shook as he removed the forceps. He had never wanted to use them again.

As he reentered the bedchamber, he stared at the woman whose life was in his hands. Her arms hung limp at her sides until another contraction descended. Pain contorted her face, her hands digging into the bedding. The look she gave him, full of need and hope, as he returned to her side, reminded him of Eliza's—only minutes before she slipped away.

* * * * *

Rachel's newborn howled.

"She has a nice set of lungs." Nathan took a cloth and wiped her child. "She's beautiful. Do you want to see your daughter?"

Words failed Rachel. With her throat clogged, she nodded.

He wrapped her baby in a blanket and laid her in the crook of Rachel's arm. Her child quieted and peered at her. Tears slipped from Rachel's eyes as she stared at *her* daughter. Tiny. Rosy cheeks. Delicate features. And a black head of hair. Like her deceased husband—a constant reminder.

Rachel took the small hand in hers and caressed the soft skin. "She is so little."

Nathan cleaned up. "I can remember when my younger sister was born. When I got to hold her, I thought I was going to drop her."

"Where is your sister now?"

"She lives near here with her husband."

"Does she have any children?" Her gaze transfixed on the tiny bundle in her arms, Rachel smoothed the fine dark hair away from her daughter's face.

When he didn't answer her, she glanced up. His eyebrows slashed downward. His lips pressed together. He turned away.

"I'm sorry. I should not have asked." Exhaustion weaved its way through Rachel, weighing down her limbs.

He peered over his shoulder at her as he tossed dirty cloths into a bowl. "Yes, she has a son. But she almost died giving birth. I was not…" He shifted around, a shadow in his stormy blue eyes. "I was not here to help her."

"Where were you?"

"In New York. Fighting the English."

The English. Her heartbeat slowed. Her mouth went dry. "In the recent war?"

"Yes. I was a physician with our troops." The rigid set to his shoulders and the nerve that twitched in his cheek attested to suppressed anger.

Against the English. Rachel bit into her bottom lip. At the Charleston harbor she had heard others who spoke with her accent but had been in this country at least long enough to set up shop at the wharf and surrounding area. *How do I tell him I am English, newly arrived? Does he already know? He hasn't said anything.*

The war had ended a year ago. Her husband had proclaimed that this young country was the place for them to go, that opportunities abounded for him to make enough money to give her the lifestyle she was accustomed to. Tom had not cared that she was happy in England and feared traveling so far from all she had known.

The broad-shouldered doctor gathered up the rags, bowl, and bucket of heated water used to clean her and her daughter. "I will send in Maddy. Now that the baby has arrived, she should be of some use to you."

Rachel pressed her lips together to keep from blurting that she had recently arrived from England. The sound of the thunder in the distance reminded her of her predicament—several miles from Charleston, in the woods, with a storm raging.

While her daughter nursed, Rachel fought the exhaustion that claimed her. She had to stay alert. What if he discovered she was newly arrived from England, the country he had recently fought against, and threw her and her baby out? Rachel hugged her daughter even closer, peering out the window. Pitch black greeted her. *In the rain at night?*

Two

Cries penetrated Rachel's dreamless sleep. They meant something. She was sure of that, but for a moment she could not recall what. The thundering in her head momentarily drove the noise into the background. Then the memories flooded her mind, propelling her toward wakefulness with a jolt.

Her eyes flew open. The first thing she realized was that it was morning. The second thing was that her baby was gone.

The cries continued from the other room. Ignoring the pounding in her head, Rachel threw back the covers and slipped her feet to the wooden-planked floor. When she stood she gripped the bedpost to steady herself. She peered down at her attire, her own muslin nightgown. All she could remember from the evening before was the stranger who delivered her baby leaving the room to get Maddy. Did her maid undress her? Vaguely she recalled Maddy stripping off her dirty clothes and making sure the rest of the filth of the trip was washed away as best as she could under such primitive conditions.

Where are the rest of my clothes? Where is my baby? Rachel scanned the small room and found her chest against a wall made of logs then her robe lying across the covers at the end of the bed. Snatching up her robe, she started for the door, the cries of her daughter demanding her attention. But her sudden movements caused her to stop a few feet from the bed. Lightheaded, she teetered. The bed, the table, and a chair in the corner spun like a twirling prism. She sank to the cool floor, squeezing her eyes shut. The blackness swirled while pain struck against her skull like the clang of the bell on the ship. She grasped her head and pressed her fingers into her scalp. The sound of her baby's wails grew nearer. When she peered up, the doctor named Nathan Stuart stood in the doorway with Maddy right behind him. He cradled her daughter in the crook of one arm against his chest. The sight of such a large man, rugged looking in buckskin leggings, took her breath away. She blinked rapidly, trying to still the spinning room. She could *not* be ill right now. She had a child to care for.

"You have a bump on the side of your head the size of a goose egg." His deep, gravelly voice cut through the haze clouding her mind.

"I do?" She felt for the lump, her fingers grazing over it. A jolt of pain threatened to rob her of clarity.

He moved to hover over her. After passing her crying daughter to Maddy, he bent forward and wrapped his arms about her middle. "You need to stay in bed. You were hurt in the accident."

The warmth of his body heat soothed the anxiety building in the pit of her stomach. He helped her to her feet and then guided her to the side of the bed.

With his assistance she sank down onto the soft bed. His scent of soap, burning wood, and maleness assailed her. Heat infused her cheeks. She averted her gaze.

"Thank you for procuring my trunk." She hated being beholden to a stranger, but she didn't have much of a choice. She knew no one in South Carolina and only had a few distant relatives in the Boston area—ones who had migrated to this country before the rebellion in 1776.

"Ma'am, Dr. Stuart did much more than that." Maddy cuddled Rachel's daughter to her chest, rocking her in her arms, but nothing quieted the baby. "He brought my bag too."

"The cart is ruined, but I managed to retrieve some of your crates. Some of your belongings are broken."

Rachel sat back against the headboard, lifting her arms to take her baby. "Did you see a horse nearby? Brown, with a white mark down his nose?"

"No."

Her daughter nuzzled against her, her cries calming as she searched for her nourishment. "Is she all right?" Rachel asked, watching her child with wonderment.

"Yes. She's beautiful and hungry. I tried to keep her satisfied so you could rest, but alas, I am not what she wants."

Embarrassment heated Rachel's cheeks. She was learning American men were different from Englishmen. More rugged. Less refined.

He grinned, his attention focused on her child. "I will have Maddy bring you something to eat and willow bark tea for your headache."

When he and Maddy left her alone with her child, Rachel released a long breath. While her daughter nursed, she rested her head against the backboard and assessed the room. The sturdy, well-made furniture surprised her. What little she remembered of the outside of the cabin had not prepared her for the homey, neat interior. Nathan Stuart's bearing and his attire the day before attested to his upper-class background. But today she had seen another side to him, more in line with some of the men on the dock.

FROM THIS DAY FORWARD

A sucking sound fastened Rachel's gaze on her daughter. So tiny, so defenseless. She was her child's sole protector. *I shall not let anything happen to you.* Tears welled in Rachel's eyes. How was she going to fulfill that promise? The sense of being totally on her own swamped her as it had so many times since she stepped foot on American soil. A wet track rolled down her cheek and fell onto her baby.

Rachel studied her daughter's small features, delicate like the petals of a rose, the mop of curly black hair, so like her husband's. Her heart slowed to a throbbing ache. Her daughter was totally dependent on her for everything. That realization unnerved Rachel more than when the captain of the ship had told her that Tom had drunk too much and fallen overboard. Her first thought had been relief, that she was finally free of Tom. Only later had reality sunk in, and she had discovered how serious her predicament was. Then terror struck her. Somehow she would find the means to keep her daughter safe.

After switching the baby to her other side, Rachel closed her eyes, content for the moment to listen to the little noises her child made as she suckled. She needed to name her. Her mother's name was Margaret. Perhaps that could be her one connection to home. Perhaps… The thought faded as weariness weaved its way through her.

* * * * *

"Sir, is she well?"

The sound of Maddy's high-pitched voice floated to Rachel, drawing her from the blackness that embraced her in comfort. She stirred, opening one eye, to find Dr. Stuart leaning over her to take her child from the curve of her arm.

She clasped her daughter tighter, quickly glancing down to

make sure she was covered as she sat up straighter. "I'm fine." The moment she said those words she became aware of the persistent throbbing in her head.

"Here, drink this." He picked up a cup sitting on the small table next to the bed. "'Tis willow bark tea. You should feel better after you do."

Rachel passed her sleeping child to Maddy then took the drink and sipped it. "Thank you."

"I have chicken soup as well as bread and cheese." He took the cup she had emptied and set it next to a bowl on the table. "'Tis not much. I was not prepared for a…guest."

As the tea began to take effect, the pain subsided to a dull throb. "I appreciate what you have done for us. As soon as I can, I shall be on my way. Perhaps later today."

"Nonsense." He picked up the bowl and gave it to her along with a spoon. "You cannot go anywhere till you have regained your strength. Is there anyone I can notify?"

She stared down at the liquid in the bowl with bits of chicken and vegetables. "No, there is no one. My husband died recently." When she lifted her gaze to his, she saw the kindness in his tired features, the warmth in his blue eyes like the sun on the lake at Mansfield Manor. He had done so much for her already. The sense she could trust him spread through her to calm her anxiety. "He died on the voyage over here from England." Breath held, she waited for his response.

His mouth tightened for a moment before straightening into a neutral expression. "I thought as much. Do you know anyone in South Carolina?"

The realization of how utterly alone she really was shuddered down her length. A stranger in a strange land with little money and a new baby. "No one." Her hands holding the bowl trembled, sloshing the broth onto her.

He cupped his hands over hers to steady the quivering. Again a softness entered his eyes as they roamed over her. "That's not true. You know me."

She attempted a smile that fell. "I don't want to be a burden to you. As soon as I can travel, we will leave for Dalton Plantation."

His hands slipped away from hers. "Plantation?"

"You don't know of it? I thought I was near it. Am I lost?"

"What do you know about this…plantation?"

Rachel set the bowl of soup in her lap, its aroma stirring the hunger pangs in her stomach. "Only what Tom, my husband, told me. The location. That it would be a new start for us. We would have a large house to raise our children in. Plenty of land to grow crops. There would be servants, field hands to help us." She dipped the spoon into the liquid and sipped the broth. "This is delicious."

A frown creased his brow. "I don't know where your husband obtained his information about Dalton Farm, but 'tis not anything like that. There are a hundred fifty, maybe two hundred usable acres, uncultivated, and a house on the land, a small one that needs repairs from the great storm of 1811. There's a barn. It needs repairs too. There hasn't been anyone to look after the place since the war. The Daltons left for England a few years back. The farm is run down, but what is not swampland is good for planting crops."

"If a person knew how," she whispered, more to herself than him. *What has Tom done?*

She stared down at her cooling soup, fighting the tears that demanded release. Swallowing the lump in her throat, she blinked to rid her eyes of them. But one dropped into her broth.

"I'm sorry to have to tell you about the farm."

Concern threaded through his voice and immediately reminded Rachel she had an audience. She peered up at him. He stepped back, rubbing his nape and looking about him as if he were searching for a place to disappear.

"Coming to America was not my dream. Now I don't know what to do."

His gaze settled on her. "I can take you back to Charleston. There is bound to be a ship leaving for England soon."

"No!" The one word flew out of her mouth so fast it even surprised her. "I cannot do that." She raised her chin a notch. "I shall make do with what the Lord has given me."

His expression darkened. He clamped his jaw shut and glanced at Maddy, who held Rachel's daughter. "What about your child?"

"We shall be fine," she said with as much determination as she could muster, but her voice cracked.

He frowned. "How?"

"God will provide."

He snorted. "He will? That naïveté will get you killed."

She sucked in a deep breath. "I don't have a choice. I cannot return to England. My parents disowned me. Dalton Farm, in whatever condition, is all I have. It will be my home now." She dropped her gaze to the bowl of chicken soup and picked up the spoon to take another taste of the broth.

"Where did you grow up?" Tension poured off him, from his taut posture to the intense glint in his eyes.

"Devonshire. My family owns an estate there. Mansfield Manor."

"Why did your parents disown you?"

"Because I married Tom Gordon, a man they did not think worthy of me." It wasn't until after her marriage to Tom that she had discovered how right her parents had been. She wrote a letter and told them how sorry she was for defying them. She never heard back from her parents.

"Surely now that your husband has died and you have a child—"

"My father made it quite clear he never wanted to see me again. He had arranged a marriage for me. No one goes against him."

His look turned to ice, his jawline sculpted in stone. "I know how that is."

"You do?"

"Yes."

Someone who understands what I am going through. The feeling of kinship with this man heightened the intimacy she felt between them. The room shrank in size, her heartbeat increasing. "What happened?"

"My grandfather insisted I do what he wanted…to run Pinecrest, to learn how from my father. I didn't want to be a planter. I wanted to help others as a physician. I had already started to train when…" His gruff voice faded into silence. He peered away, swallowing hard. A war of emotions played across his features, as though he were reliving a bad memory.

The connection she felt to him strengthened. The urge to help him as he had her prompted her to say, "So you went against your grandfather's wishes as I did my father's. Was there no way you could do both?"

"I tried, with my father's support, but five years ago we lost many people on the plantation to yellow fever. My father tried to help and succumbed to the fever. I could not do anything to save him. After my father's funeral, I stood up to Grandfather. He didn't take kindly to that. He really does not understand…." He snapped his mouth closed, a nerve jumping in his jaw.

"What does he not understand? That being a physician is important to you?"

"If I had completed my training as I had planned, I might have been able to do more to save my father."

"You were upset that your father died. How could your grandfather disown you for speaking what you felt?"

Dr. Stuart rubbed the back of his neck. "There was more to it than that. Looking back now, I believe my grandfather would have accepted my learning to be a physician as well as a planter." He sucked in a deep breath and looked right at her. "Soon after my father's funeral, my grandfather sent my mother back to England, telling her she was not welcome at Pinecrest ever again."

His expression was solemn and hurt dulled his eyes. Her throat swelled, tears close to the surface. "Pinecrest was your mother's home." Like Mansfield Manor had once been hers.

"That's what I thought. But when I spoke up, my grandfather became very angry with me."

"He threw you off the plantation then? For standing up for your mother?" Rachel never wanted to meet this man who could not understand a son speaking up for his mother.

"Not right away, but our relationship became very difficult after that. I know he hated the English because they killed his eldest son and youngest brother in the Revolutionary War, but I thought he had reconciled himself to Mama. But for some reason my father's death set off a tirade."

Is this kind of hatred widespread? The fact that she was in a country that had been at war with England only a year before underscored the perils she might face, but at least here she had some land. Back home she would have nothing. "I am so sorry. I know what it feels like to lose family."

"Not long after my mother returned to England, I left to further my training as a physician. Grandfather made it clear he did not want me to return to Pinecrest either. Later he disowned me and refused to talk to me after that, even though my brother and sister tried to end the dispute between us. I thought when I came back from the war he would have changed."

"But he hadn't?"

Nathan laughed, but the sound held no humor. "Hardly. The war between us and England, the burning of our capital, only fueled his anger against the English and for some reason against me too."

"But you fought against my…England."

"I know. He welcomed my sister's husband but would not talk to me." He curled and uncurled his hands at his sides. "I am done with him. He can live in his hatred and misery. I don't need him or his money."

Silence reigned in the small bedchamber.

The sadness she glimpsed in Dr. Stuart's eyes mirrored what she felt every time she thought of never seeing her mother and siblings again. Emotions crammed her throat. She would not cry again in front of him, even though they had shared the same fate with their families. She had to remain strong if she were going to make it here. "This soup is wonderful. My compliments to you."

One corner of his mouth tilted upward. "It could have been Maddy who made it."

"Ack. Not me. Ma'am knows I don't know how," her maid said, rising from the chair in the corner. "The baby is getting fussy."

Rachel finished the last bit of her meal, passed the bowl to Dr. Stuart, and took her child from her maid.

Maddy gathered up the dishes. "I can wash these."

When Maddy left her and the doctor alone, Rachel's nerves tingled with an awareness of the man only feet from her. *What do I do now?* "Who taught you to cook?" she finally said to cut into the uncomfortable silence between them.

"The camp cook. Do you know how to cook?"

She shook her head. "We had someone who took care of all that. Mama would have fainted if she had found me in the kitchen, learning to cook."

His attention slipped to her daughter, who had fallen asleep almost instantly when Maddy gave the child to her. "She's one beautiful and determined little lady already."

"How so?"

"She immediately spit out the cloth I gave her to suck on earlier. She knew it would not give her the milk she needed. Your daughter knows what she wants. She began howling right after that this morning, only to stop for a few minutes while I washed her. That did not satisfy her long, however."

"You washed her?"

"I wanted to clean her up."

"But Maddy could have done that."

He chuckled, the sound of merriment luring her to him. His very presence dominated the room, as though the man had complete command of himself. He seemed so capable, even to the point of cooking for himself—a man who had come from a wealthy family. The rich men she had known in England probably did not even know where the kitchen was in their big houses. *Does he have regrets like I do? Does he wish he hadn't stood up to his grandfather—that he hadn't been disowned?*

"I found Maddy curled asleep in front of the fireplace. I didn't want to disturb her. I enjoyed holding your…what are you going to name her?"

"Faith." *I am going to need a lot of it in the coming months.*

"I like that name." He held her gaze, the silence falling again between them.

Heat flushed her cheeks.

He looked away and said, "I can show Maddy how to cook some simple dishes, if you want."

According to Dr. Stuart, there were no servants at the farm that was to be her new home. "We both need to learn."

"Then I will teach you both at least what little I know." With a warm smile, he glanced down at Faith. An unreadable expression flitted into his dark blue eyes. "I will not be responsible for turning you out to fend for yourselves. I can imagine what it is like to be among strangers without a family."

Could she put her trust in a man again? She had put her trust in Tom. She should have realized Dalton Plantation—no, correction, Dalton Farm—wasn't what her husband claimed it was. He had been a schemer, dreaming of how to get rich quick with as little effort as possible. If only she had known his true character.

After Tom, she was reluctant to get close to anyone. She shook those thoughts from her mind. Regrets would not feed them. She didn't have to get close to learn to cook.

Rachel cuddled Faith close to her. "I appreciate your kind offer."

"You should stay here for at least a few days while you regain your strength. I will show you what little I know during that time."

Afraid of what he could read in her eyes, she lowered her gaze to Faith, unable to meet his direct look. He flustered her. She had never been in a situation like this. She should not stay, and yet she really did not have a choice—had not since she married Tom. Exhaustion clung to her after only a little bit of exertion. "Fine, but only for a day or two," she murmured, feeling torn between not becoming dependent on anyone and getting the rest she needed.

Three

"Rachel, you need to wake up."

The words penetrated Rachel's foggy mind, insisting she leave the warm comfort of the dark. She burrowed deeper into the covers. Then she became aware of a hand on her shoulder, shaking her. Imploring her attention. And cries. Faith's. Wrenched from sleep, Rachel opened her eyes to find Dr. Stuart bending over her with her baby in his arms. The sight struck every word from her mind for a moment.

He smiled. "I believe your daughter is hungry again."

Rachel knuckled the sleep from her eyes and pushed herself to a sitting position. "Where is Maddy?"

"When she could not wake you, she came and got me." He passed Faith to her, the baby's wails echoing through the room.

"Ma'am, I tried. You were dead to the world," Maddy said from the entrance, chewing on her lower lip.

Rachel took her child and settled her in the crook of her arm, rocking her. "You would think I hadn't fed her in days, not hours."

Dr. Stuart chuckled. "You would think."

Watching Faith nuzzle against her made Rachel's heartbeat slow. *This is real. I am a mother and this baby depends on me for everything.* That realization was still hard for her to grasp. Tightness in her chest threatened her breathing.

"How are you feeling?" Dr. Stuart backed away from the bed while Maddy moved into the small bedchamber.

"Tired. I could sleep for days…." She stopped and looked toward him. "I mean, as soon as I get to my home, I can rest then."

"You can stay as long as you need," he said then disappeared into the main room, closing the door.

For one wild moment Rachel wanted to tell him she did not want to leave. Ever. Uncertainty about her future gripped her. He made her feel safe, protected. *I cannot give in to my fears. The Lord is with me. He will protect me and give me the strength I need.*

Rachel positioned Faith to nurse, bolstered in her belief she could stand on her own two feet. "Maddy, I need you to let me know what supplies we have left. Check the wreck and see if there is anything we can salvage. I know Dr. Stuart brought some of the items to the cabin, but we need everything that was in the cart." And more—more than she had money for—but she did not want to say that to her maid. "The plantation is not like my husband thought. As you heard Dr. Stuart say, the house is small, but we do not need a lot of room. There are no other servants. It will be just you and me."

Maddy's eyes grew round. The color leached from her face. "I thought perhaps we would go back to Charleston."

Rachel shook her head. "I know that sounds frightening, but we shall make our home at Dalton Planta— Farm."

"How?" Her maid's voice quavered as much as her hands did.

"We have the Lord on our side. He brought us here. He has a plan for us."

"To be killed. There are Indians. There are wild animals. There…" Maddy's words petered out in a squeak.

Rachel caught her attention. "We shall be all right." *Please, Lord.* "While you are in here, I need you to help me dress. It is time I learn what I will need to do when we are at the farm."

Maddy scurried to the trunk and rummaged in it for a proper gown for Rachel.

Rachel shifted Faith to the other side and tried not to think about the man in the other room. But her thoughts refused to cooperate and strayed to him. Nathan Stuart had fought in the recent war with England. Against her country. He had seen much death and destruction. That would obviously influence a person. Her older brother had fought against Napoleon and had come home a changed man who rarely smiled or laughed.

By the time Faith finished feeding, she had fallen asleep in Rachel's arms. Rachel laid her in the middle of the bed then rose slowly. After taking a moment to adjust to standing, she removed her nightgown and allowed Maddy to slide a chemise then a petticoat over her. When her maid held out a simple morning gown of dark blue muslin with a high empire waist she had worn when she was first pregnant, Rachel slipped it on and buttoned it up the front.

Looking at the color of her dress, Rachel realized how limited her wardrobe was for a woman in mourning. As a widow, people would expect her to mourn her husband. But she refused to mourn him long, not after his cruel treatment of her. She didn't have any black and only a few gowns that were a darker color. She didn't have many coins and certainly couldn't afford to buy material for a new gown. Another dilemma she had to deal with on top of all the other ones.

Maddy insisted on brushing Rachel's hair. Rachel sat on the bed and watched Faith sleep while she indulged in the luxury. Her head still hurt from the accident, but the willow bark tea she drank earlier had alleviated the pain to a dullness she could bear. A simple headache would not keep her abed. If she were going to leave soon, she needed to start doing things for herself. After all, when she reached her new home, she would have to open up the house to air it out and would probably have to dust everything while Maddy swept. And then what?

I do not know. I know how to run a house with servants. I know how to sew. I know how to paint and play the pianoforte. None of which would get her very far in this new country.

Doubts taunted her as she made her way into the main room.

Dr. Stuart stood at the table. "What are you doing up?"

"I hate staying in bed. Mama always had a hard time keeping me there when I wasn't well."

"'Tis sometimes the best thing to do." He held a bowl and a spoon.

"What are you making?" Rachel asked as Maddy, with her shawl pulled around her shoulders, hurried toward the outer door.

"Boiled pudding." The doctor's gaze followed Maddy. "Where is she going?"

"To check the wreck. Even if something is broken, perhaps I can fix it."

He arched a brow. "The crate with china fell apart when it hit the ground. The dishes were shattered."

"There is no time like now to learn to cook. May I watch you?"

He studied her for a long moment. "If you sit on this stool."

A blush scored her cheeks at the assessing look he gave her, as if he were inspecting her for damage. She supposed he was, being a physician. *What would it be like if he looked at me with more than a doctor's sympathy?* She shook her head, clearing her thoughts. That was not her concern. Taking care of her daughter was her *only* concern now.

Easing onto the stool, she propped her feet on one of its slats. "The quicker I learn how to cook, the better off I shall be."

He stared at her with a somber expression. "Yes, starving has its disadvantages. And you have Faith to consider."

She chuckled, something she had missed since leaving her home. Tom had quickly quenched her desire for laughter, and on the sea voyage she'd had her hands full just keeping her food down. "The advantage to not knowing how to cook is that I shall get my figure back sooner." The moment she made the reference to her body was the moment she regretted her comment. She did not usually speak without choosing her words carefully, but Dr. Stuart had a way of making her relax around him, of making her forget to be cautious when it came to men. In a short time a bond had been forged between them that she could not deny. Without his assistance, Faith probably wouldn't have made it into this world.

His regard skimmed her length, leaving a heated trail where it traveled. "I don't think you should worry about that."

His gaze returned to hers. The intensity in his eyes, all male, stole her breath. She did not have to wonder any longer what it would be like to have him look at her as a man would a woman. She lifted her hand to smooth away from her face a strand of hair that had escaped her cap. Dr. Stuart glanced to the side, and everything returned to normal, as though they hadn't exchanged a look that affected her pulse, her breathing.

He placed the large bowl on the oak table and began to add ingredients. "You beat six eggs then add a pint of milk, some flour." He dumped in two spoonfuls. "Next you add a little nutmeg, salt, and sugar."

She focused on his long fingers grasping the spoon as he stirred the mixture. Those fingers had cradled her daughter, had assisted her to stand when she collapsed to the floor. Goose bumps rose on her skin. She rubbed her hands up and down her arms.

When he started filling a cloth bag with the pudding, Rachel asked, "Why are you putting it in there?"

"The bag will go into a pot of boiling water for half an hour. Then we can eat the pudding." He carried out the last step then turned over an hourglass.

Her inadequacies came to the foreground. This would be so different from managing a large household. She was not afraid of hard work but of not knowing what to do. She massaged her forehead, her headache intensifying.

"Do you want more willow bark tea?"

"That would be lovely, please."

The aroma of nutmeg infused the room, mingling with the smells of burning wood and the clean, fresh scent after the rain yesterday. Rachel sighed, content for the moment, even though her head pounded.

Everything would be fine once she was in her own home. If Dr. Stuart had learned to cook, she would be able to also.

He swung a crane that held a kettle from the fire, then using a rag, lifted the pot off the hook. His movements were efficient, precise, as if he never wasted a gesture. He exuded a quiet strength that appealed to her. Nothing like her deceased husband. Dr. Stuart was a large man, perhaps six feet, with short black hair. The buckskin breeches he wore today appeared primitive, in stark contrast to his attire of tan pantaloons, burgundy tailcoat with velvet trim, a black vest, and boots the day before.

After he poured hot water into a cup with willow bark in it, Rachel took it from him, her hand brushing against his fingers. The touch sent tingles up her arm, and she nearly dropped the tea onto her lap. She clasped the china cup and brought the steaming liquid to her lips.

He laid his palm against her forehead, their gazes bound. "You don't have a fever, but I imagine you will have a headache for a while. You must have hit your head when you were thrown from the cart. Hence the bump the size of a goose egg."

When he did not withdraw his hand immediately, she shivered. A sense of peace descended, as though she knew everything would be all right for her and her daughter in South Carolina. He would see to it. His calm aura reached out and encompassed her, and their connection strengthened beyond the mere physical touching of their skin.

She blinked, shattering the surrealistic moment. "It is nothing," she murmured, averting her gaze.

He lowered his hand and stepped back. "Still, you need to be careful. You shouldn't do too much too soon."

As Rachel sipped the tea, Maddy returned to the cabin, carrying a few pieces of the china Rachel had brought over from England.

Chewing on her bottom lip, her servant put them—three cups without handles and four plates with chips in them—on the table. "This is all."

Rachel's hand trembled as she inspected what little was left from a place setting for twelve. "We shall make do."

"I will put them in the chest." Maddy gathered the dishes and carried them into the bedchamber.

Through the doorway Rachel spied her servant lifting the lid on the second trunk, next to the one that held her clothes.

Rachel finished the tea and rose, swaying into the table. With a grip on its edge, she steadied herself. "I had better lie down."

"When the pudding is done, I will bring you some."

Mumbling her thanks, Rachel walked as fast as she could into the bedchamber. Tomorrow she needed to go to Dalton Farm. She lay down next to Faith and closed her eyes, drawing in a deep, calming breath to still her hammering heartbeat. But Dr. Stuart's scent clung to the bedding, teasing her nostrils as though he were standing next to her. So close she could touch him.

Her weakened state made her react to his nearness. *That is all it is.* She determinedly pushed the man from her thoughts.

Almost instantly memories of Tom filled her mind. She latched onto them rather than shoving them away as was her custom. All his lies paraded through her thoughts—especially the biggest one of all, that he loved her. Then she thought of his brutal manhandling, the slaps that came if she did not do as he said, the cross words like sharp knives thrust into her chest that were meant to belittle her into submission. Never again would she place herself under a man's control. To strengthen that resolve, all she had to do was recall Tom's treatment of her.

When Dr. Stuart brought her the pudding topped with melted butter, she had hardened her heart to any thought she needed a man in her life.

She took the offered bowl and said, "Thank you. This smells delicious." She only let her regard touch him briefly before she concentrated on eating the treat.

"Tomorrow I will let you do the work while I instruct you."

Her husband's instruction on how to please him resounded in her mind. Icy tentacles wrapped about her, squeezing. "Tomorrow? I need to leave by then."

"I will not hear of it. Your head still hurts and you became dizzy a little while ago. You are weak. How are you going to care for Faith and put food on the table? Your maid is as inept as you are."

Clasping the bowl so tightly her hands hurt, Rachel lifted her chin and stabbed him with her gaze. "I shall manage. I have no choice."

"How?"

She gritted her teeth. "Somehow." She could not imagine the farm being so bad that a little work on her part would not take care of it. She had seen the farmhands on her family estate and was not afraid of work. She had to make this succeed.

"I would never forgive myself if I let you leave and something happened to you or Faith."

"I am not your responsibility."

"Yes, you are. You became my responsibility when I found you on the road."

"No!" Anger quivered through her. She would take care of herself and her child.

His eyes narrowed, his arms rigid at his sides. "This does not have to be a contest of wills."

Faith stirred, but her eyes remained closed. "Then do not make it one," Rachel said in a lowered tone.

"Why can you not accept my help?"

For a moment she thought she heard hurt in his voice, but when she looked at him, she met a totally neutral expression. "Why can you not accept my answer?"

"Because I know what Dalton Farm looks like. Because I know how hard it would be for a man, let alone a woman with a baby. Because I know that you gave birth just yesterday and were in an accident too."

"I am not helpless. I know there will be some work involved." She fought to erect a barrier of polite formality between them.

"Some work? You have no idea, Rachel."

His use of her given name wiped all her intentions away. The very situation they were in made a mockery of her denying the connection between them. He had possibly saved her life and that of her daughter's.

He towered over her, his hands balled at his sides, his expression no longer bland but full of frustrated anger. Then suddenly it evened out. "How are you going to get to the farm?"

"I'm going to…" She remembered the broken cart; she remembered her horse running away.

"To what? Walk?" He folded his arms over his chest. "How are you going to get your trunks there?"

She bit her lower lip, set the bowl in her lap, and clenched her hands. "Perhaps you could give me a ride." The words tasted like bile on her tongue. She hated having to ask any more of him.

He mumbled under his breath something she could not hear. Flexing his hands, he glared at her. "The only help I'm going to give you is the use of my home. At least until you are well enough to be on your own."

"You cannot force me to stay against my will."

"I'm not. You can leave at any time, but I will not contribute to putting you in danger."

"I have to learn to do for myself."

"Fine, when you are physically up to it."

Impotency washed through her. She chewed the inside of her cheek. Her hands shook with exasperation. After the last time Tom had taken his pleasure out on her, she had vowed no one would force her to do anything she did not want to do. "You promise you will take me to Dalton Farm when I am better, not one day later?"

"Yes, I will see you settled." Relief eased the tension etched into his face.

"Then I shall stay." *As if I really have a choice.*

"Good. Rest. Your lessons begin tomorrow morning bright and early."

* * * * *

Nathan stormed outside, welcoming the coolness of the pine-scented air in the woods. *That woman is impossible. There is no way she can run the farm with only herself and her maid.*

Visions of all the things that could happen to her berated his thoughts. In town there had been talk of a gang of unsavory men hiding out in the forest north of Charleston. Although they were west, that was still too close. Her farm edged the swampy land near the river. What would she do if she encountered an alligator? In the spring the beasts became more active.

He picked up his ax and positioned a log on the stump to be split. Putting all his energy into it, he struck the piece of wood again and again. One blow after another, until he had a pile of logs for the fireplace. How was she going to chop wood for the fire?

Finally, sweat drenching him, he sat on the stump, his ax resting on the ground near his booted feet. He needed to solicit his sister's help to persuade Rachel that Dalton Farm was no place for her. If he could not convince Rachel to return to Charleston tomorrow after he showed her a few things she would need to be able to do, he would contact Sarah.

He walked down to the stream that flowed a few hundred feet from his cabin and splashed cold water on his face and neck. Then he headed back up the slope, hoping he could maintain his patience long enough to get the point across to Rachel. She did not belong here. He did not want to be responsible for another human being.

As he approached the cabin, Faith's cries reverberated through the air. He smiled. She was a hungry baby. He recalled when he brought the beautiful little girl into the world. The excitement and awe he experienced shadowed momentarily the last few years of the war, toiling to save lives. But in the end he had taken a life. He had never before been faced with the decision to kill or be killed. Now the English soldier's face haunted his sleep. He couldn't have been older than eighteen.

Very definitely, both Rachel and Faith needed to go home to England.

Four

Looking out the window the next morning, Rachel noticed the bright sunlight bathing the leaves of the trees that surrounded the cabin. It streamed through the glass and warmed the bedchamber. The day promised to be beautiful. And, no doubt, frustrating. As she prepared to go into the main room, the idea of her first cooking lesson tightened her stomach into a knot. Her maid closed the trunk lid behind her and Rachel turned toward her.

"Maddy, when you wash our muddy dresses, also do any clothes that Dr. Stuart needs cleaned."

"Yes ma'am. He has already set a tub outside for me and built a fire to heat water." Maddy left the bedchamber with her arms full of dirty clothing from their travels.

From the bedchamber doorway, Rachel spied Nathan standing by the large fireplace, stoking the fire with a poker. He stared into the flames, a faraway look on his face. Sadness lined his features. Her heart twisted at the sight of him, so alone. Again she felt an affinity with him, as though they were kindred souls.

He pivoted toward her, wiping his expression blank. "Are you ready?"

With a last glance at Faith sleeping on the bed, Rachel stepped into the main room. "The real question is, are *you* ready?"

He chuckled. "I thought I would teach you to bake bread first. How is Faith? I heard her earlier."

"As did probably everyone else for miles around. She has a nice set of lungs. She is sleeping for the time being."

He crossed the main room to the kitchen area. "The brick oven should be hot enough by the time we have the first batch of dough ready to bake. I will also show you how to make a cake. We will have it tonight in celebration."

"Celebration?"

"Yes. Faith's birth and your first day of lessons. I fancy sweets, so it does not take much for me to celebrate."

The expression on his face earlier made her doubt that last sentence. At one time perhaps it was true, but the man she saw by the fire was troubled. Grieving for his father? His mother, thousands of miles away? Or the lost relationship with his grandfather? She really knew very little about him. More questions tumbled through her mind. Had he been married before? Did he lose a friend in the war? Why was he all alone out here? Why was he not practicing medicine in Charleston?

When Dr. Stuart cleared his throat, her face flushed at the directions her thoughts had taken her.

"Are you confessing to a weakness?" she asked, desperate to quiet the barrage of queries concerning him. *Too dangerous to know.*

"Only to a sweet tooth."

"We could make the cake first then the bread."

He shook his head. "Work first, pleasure second."

The somber look that entered his eyes reinforced the sense she had that he'd had little fun in his life of late. "You are indeed a hard taskmaster. What do I have to do first?" She grinned, wanting to bring an answering smile to his mouth.

"You will need to gather the ingredients." He gave her an apron. "Here, put this on to protect your gown."

"Are you saying I will be a messy cook?"

He smiled, a twinkle sparkling his eyes like light captured in a blue sapphire. "Prove me wrong."

"That is a challenge I shall take up."

She slipped the apron over her head and started to tie it behind her when Nathan brushed her fingers away and secured the garment for her. Her pulse reacted to his nearness, inches from her back. A constriction in her chest prevented her from taking deep breaths.

She quickly stepped away, inhaling. "Where is your apron?"

"This is not my first time. Besides, I borrowed only one from my sister's cook."

"Your sister? Is that where you went earlier? Back to Charleston?"

"No, this cabin is near their plantation, Liberty Hall. Sarah and her husband also have a house in Charleston. They travel back and forth between the two homes. Your farm is on the other side of their land, along the river. I didn't see my sister this morning. She's still in Charleston."

Rachel had more questions, but Nathan pointed to a sack and said, "You will need flour."

By the time the bread was made, Rachel understood the need for an apron—at least for herself. She was not sure if more flour was on her or in the bowl. With Nathan dogging her every step, often correcting her, she did manage to put together some dough for baking bread.

Rachel inspected what she had mixed together. "This does not look very big for several loaves of bread. Perhaps one, but not two. Are you sure you told me everything?"

"The dough has to rise first then we bake it." He moved to stand next to her at the table. "Here, let me show you how to knead it. Then we will place it by the fire to rise."

Nathan put his large hands into the dough and began to press and fold it. Looking at his fingers working the mixture, she could imagine them doing the same to her taut shoulder muscles, easing the stress and ache from them. Also the knot at her nape where her spine throbbed with tension. Her eyes slid closed.

"Rachel, is everything all right?"

His deep gravelly voice intruded on her daydream and yanked her back to the present. She swallowed and tried to smile, wishing for once her cheeks did not flame with her embarrassment. Her mother had always told her it was easy to read her feelings on her face. She hoped Nathan—she had given up calling him Dr. Stuart halfway through her baking lesson—could not.

He veiled his expression. "'Tis your turn." He stepped to the side to allow her to stand in front of the bowl.

"This is a lot of work for two loaves of bread," she mumbled and touched the dough with the tips of her fingers. She pressed down, and her hands sank into the gooey mixture. The strange sticky substance clung to her skin. She wrinkled her nose and brought her hands up, globs hanging from them.

"Do it again and again."

She followed his instruction, submerging her fingers back into the dough. This time she tried putting more strength behind the effort.

After a few minutes of observing Rachel, Nathan chuckled and moved behind her. "At this rate, we will starve." His arms came around her, his hands covering hers in the bowl. "Here, let me show you what I mean by kneading."

With him guiding her, she smashed and squeezed the dough over and over. Caged by his embrace, Rachel tried to calm her heartbeat, but it had a mind of its own. Surrounded by Nathan—or so it seemed—she hardly knew what she was doing. His scent of the outdoors toyed with her senses, shoving away the aromas coming from the bread mixture and focusing her awareness on the man inches behind her. The feel of his body as it bumped against hers lured her. She wanted to lean back against him—an impulse that had nothing to do with being tired.

Abruptly he stopped, whisked the bowl off the table, and took it to the fire. "That should do it."

All she saw were the strong, tall lines of his back. Her legs went weak, as though her energy had drained from her instantly. Oh my! Resisting the urge to fan herself, she wiped her hands clean on a cloth then sat on the stool lest she collapse. She gripped the edge of the table to steady herself and leaned into it for support.

He turned from the fire, his expression unreadable. "Now for the cake."

"What do I do?" she managed to ask in a whisper—a weak one at that.

"Nothing. You are going to sit and watch this time."

She struggled to her feet and prayed she did not sink to the floor. Determined not to let this man get to her, she stood straight even though her hands locked about the table's edge. "Chicken. Afraid of what I shall do?"

When Faith's cries pierced the air with her urgency, he said, "You had better see what your daughter wants."

We both know what that is. Rachel shuffled toward the bedchamber, barely able to pick up her feet. "This does not mean you don't have to answer my question. Don't do anything until I come back."

"Yes ma'am," she heard him mimic Maddy. A tinge of laughter followed his statement.

After changing Faith's nappy, Rachel scooped up her child and returned to the main room. "I know this is surprising, but she is hungry. I shall be back in a while," she said over the cries of her daughter, "to make that cake. I need to learn to cook. Not watch you." Especially that. It sent her thoughts in a direction they did not need to go.

"You can sit in here by the fire. I have a few chores I can do before *we* make the cake."

He pulled a chair in front of the fireplace then snatched up a bucket and headed for the door. Rachel patted Faith on the back and whispered soothing words that she doubted her daughter could hear over her renewed wails. The moment she was alone, Rachel sank down onto the seat and unbuttoned the front of her gown. Faith quieted immediately when she started nursing.

Rachel leaned back and relaxed, a sigh escaping her lips. *Cooking is hard work.* Now that she had stopped she could acknowledge that kneading, stirring, and beating were exhausting. No doubt that was why Nathan wanted to bake the cake. She was discovering that Nathan was very perceptive, something Tom had never been.

For a short time she forgot about her circumstances and relished the peace of the moment. The aroma of burning wood laced the air and mingled with the scent of the different ingredients she had used. The warmth of the fire chased away any chill in the cabin. The emotional satisfaction of holding her baby in her arms fulfilled her as nothing before had. The knowledge that she, Faith, and Maddy were safe for the time being left a contented glow deep inside. The Lord had sent her a protector, Nathan, when it seemed all had been lost. Her plight could have ended differently if he had not come along.

But as much as I owe him, gratitude is all I can give him.

"Nathan." The door opened, and a beautiful woman with a bonnet that did not hide her blond curls sailed into the cabin, coming to a halt when she spied Rachel by the fire. The young woman's jaw dropped for a brief moment before she snapped her mouth closed then asked, "Who are you?"

Rachel's surprise matched the lady's. She quickly turned away and adjusted her dress, thankful that Faith was all but through nursing. Pushing to her feet, Rachel faced the woman, who was dressed in a rose muslin morning gown with a brown spencer. The lady's mouth pinched with puzzlement. Tension seized Rachel, the momentary peace she had experienced shattered. "Who are you?" she countered.

The tall lady came farther into the main room. "I'm Nathan's sister, Sarah McNeal. And you?" One eyebrow rose, reminding Rachel of Nathan.

She could just imagine what was going through the woman's mind. Rachel hugged her daughter to her. "I am Rachel Gordon. I had an accident with my cart two days ago, and your brother rescued my maid and me then helped deliver my baby."

"He did?" Sarah clapped her hands, a smile appearing, along

with two dimples in her cheeks. "That is wonderful. If he delivered your baby, that means he has reconsidered his decision."

What decision?

Sarah crossed the room to peek at Faith. "She's beautiful. Are you from around here?"

Rachel relaxed the taut set of her shoulders. "No…yes." She laughed. "I mean, I have newly arrived in Charleston and was heading to my plantation." Her face heated. "My farm, when I had the accident."

"So that cart in the ditch is yours?"

"Yes."

"Where is your husband?"

Rachel met Sarah's direct gaze. "Dead."

"When? How?" Sarah's eyes brightened when they latched onto Faith. "May I hold your daughter? I hope I have a little girl."

Rachel nodded while she tried to decide how much to tell this woman. She placed Faith in Sarah's arms. "He died on the ship from England. I have only been here a few days."

"Aha, I thought you were English. That is awful, being left stranded here. Do you have any family in Charleston?"

"What are you doing here, Sarah?"

Gasping, Sarah whirled around with Faith cradled against her. "May a sister visit her brother?"

Rachel glanced toward the open doorway. She had not heard Nathan come in either. Her pulse kicked up a notch.

"Yes, but since we saw each other a few days ago, there must be a reason for this visit. Did you come from Liberty Hall? I was there this morning and you were not."

"You were? Why?"

"To borrow a few items to help Rachel. So you came from Charleston. I am surprised you came here before going to Liberty Hall. Where's John?"

"In Charleston. He was at the docks when I left." Sarah fussed with the blanket around Faith then handed the baby back to Rachel. "Patrick wants to see you."

"He knows where to find me."

"At Pinecrest."

"No."

"Grandfather is sick."

"Then Patrick should have a physician see him."

"He will. *You.*"

Nathan strode toward a cabinet and withdrew another large bowl, placed it on the table, and then poured sugar into it, along with other ingredients. After he added the flour, he began stirring the cake mixture, his features set in granite.

Sarah stamped her foot. "Nathan Stuart, don't you ignore me."

"If you two will excuse me…" Remembering squabbles she'd had with her siblings, Rachel sidestepped toward the door of the bedchamber.

Nathan trapped her with an intense gaze, burning with suppressed anger. "Stay. I promised I would show you how to make a cake."

"But—" The protest died in Rachel's throat. From across the room, Nathan's distress beckoned to her. She wouldn't leave if he wanted her to stay. She owed him that much.

Nathan swung toward his sister. "Sarah, you are welcome to stay and enjoy a piece of cake when 'tis ready, but if you do, not another word about Grandfather."

"You are as bad as he is. We are a family, whether you two want to acknowledge that or not. You used to follow him everywhere and hang on his every word. How can you turn your back on him?"

His jaw clamped shut, a muscle in his cheek twitching. "I didn't throw him off my land nor threaten him at gunpoint. When I returned from the war, I wanted to mend the rift between us, but obviously he didn't."

"Please go see him. He can be stubborn but—"

"It will not do any good." Nathan picked up some patty pans and buttered them.

His sister threw her hands up. "Men and their pride." She turned toward Rachel. "Perhaps you can talk some sense into him. I give up."

"I have found it is hard for some men to admit they may be wrong. Pride is a convenient excuse for them." Rachel shifted her sleeping baby in her arms. "I need to put Faith down."

Sarah removed her hat. "I will come with you."

* * * * *

The women disappeared into his bedchamber. Nathan poured the batter into the pans and put them into the brick oven next to the fireplace then checked on the rising bread dough. He quaked from trying to hold in his intense emotions. They demanded release.

Sarah was asking too much of him. He had loved his grandfather, but the stubborn old man had turned him away from Pinecrest merely because he had not wanted to be a planter but a physician. He had tried to do his duty to the family and take his father's place after he died, but his heart had not been in it, especially when his grandfather sent his mother away.

He listened to his sister and Rachel chattering in the other room as though everything were normal. It was not. Guilt ate at him, just as Sarah knew it would. Even though his grandfather wanted nothing to do with him, he knew he would end up at Pinecrest. As much as he wished he could turn his back on his grandfather, he could not.

The walls of his cabin pressed in on him. He strode to the door and stepped outside. To the left, near the stream and down the slope, Maddy labored to wash the clothes. Sarah's driver strolled toward Rachel's maid and spoke to her. Maddy smiled up at Moses, a husky, muscular black man in his late thirties who had been working for the McNeal family most of his life. Trustworthy and protective of Sarah. His brother-in-law would not let her gallivant all over the countryside without Moses. But knowing his sister, she probably did not inform John that she had left Charleston.

Stubborn women. That described his sister—and Rachel.

* * * * *

The sun beat down upon Nathan as he rode toward Pinecrest. Nearing his childhood home, he spurred his horse faster. He did not want to be away from Rachel, Faith, and Maddy too long. They were safe on his land, next to Liberty Hall, because no one would cross John McNeal, but Nathan hated leaving them alone. When Sarah had invited Rachel to stay at Liberty Hall while he was gone, he had tried to persuade her to go, but she had insisted on staying where she was and practicing what he had taught her. He hoped not to be gone long—certainly not overnight. He wasn't even sure his grandfather would let him inside.

The large, two-story house loomed before him. He paused at the edge of the forest that surrounded his childhood home. Sunlight made the bricks seem as though they were on fire. The veranda, with tall white columns standing sentinel, ran the length of the front of the house. A once lush garden on the left remained a jungle because only his mother had kept it up. When she had left and gone back to her family in England five years before, his grandfather had ignored the myriad flowers as he had refused to mention Nathan's mother's name. That was the beginning of the end of his relationship with his grandfather.

Determinedly shutting the lid on his memories, Nathan prodded his horse forward. Dread encased him in a fine sheen of sweat. When he mounted the steps to the front door, he almost spun on his boot heel and left. But he had ridden for over an hour to appease his sister and to reassure her—no, himself—that his grandfather was as healthy as he had always been.

Patrick opened the door before Nathan had a chance to knock. "I saw you coming from the bedchamber window upstairs."

"His room?"

"Yes, I haven't wanted to leave his side."

Nathan studied his younger brother's unshaven face. His brown eyes were dull, his blond hair a mess, as if he had run his hand through it again and again. "You are worried?"

Patrick nodded. "He hasn't eaten in days. He has a fever. He sleeps most of the time. Grandfather is usually up with the sun and does not go to bed until well after the sun has gone down."

"Has he seen a doctor?"

"Dr. Ellsworth came the other day and bled him. Grandfather has gotten worse since the doctor left. He has little strength even to talk when he is awake. I don't want that quack seeing him again."

"I will see what I can do, but I may not be able to help him. He is seventy-five years old." It wasn't until he said his grandfather's age out loud that Nathan realized how old he really was. Grandfather had always been so invincible to Nathan. The thought that he wasn't did not settle well with him. It would be so much easier if he could hate the old man—less painful. But snippets of his past always intruded. The time Grandfather taught him how to fish. Or the first time he rode with Grandfather across Pinecrest land.

"Please take a look at him." Patrick, five years younger than Nathan, headed for the stairs.

"He may not see me."

"You have to try. I don't know what else to do."

The plea in Patrick's eyes scared him. Perhaps this was worse than he thought. A world without his grandfather seemed inconceivable, even if the old man wasn't talking to him. "Fine. I will do what he will allow me to do."

He followed Patrick to their grandfather's bedchamber. The drapes were open and light poured into the room, but the air smelled of sickness. Nathan took one look at the shrunken figure in the large bed, and his worry intensified. There was not anything invincible about the man lying there, still, his eyes closed. Lines of age carved deep into his grandfather's craggy features, almost all the color gone from his face.

Nathan inhaled a deep breath to ease the contraction about his chest. He moved to the bed and put his bag of medicines on the table next to it.

When he lifted his grandfather's hand, the old man's eyes fluttered open. For a moment he did not seem to recognize Nathan. Then a light dawned in his eyes. He slipped his fingers from Nathan's grasp. The action only increased Nathan's concern. In the past his grandfather would have yanked his hand away, with anger immediately invading his expression. The frown finally appeared, but slowly, as though Grandfather did not have the strength to be fully mad at him.

"Leave," his grandfather whispered, a touch of fury behind the one weak-sounding word.

"I will leave when you can get up and make me."

The old man tried to rise and fell back the few inches he had managed. "I will—soon." Coughs racked his body.

Nathan laid his palm on his grandfather's forehead. Heat burned into his hand. "As soon as I get you well, you can personally throw me off this land."

The old man's eyes closed, and he did not reply to the challenge. That worried him more than anything else. His grandfather never let anyone get the last word in, especially his disowned grandson. Nathan went to his bag and searched for the chamomile and feverfew. As he treated Grandfather, the powerlessness he had experienced in the war when caring for wounded soldiers mantled his shoulders as if hundreds of pounds pressed down on him.

His hands shook as memories assaulted him. The echoes of the soldiers' screams rang in his mind like a death toll. He had tried to help many men—some lived, more died. He had become a physician to save lives and ease the suffering. He had failed with his father and Eliza and her child. The sense that he could not help them had been confirmed during the war.

Nathan assisted his grandfather to sit up so he could sip the brew he had mixed for him. Nathan's determination hardened. He had already lost too many people he cared about. He would not lose his grandfather.

Five

A knock sounded at the cabin door. Rachel jumped and gasped. Maddy's eyes widened, and she scanned the main room as if she were searching for a place to hide. As Rachel moved toward the front window to see if she could spy who was outside, another rap filled the cabin. Although the noise was not that loud, Faith started crying in the other room.

"I will get the baby." Maddy scurried into the bedchamber.

Rachel peeked outside and glimpsed a tall, thin man, dressed in black pantaloons and tailcoat with a tan vest and boots. He reminded her of a gentleman she would have seen on the streets of London. Beneath his black top hat that partially shadowed his face, she saw a strong jawline and a cleft in this stranger's chin. Both features reminded her of Nathan.

His brother?

When the man turned away to leave, she caught a better look at his face—a kind one that resembled her benefactor. *Is something wrong*? She hastened to the door and opened it when the man was halfway to his carriage.

"May I help you?" she asked in a breathless rush.

He swung around and faced her, removing his hat. "I'm Patrick Stuart, Nathan's brother. He has sent me to bring you to Pinecrest."

The solemn lines on his face prompted her to ask, "Is his grandfather well?"

"With my brother tending him, he will be. But Nathan cannot leave his side right now and he didn't want you to stay alone here overnight. I have brought the carriage." He waved his hand toward it on the road down the incline. "He told me you have a baby and a maid accompanying you."

"Yes, but we are perfectly fine here by ourselves." As she spoke, she took in the forest nearby with the dark shadows of evening beginning to lengthen over the terrain. A bird flew overhead, screeching, declaring her foolishness in remaining in a strange place with night approaching.

"I cannot leave you alone. Nathan would never forgive me if I did. Please. I'm worried about my grandfather and need to be at Pinecrest, but I will stay if you do."

The gentle threat made up Rachel's mind. "Very well. We shall go with you. Let me get Faith and Maddy."

"Thank you for understanding, Mrs. Gordon."

Thirty minutes later, Rachel sat beside Nathan's brother while in back Maddy held Faith, who had fed before they left and returned to sleep. "How far is Pinecrest?"

"An hour and a half by carriage."

While night settled over the landscape, lanterns on the sides of the chaise afforded some light. Apprehension blanketed Rachel as the dark did the forest. Nathan and his grandfather were estranged. She didn't feel comfortable going to his plantation, uninvited by the older man.

As Patrick handled the team of two horses pulling the carriage, he glanced her way. "Nathan explained your situation."

"I am indebted to your brother for helping me. I don't know what I would have done if he hadn't come along when he did."

"The Lord provides."

"Yes, He does." That was the only thing she had to count on at the moment. If she stopped to think about her future, fear took over. She could not afford that. Fear would weaken her, and she needed all her strength in the days to come.

By the time Patrick Stuart pulled up in front of a massive house, Rachel's shoulders slumped from the trip over a road rutted from the recent rains. Nathan's brother had apologized for the rough ride. Maddy had managed to keep Faith calm in the back, although once a large bump had aroused her daughter from sleep for a moment.

Mr. Stuart jumped down from the seat and assisted Rachel to the ground. Then, she took Faith from Maddy while he offered her maid his hand. Soft light streamed from the large house. The front door swung open, and Nathan came out, carrying a lantern, followed by a servant who took care of the horses and carriage.

"I was worried something might have happened to you all on the road." Nathan's gaze swept from Rachel to his brother. "No sign of trouble?"

"No. It took longer than I anticipated."

"Faith was hungry. I fed her before we started the journey." In the glow of the oil lamp, the sober lines on Nathan's countenance concerned Rachel. Was it his grandfather's health or something else that put that expression on his face?

"How is Grandfather?" Mr. Stuart carried in the bag of clothing Maddy had packed.

"He's sleeping more comfortably now. His breathing sounds better."

"Good." Nathan's brother paused on the threshold and shifted toward Rachel. "I will show you to your room."

She transferred Faith to Maddy. "I need to speak with Dr. Stuart. I will be there shortly."

As Maddy entered the house with Faith, Mr. Stuart peered back and said, "I am putting them in the Rose Suite."

Nathan nodded to his brother. When they were alone, he turned to Rachel. "Is there something wrong?"

"I was going to ask you that very question."

"I am perfectly fine and will be even better when I can get back to my home." As he said the last word, his gaze swept the façade of the house.

The brief longing she glimpsed in his eyes formed a bond between them. She wanted to go back home to Mansfield Manor, to talk with her mother about Faith, to feel her love, to listen to her advice about child rearing. But that was not going to happen. When Nathan returned his attention to her, all evidence of that look vanished, to be replaced with a stern one. "It didn't go well with your grandfather?"

"If you enjoy wrestling a bear, then everything went fine. The first word out of his mouth to me was 'leave.'" Although Nathan scowled, his tone conveyed more hurt than anger.

She laid her hand on his arm. "I am sorry about that. Obviously he changed his mind. You are here."

"Only because he didn't have the strength to personally kick me off his land."

"Is he letting you tend to him?"

"Yes. Barely. Fighting me as much as he can."

"Which is what concerns you?"

"He's not the man I saw six months ago."

"Perhaps your grandfather is like my papa. He is the worst patient. He does not want anyone to know if he isn't feeling well. He sees sickness as a sign of weakness."

"The same. Grandfather has never understood why healing people is important to me, and yet when a horse or one of his dogs becomes ill, he tends to them personally until they recover."

"Probably because you are not doing what he wanted." The same reason she was in this predicament right now. She refused to follow her father's plan for her future. She thought she knew best.

"Probably." He turned toward the front door still standing open. "Let's go in. I know it has been a long day for the both of us."

When she entered the house, the foyer spoke of the Stuart family's wealth. Highly polished wood gleamed in the soft lighting of the interior. The richly ornate carpet beneath her feet matched some of the ones she had seen in the houses of the peers of the realm. Portraits in gilded frames adorned the walls as she climbed the curving staircase to the second floor.

Nathan gestured toward the last picture at the top. "That's my father."

She paused and studied it for a moment. The young man had blond hair like Nathan's brother and sister and the same kind, dark brown eyes as well. His smile made her feel welcomed to Pinecrest.

She looked to the right at the one before his father's. "Is this your grandfather?"

"Yes."

The same kind eyes as his son's contradicted what she had heard about the man. What happened to change him? "When was this painted?"

"Each one was done when the eldest son was about thirty."

"How old are you?"

"Thirty-five."

"So yours should be up there."

"It had been commissioned when"—Nathan swallowed hard—"when my father died and everything changed."

The heaviness in her heart swelled into her throat. "It was not done?"

"No. I understand from Patrick that Grandfather has an artist coming next month to do his portrait. Patrick is now considered the eldest son." The sense it did not matter to him didn't carry over into the expression in his dark blue eyes.

"All you can do is offer your forgiveness. Perhaps, in time, he will see the wisdom in forgiving you."

"It has been nearly five years. I don't think time will make a difference, nor the fact that I forgave him years ago. He's a hard man who does not bend to anyone."

"Now you see why I cannot go home. My father and your grandfather have a lot in common."

"Come. You need your rest."

"You do not have lessons for me tomorrow, do you?" She infused humor into her voice, needing to lighten the mood.

"We may be home by afternoon." He started down a long hall-way, decreasing his pace in front of a door as he threw a glance toward it then picking his step back up. When he came to a halt at the far end, he faced her. "This is your room. I will be staying for the time being in my grandfather's." He gestured toward the door. "In case you need me."

"I will be fine. Don't worry about me."

"Thank you for coming. I couldn't leave you in the cabin by yourself overnight."

The softness in his look doubled her heartbeat. Seeing him after being apart all day uplifted her spirits, which immediately fright-ened her. In a very short time, she had come to care about this man who had saved her on the road. She shouldn't. "Well, you will have to leave me alone when I go to Dalton Farm."

A frown descended. "About that—"

She raised her palm to stop his words. "Don't. I will be going to my new home." Then she fumbled for the handle and quickly slipped into her suite of rooms. A fire blazed in the fireplace, Maddy rocking Faith in front of it as she sang a lullaby to her.

This bedchamber was so different from the one at Nathan's home. Its size alone rivaled the total size of the cabin. Heavy wine-colored draperies of damask were pulled closed over two large windows. Wallpaper with tiny roses covered the walls. A massive, four-poster bed of walnut dominated all the other pieces of furniture. Next to it sat a table with an oil lamp that made the room much brighter than candles, as though a dark shadow was not allowed in the bedcham-ber. A cozy warmth, which did not carry over into the rest of the house, suffused the area.

Maddy looked up and gave Rachel a huge smile. "Mr. Stuart told me he had a servant bring in a cradle and this rocking chair for us. Perhaps we can stay here for a while."

Rachel crossed to the bed and pressed her hand down into the softness of the mattress, the feel of the brocade coverlet luxurious beneath her fingertips. "Don't get used to this. We shall not be here long." But looking around the room only underscored her longing to go home to England.

* * * * *

"How is he?" Patrick came into the dark bedchamber, stopping next to Nathan beside their grandfather's bed.

"Better." The raspy sound of the old man's breathing mocked his words. "He's now sleeping well. I put a poultice on his chest that seems to help some."

"You need to sleep. I can stay with him. If he becomes worse, I will come get you."

"No, I cannot sleep." Although weariness dogged Nathan's every step, being home brought back too many bittersweet memories for him to rest.

Patrick pulled a nearby chair closer to the bed and sat. "I miss talking to you. I wish you and Grandfather would—"

"Patrick, if you stay, I prefer not discussing what happened five years ago. It will not change the facts."

"Have you ever tried to contact Mama?"

"Yes. The first year she was gone I wrote to her. I finally received a letter telling me that it was better she left before war broke out between our countries. She is English and wants to live in England."

"I wrote her, too, and received the same type of letter. It is as if with Papa's death and what Grandfather did, we don't exist to her anymore. How can she do that? I saw Mrs. Gordon holding her baby, and I just don't understand."

"I cannot answer that." A picture of his mother climbing into the carriage the day she left Pinecrest for good filled Nathan's heart with the deep ache he had felt at the time. She wouldn't listen to him when he pleaded for her to stay. She told him she wanted to go home to England, and now that her husband was dead, she finally could. It was not until later he had discovered that his grandfather had ordered her off the plantation. "I wish I had arrived at the dock before her ship sailed. I might have been able to do something about what occurred."

"Defy Grandfather?"

Nathan twisted toward his younger brother. "Yes. I ended up doing that anyway." The final incident with Eliza and her baby that had caused the rift completely to tear between Grandfather and him nudged forward in his mind. He shut it down lest he refuse to sit at the old man's bedside and nurse him back to health. "I could not stay at Pinecrest, knowing that he had sent our mother away. She was the mistress here. Our father had been buried the day before."

"What kind of man does that?"

A murderer. No, you shouldn't think that. He is your grandfather, your kin. This discussion has to end. "Tell me about the plantation. Do you like running Pinecrest?"

Patrick's face transformed into a smile that glinted in his dark brown eyes, so like their father's. "Yes. These past few weeks, with Grandfather not feeling well, I have been doing most of the managing. We are expanding our cotton fields. We will need more field hands. I'm going to Charleston to purchase ten more."

"Purchase?" Nathan sprang to his feet. "I thought you felt as I do about slavery."

"I do. I have convinced Grandfather to try a new way. I will pay the workers a wage, and they can buy their freedom. I wanted to give them their freedom, but Grandfather wouldn't listen to me. He did agree to this. I will keep an account for each slave, and then if they want to stay on and work here, they will continue to be paid a fair wage for their labor."

Nathan's tension melted away as he stared at his little brother, a man of thirty. This very issue had driven him and his grandfather apart, leading to Eliza and her child's death, and now Patrick had accomplished what he had tried to five years ago. "I'm glad one of us could make Grandfather see that owning slaves is wrong."

"I wish he had listened to you. He has mellowed with age. With both Sarah and you gone, I think he's lonely, but he will not admit it. He nags at me to find a wife and start a family before he dies."

"Not a bad idea. Have you met anyone?"

"I have been too busy to look for a wife. Once I get the new fields planted and this new system working, I plan to. Seeing Sarah with Sean and now expecting another baby makes me want a family."

Not me. Then he would be responsible for them, and if he lost them, what would be left for him? He didn't want to care for someone—not with all the people he had lost over the years, not with the fact his own mother would rather be in England than here with her family.

* * * * *

70

"There you are," Patrick Stuart said, approaching Rachel in the over-grown garden at the side of the house. "What are you doing out here?"

Rachel pointed at a bright red flower poking its way out of the wild greenery covering the ground. "Look. This plant is trying to live even though it is being choked out by the weeds." She bent and smelled its sweet fragrance. "Your mother had roses?"

"Yes, brought over from England. This one is blooming early. Usually I will see the flowers from it in late April."

"I hope at my farm I shall have a place for flowers. When I look at them, it gives me such hope. What beauty in a sometimes ugly world. At Mansfield Manor I used to spend hours in our gardens. Mama always knew where to find me if I wasn't in the house." She straightened. "How is your grandfather this morning?"

"Much better. I'm sorry you had to delay your plans for two days, but I believe Grandfather is recovering because of Nathan's presence."

"So he can throw him off the plantation?" Rachel asked with a smile. "At least that is what Nathan thinks."

"Partially that, but also because Nathan is a good physician. He pours everything into his patients. He's determined that Grandfather is not going to die, and he isn't—at least not from this illness." Mr. Stuart glanced around him. "We really need to do something about this garden."

"Nathan told me your grandfather did not want anyone to touch it."

"Perhaps I can change his mind. If I find a wife, she will not want such an eyesore of an untended garden staring at her whenever she comes outside. That ought to motivate my grandfather to do something."

"He wants you married?"

"Yes, so he knows his name will continue."

"What about Nathan?"

"I guess he doesn't think Nathan will ever marry. He may be right."

Mr. Stuart's statement bothered her. Rachel didn't want to marry again either, but that was because she had once. Nathan had never wed. Perhaps marriage would agree with him even though it did not with her. "What has brought you out here?"

"You."

She lifted her head and looked up into his dark brown eyes. "Me? Why?"

"'Tis time to break the fast, and Nathan is going to join us this morning." He offered her his arm.

Rachel slipped her arm in his. "I was beginning to wonder if he had left Pinecrest after that first night."

"You have kept yourself entertained?"

"Yes, I have been pestering your cook. She has shown me some of the dishes she prepares. I even walked to the stable to ask some questions of your workers."

"Good. I don't think Nathan would have stayed if you had not agreed to come to Pinecrest." Mr. Stuart strolled with her toward the veranda.

"I have enjoyed myself, but it is time for me to go to Dalton Farm."

After opening the front door, he swept his arm across his body, indicating she should go in first. "I have a gift for you to take with you."

"I cannot take a gift from you."

He crossed the large foyer to the dining room. "I am sending

Amos to repair your cart. You will need one. Nathan said one of the wheels on yours is broken. Amos can replace it."

Rachel opened her mouth to refuse the help but realized she was not in a position to decline someone repairing her cart. "Thank you." Now if it were only possible for her to find her horse. If not, she would have to use her meager coins to buy an animal for the cart and a plow that one of Mr. Stuart's workers showed her needed to be used for the fields.

She moved into the room and picked up a china plate to serve herself at the sideboard. The aromas from buckwheat cakes, cold bread, sausages, and mush whetted her appetite. As she took a chair, Nathan appeared in the entrance. His gaze snagged hers and held it. Dark shadows under his eyes attested to the long hours he had spent at his grandfather's bedside. One corner of his mouth lifted, his look sparkling to life.

"I'm starved." Nathan filled his plate with a taste of every food laid out for their pleasure. When he sat across from Rachel, he asked, "Have you been resting well?"

She nodded. "Mostly."

"Mostly?"

"I learned how to make Johnny cakes, and this mush is my contribution to the meal."

"You cooked?" Nathan glanced toward his brother. "I told you she needed to rest. It hasn't even been a week since she delivered her baby."

"'Tis clear you have not tried to stop her from doing as she intends." Mr. Stuart waited until the young black girl filled his cup with tea then took a sip.

The servant poured tea for Rachel too. Steam wafted from her drink, the heat rivaling the look Nathan shot his younger brother. "I am most reasonable when it is warranted."

Mr. Stuart chuckled. "You see what I had to deal with."

Nathan lowered his head and took a bite of his buckwheat cakes.

Rachel sipped her tea while waiting for the men to sample her mush. Finally, after Nathan ate all his cakes and sausage, he dipped a spoon into the creation she'd made by herself while the cook went about her usual duties. When Nathan slid the utensil between his lips, she held her breath. It was a simple recipe the cook had said would be hard to mess up.

With his mouth puckering and his eyes watering, Nathan gulped down the bite and quickly followed it with several large swallows of tea. He coughed and drank some more.

"What is wrong?" Rachel peered from Nathan to his brother, who placed his spoonful of mush back onto his plate.

"Salt. How much did you put in this?" Nathan asked in a strained voice.

"Cook said to salt to taste. It was bland, so I thought it would need a lot." Rachel took a small taste of the mush, lumps and all, not completely prepared for the salty assault on her tongue. Tears, more from her failure than the salt, glistened in her eyes, making Nathan's image blurry. "I am sorry. Next time I will add only a pinch or two." *Not a palm full.* "One pinch did not seem to do anything."

"Perhaps you should stay a little longer so the cook can instruct you again." Mr. Stuart finished his meal, all except the mush.

Nathan yanked his head up. "Grandfather is on the mend. Staying longer will not set well with him."

"Nonsense. He has tolerated you." Patrick snapped his mouth closed, his gaze glued to the entrance into the dining room.

Rachel swiveled her attention to the older man with long white hair standing in the doorway, his shoulders slumped over, his hands clutching a cane. His dark eyes full of thunder.

"There is a young English girl upstairs with a baby. What is she doing in my house?" Nathan's grandfather's gaze zeroed in on Rachel, hard, relentless. "Who are you?"

"I am Rachel Gordon."

"Are you with that English girl?"

She nodded, her throat going dry as he drilled his gaze into hers.

"I told her to pack her bag and get off my land. The English are not welcome here."

Nathan bolted to his feet, knocking his chair over. The crash reverberated through the room. "We are leaving."

His grandfather directed his fury at Nathan. "You brought them here? You know how I feel about the English."

"I brought Rachel here. The war is over, Grandfather." Nathan's brother rose and rushed to his side to assist him to a chair.

The old man shook off his help. "Makes no difference to me. All English are a murdering, lying bunch." He raised his cane toward Rachel. "Get off my land."

Nathan grabbed the carved wooden weapon as his grandfather waved it in the air and stilled its movement. "We are going. I can see you don't need my help any longer."

"Never did." Mr. Stuart's eyes narrowed to slits, with his mouth set in a determined slash. He wrenched the cane from Nathan's grasp and hobbled toward the head of the table.

The older man's hatred shuddered down Rachel's length. She pushed to her feet, her legs trembling so badly she wasn't sure she would make it out of the room. Nathan clasped her arm and led her into the foyer. She wanted to lean into him for support, but as energy surged through her limbs, she stepped away from him.

I am not Nathan's problem.

Fear underlining her features, Maddy descended the stairs, with Faith cradled in one arm and carrying a bag with the other.

Rachel hurried to her maid and took her daughter, hugging Faith to her while loud voices boomed from the dining room. Without a backward glance, she spun around and headed for the front entrance. If she had to walk, she would leave Pinecrest now. Quaking, she clasped her daughter tighter against her to keep from dropping her.

Maddy kept pace with her. "Are we leaving, ma'am?"

"Yes." At the door she looked back at Nathan.

A war raged on his face—regret quickly evolving into anger. "Go to the stable. I will be there shortly." Then he turned on his heel and marched back into the dining room.

Rachel didn't wait to hear his exchange with his grandfather. The older man's fury reminded her of her father's when he heard about her marriage to Tom. But this time she had done nothing but be born an Englishwoman.

* * * * *

Nathan sat in front of the fireplace, staring at the flames devouring the logs. For a few minutes the mesmerizing blaze lured his thoughts away from what had happened that morning at Pinecrest. Until he saw Rachel standing in the doorway to the bedchamber. He did not want to have this conversation with her, but he glimpsed determination in her expression. Sighing, he leaned against the hard back of the chair.

"I wish I had not accepted your brother's invitation to stay at Pinecrest." Rachel moved toward the other chair in front of the fireplace and eased onto its wooden seat. "When you talked about your grandfather, I didn't understand the extent of his hatred toward the English."

"I apologize for how he treated you. What happened to our family was thirty-seven years ago. You had nothing to do with it. He has become unreasonable in his old age, and I told him that this morning." His grandfather's anger still gripped Nathan, coiling his gut into a hard knot.

"Does he know that Amos came to fix the cart?"

"No. Patrick insisted Amos come in spite of how Grandfather felt."

"What if he finds out about Amos? Will Amos get in trouble?" Rachel entwined her hands so tightly her knuckles whitened.

"He will not find out. When I left the house, Patrick was helping Grandfather back to his bedchamber. His outburst sapped his energy."

"Is he all right?"

Nathan bolted to his feet. "You are worried about a man who threw you off his land because you were born in England."

"He is your grandfather, and you have done so much for me."

One corner of his mouth quirked up. "It probably didn't help that you were with me."

"But you stayed by his side and nursed him for two days. Surely that meant something to him."

The fury he had faced this morning in the dining room told him otherwise. "I prefer not to discuss my grandfather anymore. It will not change his mind about how he feels about me."

"Then could you tell me when Faith should start eating solid food? She is constantly nursing. Is that normal? Is that…" She gasped, her hand to her mouth. "I should not have asked you that. I know you are a doctor, but…" Her strangled voice came to a halt.

Nathan couldn't tell if it was embarrassment or the heat from the fire flushing her cheeks—or both. He compressed his lips to still a smile. "I don't know. I realize that some physicians are delivering babies more and more, but I am afraid my experience is limited to older patients. Mostly soldiers and their ailments and wounds."

"I am sure I shall figure it out." Her expression full of doubt, Rachel yawned. "It has been a long day, and tomorrow will be another one, with you taking me to my farm." Rising, she gave him a smile. "I cannot thank you enough for helping me these past five days. Good night."

Nathan watched her disappear into the other room, the words he needed to say to her on the tip of his tongue. But he couldn't tell her he was not going to take her to her land tomorrow. He had one last thing he would try to talk her out of staying at Dalton Farm. If that did not work, he didn't know what he was going to do.

Turning back to the blaze, he stared at the yellow and orange flames. An idea began to take shape in his mind. Perhaps he should write her family in England and tell them of her plight. He gathered his writing supplies and sat in front of the fire to do just that.

When he finished, a restlessness still claimed him. He paced the main room, trying to figure out what else was nagging him. Bits and pieces of his conversation with Patrick infiltrated his mind. It had been five years since he had written his mother in England. Even if she wanted nothing to do with her children, he was going to write her a letter to let her know what was happening to them. He was not doing it for his mother but for himself. This sense of abandonment overcame him every time he thought about her. The same feeling he glimpsed in Rachel.

Is that why I cannot leave her at the farm and walk away?

Six

"I don't understand why you cannot take me to my farm today," Rachel said, cradling Faith close to her while she sat on the cart seat next to Nathan. He was so near his arm continually brushed hers as he held the reins. Perhaps she should have brought Maddy with her instead of traveling alone with Nathan, but this morning her maid had wanted to try to follow Pinecrest's cook's instruction on how to make tallow candles.

"I thought you might like to talk with my sister about raising babies."

"This is about that question I asked you last night, is it not?" Rachel stared at his strong hands clasping the leather straps and remembered again those same hands covering hers and pressing them into the dough. The memory bombarded her with a finely honed awareness of the man beside her.

Nathan tightened his grip on the reins. "My experience as a doctor has mainly been on the battlefield."

"Not the nursery?" She wanted to take his hands into hers and knead the tension from them. Ever since they had returned from Pinecrest, he had been wound so tightly, withdrawing into a place deep inside him.

"Right. I have absolutely no experience raising children. Sarah should know when to start Faith on solid foods and anything else you need to know." He guided the cart off the road onto a lane.

Through the pine trees Rachel glimpsed a red brick house much like Pinecrest except that this place exuded warmth. A profusion of flowers softened the exterior and welcomed visitors. Rachel immediately thought of her family estate in England. The beat of her heart slowed to a throbbing ache. She missed her sister and two brothers. She missed her parents and wished she were going to her mother for advice about babies, not a woman who was practically a stranger.

"Then you will take me to the farm tomorrow?"

"Look, my sister is outside in her garden. She takes after my mother and loves to spend time among her flowers." Nathan urged the horse to a faster pace and brought the cart to a stop near his sister.

Sarah got to her feet, removing her straw hat and wiping her brow with the back of her hand. "I must be seeing things. That is the only way to account for me seeing my big brother three times in a week."

Smiling, Nathan jumped down from the cart. He reached to take Faith. "Come over here and be useful, Sarah." After giving the baby to his sister, he placed his hands about Rachel's waist to help her down.

The moment he touched Rachel her pulse began to pound and her mouth went dry. She stared into his eyes, her throat closing at the gentle look he gave her. So different from Tom. When he set her on the ground, his hands lingered about her, his gaze still bound to hers. She became lost in his blue eyes, like the sky as evening approached, and for a moment no one else existed.

Sarah coughed. Instantly Rachel pulled back from Nathan, averting her look while disappointment took hold of her. She missed the feel of his hands on her waist, the sense of security she felt with him near.

Rachel took Faith from Sarah and bent to coo at her daughter. Embarrassment burned her cheeks when she caught the speculative gleam in Sarah's eyes.

"Did everything go all right at Pinecrest? You have not come to tell me bad news, have you?" Sarah angled her straw hat back on her head.

"I didn't say I was going."

"I know you, Nathan. You went. In spite of what has happened between you two, you still love Grandfather."

"But that's not enough," Nathan murmured, almost to himself. "I would say our grandfather is getting better. He had enough strength to throw me off his land yesterday. I think my presence inspired him to get well so he could do just that."

Rachel heard the hurt in Nathan's voice and wanted to comfort him as he had her. But his closed look pushed everyone away, even his sister. "He threw *us* out of the house."

Sarah swept around toward Rachel. "You were at Pinecrest, and my grandfather asked you to leave?"

"The moment he discovered I had recently come over from England."

"Our family was originally from Scotland. There's no particular love lost between my family and the English, but what really caused my grandfather to hate your country was his brother and eldest son were killed by the English soldiers in the Revolutionary War. Ever since our father died, Grandfather has grown worse in his hatred of the English." Sarah returned her attention to Nathan. "How is Patrick doing?"

"Trying to run the plantation and take care of an old man who does not want to be taken care of."

"I know it wasn't easy to go see Grandfather, but I feel better knowing he's all right now. He can be difficult, but he is family."

With a frown, Nathan folded his arms over his chest. "I need to see John. Where is he?"

"At the stable. By the way, Rachel, a horse was found loose on our land two days ago. Do you think it is your horse that ran off?"

"I hope so. Amos fixed my cart, but I don't have an animal to pull it."

Sarah smiled. "Then the gelding is yours."

Nathan's eyebrows slashed downward. "But you don't know if the horse is Rachel's."

His sister waved her hand in the air. "I will have John bring the animal up to the house for Rachel to look at. I am sure it is."

"I will leave you two to chat." Still frowning, Nathan nodded to the women then strode across the lawn.

Rachel watched him walk away, his strides as purposeful as everything he did. His movements were precise, economical. Over the past few days she had found herself watching him more and more—and liking what she saw. But then, Tom had fooled her before they had married. How could she ever trust her judgment again after being hurt so badly by Tom?

Sarah's touch on her arm jolted Rachel out of her musings. "Let me get you and Faith inside, out of this sun. It can be beastly."

"I get the distinct impression your brother does not want me to go to my new home."

"I have never been to Dalton Farm, but I understand it will require much hard work."

"I'm not afraid of hard work." *What choice do I have?*

"Good, because life on a plantation or farm is full of hard work. John wants me to slow down because I am with child, but there is just too much to do." Sarah stopped under a large live oak, dripping with grayish-green tresses. "You might consider exchanging your horse for an ox. We could use another horse and in return give you one of our oxen."

"Why?"

"An ox would be better pulling a plow than a horse. It can also pull your cart. Oxen are slow but steady and have more endurance than horses."

"How do you know so much about this?"

"John. He wants me to know as much as possible about how to run the plantation in case something were ever to happen to him. We have a good overseer, but I was in charge when John went to war."

There was so much for her to learn, but Sarah gave her hope. "Then an ox it will be."

Nathan's sister started toward the house. "Good. I feel much better knowing you will not have to deal with a skittish horse that left you in such a predicament last week."

Rachel strolled next to Sarah into the coolness of the house.

In the parlor Sarah indicated a sofa for Rachel to sit. "I need to check on my son."

After Sarah left, Rachel inspected the room. A sense of welcoming warmth permeated the parlor, from its blue brocade sofa and chairs to its yellow accents. Sunlight poured into the room from two large floor-to-ceiling windows with blue velvet draperies. The wooden floor was polished to a gleaming sheen and covered partially by an ornate blue and gold rug.

Sarah returned. "I have asked Bella to bring Sean down as soon as he is up from his nap."

"How old is he?"

"Three, and into everything. He gave us a terrible fright this morning when he climbed on top of the chest of drawers in the nursery. He wanted to jump down. Thank goodness, Bella, his nanny, reached him before he leaped."

"So I have that to look forward to."

Sarah laughed. "I hope not. I am praying my next one is not quite as adventurous as Sean. He takes after his father." She placed her hand over her stomach.

"How many more months until your new baby is here?"

Sarah's look softened. "Too long. Four months. I think John is more eager than I am."

A memory flashed into Rachel's thoughts. She had been so excited to share the news of expecting a child with Tom. That feeling had died quickly. Now all she remembered was Tom's anger when he had discovered she was going to have a baby, his disgust at her shape as she had grown big with child.

"I know Nathan wanted to see John, but I have the feeling there is more to this visit than that."

Rachel glanced down at Faith still sleeping in her arms. "Nathan thought you could help me. I have a few questions about raising children."

"I will try, but with Sean, it has been trial and error. Sometimes more errors than I care to admit. 'Tis times like this when you wish you had a mother around to ask. Alas, that is not possible for me or you."

"No." But that didn't keep her from wishing it were so. Rachel leaned back on the sofa. Seeing Sarah made her miss her own sister all the more. "When do you start feeding solid food to your baby? Faith wants to nurse all the time."

Sarah smiled. "It was the same with Sean. He has quite an appetite even now."

A noise in the hall drew Sarah's attention. A little boy with dark hair and sparkling eyes came running into the parlor. He flung himself at his mother, his chubby arms squeezing her, laughter sprinkling the air.

"This is Sean." The boy climbed up onto his mother's lap, and Sarah kissed him.

Rachel's heart swelled. She wanted more children. She had dreamed of having a house full, but that didn't seem possible now. She would have to content herself with learning to take care of herself and Faith and never be beholden to another.

"As you can see he is quite exuberant." Sarah's chuckles assuaged the anxiety taking root in Rachel.

* * * * *

"Do you need any help?" Nathan swung the stall door open and entered.

John looked up from checking over the foal. "No, I think everything is fine here. I didn't realize you were coming by today."

"I wanted Rachel to spend some time with Sarah."

"This sounds serious."

"Not for me."

His brother-in-law stared at him long and hard. "Of course not," he murmured, then he stepped over to the mare and began inspecting her.

"Married life might be good for you, but that does not mean it is for everyone."

John glanced up. "Who said anything about marriage?"

"What Rachel needs is to return to her family in England." *Like my mother has.*

"I gather Rachel does not feel that way," John said with a chuckle.

"No." Nathan plowed his hand through his hair, picturing the woman who came to within inches of his height, her long hair hanging loose beneath her cap, her brown eyes dark with the emotions she did not hide well from others. "She is one stubborn lady."

John continued his inspection of the mare, his hands running down her hind legs. "You have discussed it with her?"

"What, that she is stubborn or that she does not want to go back to England?"

His brother-in-law stared straight into his eyes. "I think you know."

"I tried to, but she refused to talk much about her family other than they disowned her when she eloped with her husband."

"So you have something in common with the woman."

"Believe me, that is all."

Again John's sharp gaze sought Nathan's. "Then why are you helping her?"

"Because I can." He could remember all the times he'd had to stand by helplessly and watch a man die because there was nothing he could do about it. He did not want to feel that way ever again.

"I'm not talking about delivering her baby. I'm talking about having her stay with you. Not something a recluse does."

Nathan shifted his weight, uncomfortable under the perusal of his former commander. "I could not turn her out to fend for herself and still live with myself."

"No, but she could have come here. Did you offer her that option? You know we would never turn anyone away in need."

Nathan remained silent, his jaw clamped shut.

After a long silence, John sighed. "No more about this woman. Did you search me out for a reason?"

"I want you to post these letters for me." Nathan withdrew the two sheets of paper he had sat up half the night trying to compose to Rachel's parents and to his mother.

John peered at the top letter. "Going against her wishes?"

"Someone has to look out for her."

"So you have become her guardian."

"I'm no one's guardian. I want them to come for her before something bad happens."

"You almost sound desperate."

"I am. Would you be able to take her to Dalton Farm and leave her?"

"No." John's brow furrowed. "What are you going to do?"

"That is the problem. Perhaps she could live here after all, since I know she cannot live with me, even with her maid." The thought of her leaving his cabin should have brought relief. Instead, disappointment washed over him. That realization unnerved him more than anything.

"Knowing Sarah, she will try to convince her to stay with us. Is that why you brought her here?"

"I woke up last night in a cold sweat just thinking about her at the farm with just Faith and her maid. She wanted to go there today." Nathan paced the length of the stall, the sense of being trapped engulfing him. "Will you post the letters?"

"I will be going to town in a couple of days. I will do your bidding." John shuffled the bottom letter to the top. His eyes widened when he saw to whom it was addressed. "Does Sarah know you wrote your mother?"

"No, and I would like to keep this between us. I know how she feels about what happened five years ago. I will not add to her distress."

"Then why did you write your mother?"

"After talking with Patrick, I felt I had to try one more time to understand why she walked out on us." *I need to find out why she abandoned us.*

"I don't like keeping secrets from Sarah, but I will not add any stress to her, especially since she is with child. I cannot take the chance of something happening to her. She almost died giving birth to Sean. I often wonder if my being away fighting during the war had something to do with that."

Nathan knew the dangers of childbirth for both the woman and the baby. Like John, he didn't know what he would do if he lost Sarah. The difficulty with Rachel's delivery only reinforced that. She could have died along with Faith if he had not been there to help.

John straightened. "Let's join the ladies. I want to get to know this woman who has you so agitated."

Nathan started to deny his brother-in-law's last comment then realized it was true. He didn't want to feel responsible for another human being, and yet he did for Rachel and Faith, even Maddy. Somehow he had to convince Rachel to stay with Sarah until someone from her family came for her. Since it would be months until they did, there was no way she and Faith could stay with him at his cabin.

* * * * *

Rachel heard voices speaking as if they were in the middle of a fog as thick as she had seen on the moors. Slowly she surfaced from sleep. *Who's talking?* Then her mind flooded with memories of the past year—Tom's coldness, the ship voyage, the birth of her daughter— and she came awake with a start.

Rachel shot up straight in the chair, glancing around her at Sarah and Nathan on the sofa across from her. Warmth singed her cheeks. She smoothed the loose strands of her hair back from her face. "I am so sorry. I must be more exhausted than I thought. I have never done something like this before."

Nathan's eyebrow rose. "Sleep when you are tired?"

"I usually manage to stay awake for a conversation."

Nathan drilled his gaze into her. "What are you going to do when you are by yourself and so tired that you cannot stay awake, but there are still chores that must be done?"

The heat in her cheeks quickly flamed with anger. For half the day Nathan had been trying to convince her to stay with Sarah. In the past hour he had been trying to convince her at least to stay at his cabin. The prospect of staying at Liberty Hall was tempting, but she would not impose on the McNeals. And the idea of staying with Nathan past the next day frightened her. She did not like where her thoughts strayed concerning him, especially staying in such close proximity.

She could not become dependent on him any more than she already was. The sooner she moved on with her life the sooner she would learn to depend on only herself. Since her family had disowned her, she and Faith were alone in the world. She even felt responsible for Maddy—only eighteen, with few skills to offer another family. She was all Faith and Maddy had. She could not depend on someone else, because like Tom, that person might not stay around.

Only the Lord stayed—didn't abandon a person. "I am grateful for what you have done: however—"

Nathan surged to his feet. "What if I refuse to take you to Dalton Farm?"

Rachel stiffened, her hands fisted in her lap.

Sarah rose, sending her a fragile smile. "Now that you are awake, I will have some tea brought in and see where that husband of mine has gone."

The moment Sarah left the room and the door clicked closed, Rachel stood on trembling legs. She kept her hands curled at her sides. "Are you refusing to take me?"

"No gentleman would take you and leave you there." He covered the space between them, towering over her like a warrior preparing to do battle.

"No gentleman goes back on his word. You promised me you would." She raised her chin and stared up into his ice-hardened eyes.

"I was wrong to promise you."

"But you did."

The air vibrated with anger. His gaze bore into her with an intensity that robbed her of her next breath. The hammering of her heart thundered in her ears. She would not back down in front of him even though his fury overwhelmed her. "If I have to, I will walk to the farm."

He pivoted away, muttering something under his breath she could not hear. "Did anyone ever tell you that you are stubborn?"

"No, this is a newly acquired skill."

He slanted her an intense look that made her pulse beat even faster. "Are you saying I bring out the—"

"The best in me? Why, I do believe you do."

He paced a path from the sofa to the fireplace then back again. Halting in front of Rachel, he took hold of her arms and said, "Marry me then."

Intensity flowed from him and wrapped about her, threatening to steal her next breath. Stunned, a weakness attacking every limb, she swayed toward him. His grasp tightened on her. "I'm sure I didn't hear you right."

"Yes, you did."

For one fleeting moment the idea appealed to her. So many of her problems would be solved, and yet she never... "Do you love me?"

His eyes widened. "No. Love has nothing to do with this. I would never be able to forgive myself if something happened to you or Faith because I left you alone at the farm. With no man to protect you."

Many marriages were arranged, loveless matches. When she had married Tom, she had thought she had escaped that fate—only to find she hadn't and in the process had given up her family. She yanked herself free and backed away, her hands opening and closing at her sides. She placed the sofa between them, needing the distance to think coherently. "I am *not* your responsibility. Do I make myself perfectly clear? I don't want you caring for me. I had a husband once to do that." She could live without Tom's example of taking care of her. *Marriage is not for me.*

"But I have been caring for you."

"Beyond what you have already done for me. I owe you too much as it is."

"Pride will not feed you. Pride will not protect you. Pride will not keep you warm at night."

Rachel gasped. He wasn't implying—

"Even though 'tis spring, the nights are still cold."

"I do not need you to…" Her words faded into the silence as a picture of Nathan kissing her flirted with her thoughts. Suddenly the parlor seemed stuffy, suffocating.

"To chop wood for you?"

Flustered, she stammered out, "Yes. I am sure I can learn how. All you do is take an ax and swing it. I have seen you do it."

His laugh held no humor. "I will remember what you have said when you try."

Rachel gripped the back of the sofa, fingernails digging into the brocade material. She did not want to feel, not even this anger. Her emotions were what had gotten her into this mess in the first place. If she hadn't thought herself in love with Tom, she would be with her family right now. She raised her chin and looked Nathan directly in the eye. "You will not be around to see me do anything or not do anything."

"Yes, I will. The only way I will take you to the farm is if you let me stay and help you get settled."

"No!" The very idea of Nathan being nearby sent her heartbeat slamming against her chest. The heat in the room soared, perspiration coating her upper lip.

"Why not?" he asked in a lethally quiet voice that should have warned her of the man's own suppressed fury.

"Because—because I have to do this myself."

"What are you afraid of?"

Rachel stared into his stony features and felt as though she had hit a brick wall. She was tired of fighting, tired of not knowing what to do. She spun around, her back to him, as she stared out the window that afforded her a view of the front lawn. "Nothing." She didn't want him to see the fear she knew was stamped on her face. It would only confirm in his mind that she needed help—needed him.

Suddenly he appeared in front of her, his movements so silent she hadn't heard him approach. Startled, she stepped away and hit the back of the sofa. Trapped against him and a piece of furniture, she scoured the room for a way to escape.

"If you believe that, Rachel, then you are not only lying to me but yourself as well." So close his breath seared her face.

She wanted him to understand. She didn't have the strength to keep fighting him while trying to survive in this strange land. "I have to be able to do things for myself. All my life I have depended on others, and look what has happened. I have been stranded in a foreign country with little money and a deed to a piece of property, most of it swampland. I am ill-equipped to take care of myself now when I must."

"That's my point exactly. You—"

She lifted her hand to halt his words. "I have to start somewhere, or nothing will ever change. I have decided to start here and now." She stamped her foot. "I cannot stay with your sister, and I cannot stay with you at your cabin."

He cupped her face between his palms, his work-roughened hands warm against her cheeks. "I cannot let you do this alone. It goes against everything I am. I have to be able to live with myself. I need to make sure you will be all right. Let me stay with you at Dalton Farm. Help you. Teach you everything you need to know to run the farm. Then I will leave. I promise."

The pain that laced his voice ripped at her composure. Rachel clutched the back of the sofa to steady herself and to keep herself from leaning into him and offering solace. She was so aware of the man inches from her that she could hardly breathe. Every time she did she inhaled his scent of horse and the outdoors.

"How long will you stay?" She could not add to this man's pain, not after what he had done for her and Faith.

"Until you are settled in. Know what you are doing. A month. Perhaps longer."

"If I am going to live here, I cannot have people talking about us."

"You should have a farmhand. I will be that person and stay in the barn. That should take care of any talk. Besides, Maddy will be with you. You have to have someone help you with the spring planting at the very least."

"But you are a doctor, not a farmhand."

"I worked under my grandfather to learn how to run Pinecrest. I know enough to help you. I haven't been able to help anyone as a physician for a long time."

A contraction about her chest pulled taut at the despair she glimpsed in his eyes. "You helped me."

"Not enough."

"I'm aware I could have died if it were not for you."

His features firmed into an expression that hid the effects of her words.

She did not want to add to his hurt, but still, doubts nibbled at her. After her husband's death at sea, she could recall feeling desolation at the unnecessary loss of a human being, but quickly she experienced a feeling of freedom when she realized she would not have to answer to him ever again. On the ship she had resolved never to let a man rule her destiny a second time. It would be hard, but she was determined to make it on her own and teach Faith how as well.

"I shall agree to this arrangement as long as you allow me to pay you with a percentage of the crop. I cannot allow you to work for free, especially if you neglect your own land."

He backed away and made a low bow, sweeping his arm across his midsection. "We have a deal. One you will not regret."

The smile that brightened his face sent a warning through her body. She was already regretting her agreement to hire him. She might be wary of men and not want to get involved, but she knew it would be nearly impossible to ignore Nathan for long. Somehow she would have to find the strength to do the impossible.

Seven

Through the tall trees, Rachel glimpsed her new home. Expanses of grayish-brown wood flecked with small patches of white greeted her. As Nathan drove the cart closer over the rough ground and through high grass, more details of the framed and clapboarded structure came into view. The front door lay a few feet away from the opening into the house. Two gaping holes where windows used to be completed the façade facing Rachel.

"It looks habitable," Rachel said over the groans from Maddy. She glanced at her maid in the back. Maddy's eyes were wide, her arms hugging her body. "We shall be fine here." Rachel injected as much confidence as she could muster.

"Yes ma'am, but it looks so, well, wild."

"That is because it is wild. When the hurricane hit in 1811, it changed the course of the river and much of the farmland became a swamp. The deed might say six hundred acres, but only two hundred at best are usable for planting." Nathan brought the cart to a halt in front of the house and hopped to the ground then turned to help Rachel.

After she passed Faith to Maddy, he put his hands around Rachel's waist and lifted her to stand in front of him. She peered at him to tell him thank you, but the words crammed her throat. The brush of his gaze over her features made her knees go weak. Quickly she stepped away, her back pressed up against the cart.

He reached over her shoulder to take Faith while Rachel remained frozen only inches from him. His nearness momentarily erased the picture of her new home from her mind to be replaced with one of Nathan. His broad chest covered in a white lawn shirt. His muscular arms that had so effortlessly assisted her from the cart, the stubble of his dark beard because he hadn't shaven that morn, as was his practice, filled her vision. Until he presented her with Faith, cradled in his large hands.

A smile that twinkled in his eyes spread across his face. "At least she is not crying for food…yet."

"Give her time. She will." Rachel settled her baby against her then started for the house while Nathan helped Maddy down.

Rachel stepped up into her new home. Her breath quickened as she surveyed the area before her, the scent of dust and something rotten assailing her nostrils. Faith began to stir in her arms. She rocked her daughter while she paced farther into the large room with a fireplace at one end and two rooms at the other. One door was still hanging while the other was gone, nowhere to be seen. A crude staircase with missing steps led upward into a loft. The place, devoid of furniture, mocked her dreams of a new life in America.

"Ma'am? Where do we start?" Maddy's quavering voice penetrated Rachel's stunned mind.

She rotated toward her maid and gave her Faith. "First, I shall check the rest of this place, then we shall unload our possessions and start cleaning. Take Faith and find a place for her to sleep peacefully and safely."

Maddy nodded, her eyes still round as they skimmed over the dirt on the wooden-planked floor.

While her maid backed toward the entrance, Rachel swung around, refusing to see the grime. But nothing she did could block the smell of death emanating from the room with the door cracked open a few inches. Light poured into the house from where the windows were at one time. She crossed the large main room to see what was causing the vile odor. No doubt an animal had wandered in here and died. The prospects didn't set well with her, but she had better get used to being in the middle of nowhere with nature at her doorstep. She couldn't allow dead animals to make her squeamish. She needed to prove to Nathan she could do this.

She gripped the door and pushed it wide open then entered.

And screamed.

* * * * *

The bloodcurdling shriek rent the air, and Nathan nearly dropped the crate he had taken from the cart. He shoved it back in place and raced toward the house. His heartbeat galloped as though it were a runaway horse. He barely saw Maddy standing off to the side outside the entrance with Faith in her arms. All he could focus on was Rachel's scream and then dead quiet.

Bursting into the house, he saw her standing as though she were preserved in a block of ice brought down from the mountains. Then suddenly she whirled about and flew out of the bedchamber and straight into his embrace. Her body quaked against his.

"Rachel, what's wrong?"

She shook even harder, wrapping her arms around him while she buried her face against his chest.

The aroma of death invaded the house. "Rachel? Is there a dead animal in there?" He wanted to go look, but she clutched him with such fierceness he was reluctant to leave her.

Finally she leaned back to look up at him. Fright glazed her eyes. All color was faded from her features, her bonnet askew from pressing herself into him. She opened her mouth to say something but no words came out.

"Let me go look." Nathan tried to step away, but her fingers dug into his upper arms.

"No. Don't leave me. Dead"—she waved her hand toward the room—"man."

"Dead man?"

She nodded. "He is…" She squeezed her eyes closed and shuddered.

"Stay here. I will take care of it." At the doorway, he glanced back at her. "Better yet, go outside with Maddy."

After she hastened out of the house, he went into the room. No matter how many times he smelled a dead body, the odor nauseated him. He covered his nose and mouth and stepped closer to the man lying on the floor with a gunshot wound to his chest and his face badly beaten. He lifted the arm nearest him and estimated by the condition of the body the man had died a day or so before. Studying the craggy face, weathered by the hot South Carolina sun, Nathan didn't know who the person was, but he had seen him before in Charleston. The fact he was found on Rachel's land did not bode well for them, especially since it was obvious the man had been murdered.

* * * * *

"A dead man, Mrs. Gordon!" Maddy rocked back on her heels then forward. "'Tis not good, not good at all."

Rachel sat on a log and clutched her daughter to her in case whoever killed that man came back. She scouted the area for a place she could hide with Faith. Perhaps the barn. It wasn't too far away. Then she spied its roof with big holes in it and boards missing on the sides.

"What are we going to do?" Maddy wailed, startling Rachel and interrupting her plans to hide.

"I don't know. He looked mean. He looked…" A picture of the dead man overtook her thoughts. A black beard, straggly, oily black hair, beaten, pock-marked face, clothes of a laborer, dirty, torn, with patches on them, no shoes, his feet clad in stockings. But the worst part was the large blood-crusted hole in his chest. She had never seen a man dead from a gunshot. She balled her hands to keep them from trembling, but that did little to stop the tremors from taking over her body.

When Nathan appeared in the doorway, a grim expression on his face, she stared at him. She gulped and tried to form a coherent question, but her thoughts jumbled together.

"I saw this man in Charleston once a few weeks back, but I don't know his name," he said, stepping down from the house and covering the short distance to Rachel. "He got into a fist fight with another man. It started in the tavern and spilled over into the street."

"Do you think that man killed him? Why did he leave him here? What are we going to do with the body?" Questions tumbled from Rachel in a breathless rush.

"I will need to contact the constable about this."

"You cannot leave me alone with that body. Please."

"No. No." He squatted in front of her, his gaze beseeching her to look at him. "I will remove the body to the barn. I will not leave you alone with him."

"Then how are you going to get the constable?"

"Sarah and John are coming today."

Rachel shot to her feet, still holding Faith against her. "I cannot receive guests. Look at the house. There is a dead man inside. I—"

Silencing her words with a light press of his forefinger to her lips, Nathan grinned. "They are coming to help. And to bring the ox."

Rachel glanced at the cart being pulled by Nathan's horse then back at him. "Oh. To help? I cannot ask them to do that. I think a whole army might not be able to make this place…" She swallowed the rest of the words. She was admitting defeat before she even tried, but how could she stay when a dead man had been in her house?

"Are you ready then to leave and go to Charleston? Wait for the next ship to England?"

"No."

His intense scrutiny bore into her as if he were trying to discern her thoughts. "I will rid the house of the corpse. But that does not change the fact someone was killed here." He marched back inside.

Maddy hurried to her side. "Ma'am, I am for leaving before we get killed."

"Hush. Let me think." Rachel paced from the cart to a large live oak, holding Faith against her chest, patting her back gently.

Perhaps the man wandered into her house to die but was shot somewhere else. Or it was a hunting accident. She could remember something like that had happened on a hunt her father had participated in. A man had been mistaken for a deer and killed.

Under the shade of the tree she spun around and stared at her house. Up until today this place had been deserted for years. Now that it was occupied, surely anyone who thought they could dump dead bodies here would not use her farm. If it was dumped here, then it was a one-time occurrence. She hadn't seen any other dead bodies or bones around. Yes, it was most unusual. Not something that would be repeated.

Rachel returned to the log and sank onto it, looking at Faith, whose eyes were wide open. "Hi, little one. I dare say you are hungry." But her baby didn't cry. Instead she kept her gaze fixed on Rachel as though studying her. "We are in a pickle. I have nowhere to go in England. Papa is really angry with me, and no one crosses him."

Looking up, she spied Nathan dragging the man toward the barn while Maddy hid behind the cart. When she peeped at the dead man, she screamed and ducked back behind the wagon. The hard planes of Nathan's face sent a shiver down Rachel's spine. He was not happy. He wanted her to return to England. But she couldn't leave and stay with him or Sarah while she waited to go back home.

Lord, what do You want me to do? I need a sign that You want me to stay. That this is what I should do.

She stared at Faith's beautiful face. "The Lord will protect us. You are here because He sent Nathan to help with your delivery."

"Have you come to your senses?" Nathan said as he strode through the tall grass toward her.

"Yes." She rose. "I am much better now. You need not worry

about me. We have a lot to do to make this place habitable, but it can be done."

"Woman, are you going to stay after finding the dead man?"

"Of course. It would have been far worse if I had found a man alive in my home bent on doing me harm. What can a dead man do to me?"

"I'm not worried about him but the one who killed him."

"I have no quarrel with whoever did the deed. He should not bother me."

Nathan sighed. "You just don't understand the dangers."

She crossed the few feet to him. "Whatever I do will be dangerous. Traveling by myself back to England. Finding a place to live there. With no money by that time."

He cut the distance between them. "Contact your family. Throw yourself on their mercy."

She had to tilt her head back to look into his face because of his nearness. "It worked well for you."

A lethal look targeted her, going straight to her heart. She had overstepped her boundaries. Moving back, she murmured, "I should not have said that."

"Our situations are different."

"Are they?"

He glared at her then turned on his heel and stomped back toward the cart. For one wild moment she feared he would leave her alone with the dead man in the barn. She started forward. Perhaps she could throw herself on *his* mercy. But when he unhitched his horse from the cart and tied the reins to a nearby branch, some of her anxiety dissipated.

Rachel headed to Maddy and gave the young woman her sleeping child. "Put Faith in the cradle over there." She waved her hand toward a shady place next to the house. "Then we can unload the cart."

"We are staying?"

"Yes."

After Maddy settled Faith in the cradle, Rachel worked with her to empty the cart while Nathan took in the heavier items like the few pieces of furniture Rachel had that survived the wreck. On her third trip back outside, she saw two wagons coming toward the house. Sitting on the first one were Sarah and John. Yesterday Nathan's sister had spoken about how neighbors helped neighbors when a barn or a house had to be raised. But how would she ever be able to return such kindness?

Rachel stood at her cart and greeted her visitors with a smile. "It is good to see you all again."

Nathan came to the first wagon, which was full of supplies, and assisted his sister to the ground, kissing her cheek. Then he rotated toward John and said, "There has been a complication. Rachel found a man in one of the bedchambers, shot in the chest. I moved the body to the barn. I need one of your men to bring the constable here."

"Do you know who the man was?"

"Not his name, but I saw him in town once. Fighting. He gouged his opponent's eye out."

"That could prompt someone to pay him back." John walked to the second wagon and spoke to the driver. When the young man left on the horse tied to the back of the wagon, John returned to Nathan. "'Tis done."

* * * * *

Standing in the middle of the barn with the double doors wide open, Nathan stared up at the roof. "That should keep the rain out, which will make my life more comfortable."

John rolled his shoulders and arched his back. "We will come back tomorrow and finish the most pressing repairs. The house was not in as bad a shape as I thought it would be. I'm wondering if that dead stranger the constable took away was living here for a while before someone shot him."

"A squatter? Possibly. The bedding on the floor in the bedchamber suggests that at least he was staying here temporarily. But he could have been passing through."

"What will you do if her family does not come for her?"

Nathan hoped his words were persuasive enough. "I'm not going to think about that. I have to believe they will not leave her here. I made it clear she was in danger and ill-equipped to deal with life here." Was Rachel's father as heartless as she thought? It was one thing for his grandfather to disown him. He could take care of himself. But Rachel was a woman, brought up for a different lifestyle than what she would face here.

A white-and-brown cat that John had brought to keep the mice population under control moseyed into the barn and weaved in between John's legs. "I don't want to be around when she finds out you wrote her mother."

"That is why I'm not going to say anything to her until someone from her family shows up."

John chuckled. "Afraid she will kick you off her land."

"She might just do that, and someone has to be here to take care of her until she is rescued by her family."

"Why do you think 'tis your duty? This does not sound like a man who declared he'd had his fill of people."

Nathan stooped and petted the cat. "Faith wouldn't be here if it were not for me. Rachel has her daughter to protect, which means I have that too. I am responsible. I brought Faith into this world."

"You sound like a father."

Although John's tone held a teasing ring to it, his words stunned Nathan. A father? No. He would see to Rachel and Faith's safety, but the moment her family came for them he would reclaim his life. "I am thinking after she returns to England that I will head west."

"Have you said anything to your sister about this?"

"No, and I would ask you not to either. I have not made up my mind yet, and she does not need to worry needlessly."

"You have really given up on your grandfather."

Nathan rose. "He has made it clear that I am not part of his life anymore. I have accepted that."

"Have you?"

"What choice do I have?" Since the Lord had forsaken him, he was alone. And that was fine by him. At least his happiness did not rely on another's acceptance and love.

* * * * *

"I cannot accept all of this from you. It is enough that you, John, and your workers are helping me repair the barn and house." Rachel swept the last of the dirt from the floor out the front entrance with its newly hung door wide open.

Sarah set the rag on the table she had been cleaning and faced Rachel, with her hand on her waist. "I will not take this furniture back now. It was in storage and not being used. When you get your own, if you must, you can give this all back to me then. It will go back into storage."

Rachel locked gazes with Nathan's sister for a long moment. She was not used to accepting charity, but ever since she had arrived in South Carolina, she had been forced to do that very thing. Usually in England she was the one helping others. Uncomfortable with the turn of events, she swung away from Sarah and stared at Faith asleep in the cradle, a cradle Sarah had lent her to use. "How will I ever repay you and your husband or Nathan?"

"We don't want you to repay us." Sarah strode to Rachel and took her hands. "When you see someone in need, help them if you can. That is all I ask. That is what the Lord asks us to do."

Tears fought for release, blurring Rachel's vision. "I don't know why I am crying all the time. I didn't used to do that."

Sarah laughed. "Now *that* I can help you with. After Sean was born, I cried all the time, but gradually that lessened as he neared his first birthday."

"So I have a year of this to look forward to."

"It will go by fast. I cannot believe Sean is three years old. Before long he will be a young man following his papa around and learning how to run the plantation."

Rachel leaned the broom against the wall near the front door. "Is that what Nathan used to do until his father died?"

"Actually, Nathan used to trail our grandfather all over the plantation."

"He did? Then why did your grandfather…" Rachel attempted a smile that failed. "Sorry, I shouldn't have asked that."

"I don't know what has gotten into Grandfather's head. I some-times wonder if it was sheer grief at his only living child's death. Patrick is the one who seems to be able to reach him some, but even that is not often." Sarah walked to a basket and lifted it to place it on the table she had cleaned. "I had our cook prepare you some food for the next few days."

"You didn't have—"

Sarah raised her hand. "Not another word. You will be busy getting this place livable and will not have time to bake and cook." After removing her apron and cap, Sarah picked up her bonnet and tied it on her head. "We will be back tomorrow to finish."

Rachel bit back the words, *You don't have to come back and help.* She saw the determined look in her new friend's eyes and knew she would not appreciate her saying such a thing.

"I had better go find my husband."

"I will come with you." Rachel moved to the bedchamber. "I will be going to the barn," she told Maddy, who was making the bed. "Faith is still asleep."

"Do I have to clean the other bedchamber?" The young woman threw a wide-eyed gaze toward the room where Rachel had dis-covered the dead man.

"No, we will leave it alone for the time being." Rachel could not bring herself to go into that bedchamber either. At least she could shut the door and ignore the area until she could muster her bravery enough to go inside.

When Rachel stepped outside, the fresh, cool air with a hint of pine in it cooled her cheeks. She scanned the land around the house and realized she owned it. She had never owned anything like this. In England she had been beholden to her family for everything. What if she could make this work and have it become a productive farm? Be able to hire field hands to work her land for her and provide a home for her child? Would that rid her of this constant fear in the pit of her stomach?

"The barn is looking like a worthy barn." Sarah started for the wooden structure seventy feet from the house, between them and the swamp.

Rachel followed her, passing one of Liberty Hall's workers putting the panes in the last window. She would write down all the items the McNeals had "loaned" her and would find a way to repay them, in spite of what Sarah said. If this young country could declare its independence from England, twice, with the ending of the War of 1812, then so could she from her family. And yet as she thought that, she recalled her younger sister and wished she could be there for her coming out. Did Elizabeth fulfill Papa's wishes for her? Rachel might never know. That realization saddened her and made a mockery of her declaration of independence.

Sarah disappeared in the barn while Rachel woolgathered, rotating in a full circle. Glimpses of the river could be seen through the trees to the south of her home. Nathan had mentioned at one time there was a pier that extended from her property where boats could tie up. He did not know if it was still there.

Suddenly a ruckus erupted to her right. Her heart pounding, Rachel whirled toward the screeching sound at the moment two hens flew out of the bushes with the new cat right behind them. Out of the corner of her eye she glimpsed Nathan, John, and Sarah rushing out of the barn. Rachel dove for the nearest chicken. Her first attempt landed her in the dirt. She jumped up and ran after the bird as it raced for the house with Cat right behind it.

"Get the other one," she shouted over her shoulder while pursuing the white hen.

At the entrance to the house, the hen flapped its wings and hopped up into the main room. Rachel twirled around and blocked the cat from entering while slamming the reattached door shut. She leaned back against it and surveyed the area. Clucking the whole way, the hen headed straight for the bedchamber where Maddy was.

The young woman came to the doorway, and the chicken detoured and ran around in circles, its cackling growing louder and louder. Rachel stood in the center of the room, watching the bird until she felt dizzy. She clutched the table near her, closed her eyes for a brief moment, then refocused on the chicken. It zipped by her. She pounced on it and grabbed it up into her arms. She held the wiggling body close to her.

"I did it," she said.

"Is that dinner?" Maddy asked as Nathan came into the house clutching a brown hen.

"No." The white chicken settled down, but its heart still beat quickly against Rachel's palm.

"I agree. John found a rooster and another hen in the bushes."

"Who do they belong to?" Now that she had stopped chasing the hen, Rachel's exhaustion demanded her attention. She collapsed onto the stool nearby, still clasping the bird. She didn't have enough energy to go after it again.

"They belongs to you now."

"This means eggs." She grinned at Nathan. "Perhaps more chickens."

He nodded.

Rachel peered down at the white hen perched in her lap, the beating of its heart slowing. *The sign I asked for. Thank You, Lord.*

* * * * *

Five days later, while Maddy completed washing the clothes, Rachel hung them up on the line Nathan had strung for her. Every part of her body ached from pushing, pulling, hauling, and anything else she needed to do. But she would not utter a word of complaint to Nathan.

Today she planned to chop wood for the fireplace and show him that she could. He was out with the ox and plow, preparing a field. If she could have it done by the time he came in for dinner, it would be one more task she had learned and finished. The day before, she had finally managed to bake a decent loaf of bread. Then she thought of the dense piece she had sliced off a rather small, flattened lump. Perhaps not decent, but edible at least. Next time she would let it rise longer. At Mansfield Manor, the food was served at meal times, and she never thought of all the work that went into putting it on the table.

After a quick peek to check on Faith in the cradle under the live oak, she marched toward the stump Nathan used to chop the wood. As she had seen him doing it, she positioned the log to be split standing straight up. She picked up the ax and dropped it at her feet. All right, it was heavier than she thought. Clasping the handle with both hands and gathering all the strength she could muster, she again lifted the ax and swung it toward her target. The tool grazed the top of the log, causing it to fly off the stump—into her. Knocking her back as the ax sailed through the air. Her bottom landed on the ground with a thud.

The hard impact with the earth jolted her. Her eyes slid closed until she remembered the ax wrenched from her grasp. They bolted open to find a large man, probably the size of the bear she had heard so much about, with the tool she had flung away in his hand.

Eight

Rachel's gaze passed the dirt-covered black boots, skimmed over the brown trousers and white shirt, to the face of a giant with the reddest hair she had ever seen and bright blue eyes that wrinkled at the corners. From laughing. At her. His booming merriment filled the morning air, the ax still gripped in his hand.

"Who are you?" she said so softly she had to repeat it for him to hear her over his amusement.

Before the man had a chance to answer her, Maddy rounded the corner of the house and charged at him, tackling his legs and sending him and the ax propelling toward Rachel. She scrambled to the side as the giant hit the ground where she had been only a moment before.

Maddy yanked the ax from his hand and poised it above him.

"Maddy!" Rachel screamed, never having seen her servant so fierce looking.

The man rolled away from Rachel and scooted back from Maddy, but instead of anger lining his face, his merriment deepened the crinkles at the corners of his eyes and a huge grin, displaying a missing tooth, met Rachel's perusal.

While Maddy still held the ax as though she would use it at any moment, Rachel asked, "Who are you? Why are you here?"

A sober expression descended as he took in Maddy's ferociousness. "I came to ask ya that. You ain't a Dalton."

"No." Rachel pushed herself to her feet and towered over the man. "But I own this farm now. My husband bought it from Mr. Dalton."

"You English?" He started to get up, but Maddy lifted the ax higher and took a threatening step closer. He settled back on the ground, all laughter gone from his eyes.

"Yes," Rachel said with as much of a challenge as she could muster with her legs trembling. He could overpower both Maddy and her at his leisure. His arms were like tree stumps, his hands so big one could circle her neck and snap it.

"Mr. Dalton went to England after the storm in 1811, but I thought he would come back. I live over yonder." The giant gestured toward the northwest.

In the swamp? "No, this is my farm now." Rachel reached for the ax and took it from Maddy. "Thank you. Please check on Faith."

"But, ma'am, I can stay—"

"Please."

Maddy gave the man a narrow-eyed look then stomped off toward the oak tree. She kept her gaze glued to them while she sat next to the cradle, singing a lullaby.

"Can I git up?"

Rachel backed up a few feet. "Yes. Do you live in the swamp?"

"No ma'am. On the other side. I have a farm." He rose effortlessly to his feet for such a large man, which only reinforced the thought he could have overwhelmed them whenever he wanted.

She relaxed. "A neighbor?"

He nodded. "I didn't mean to scare ya. My name is George Baker."

"I am Rachel Gordon. Why did you come?"

"To check the pier."

"Why?"

"I do it every spring."

"Why?"

His gaze clouded for a moment. "To fix it, if need be."

"Why would you do that?"

"To use it when I need to git me to Charleston."

"But it is on my land."

Her neighbor removed his hat and scratched his head. "Uh…" He glanced away then back at her. "I have been usin' it for years. Since the hurricane changed the river. 'Tis the easiest way to git my crops to town."

Every muscle aching, Rachel seized a thought swirling around in her mind. "You can buy my farm. It is for sale." Then she might have enough money to do something other than farming.

"I ain't got that kind of money." George Baker twisted his mouth into a thoughtful expression. "But I have a pig I can give ya fer rights to use the pier."

"A pig?" Before he changed his mind, Rachel stuck out her hand and said, "A deal, Mr. Baker. Do you want to come in for a cup of tea?"

Her neighbor peered at Maddy now holding Faith in her arms. "I best be headin' back. Can I check the pier first?"

"We already have. It is in good shape."

Another furtive glance at Maddy before he donned his hat, touched its brim, and said, "I will be back with the pig."

"Good day, Mr. Baker." Rachel watched her neighbor amble away and disappear into the swampy land on the west side of her farm.

Maddy approached her. "He is coming back?"

"Yes, with a pig. The Lord is good. First chickens and now a pig."

"He might murder us in our sleep."

Rachel suppressed her laugh. "I think you sufficiently scared him."

* * * * *

"What is a pig doing tied up outside?" Nathan asked as he came into the house later that afternoon. He halted a few steps inside at the sight of George Baker sitting on a small chair that barely held his large bulk, drinking out of one of Rachel's dainty china cups, minus its handle.

George threw him a helpless look. "I brought it to Mrs. Gordon." He rose, searching for a place to set his cup.

Maddy hopped up from her chair across from him and took the dish from him. Blowing out a loud sigh, she sat back down and held his drink.

George crossed the main room, offering Nathan his hand to shake. "I heard you were back in the area."

"Yes, since last summer."

"Mrs. Gordon told me you are helpin' her with the farm."

Nodding, Nathan moved toward Rachel, her hair caught up under her mobcap with a few curls framing her face. All day while preparing the first field nearest the house for corn, he couldn't get the picture of the woman out of his mind. The smile she gave him before he left to plow, her saucy walk when she had brought him dinner in the field at noon, a flush to her cheeks because she had forgotten to wear her bonnet. Her cap exposed her face to the strong sun, especially at that time of the day. The rosy hue still graced her skin, giving her a healthy glow.

"Why did you bring Mrs. Gordon a pig?" Nathan positioned himself slightly to the left of Rachel's chair and behind her.

Rachel straightened her shoulders and raised her chin. "It is rent for using the pier."

"Do you know what to do with a pig?" Nathan asked, seeing the smug expression fade at the question she had not considered.

"Well, no, but I figured you did. Don't you?"

"If'n he doesn't, I will show ya."

Rachel beamed her pleasure at George's offer. "Why, thank you, Mr. Baker. I appreciate the help."

"'Tis not needed, George. I know what to do. So are you the reason the pier was in such good shape?"

"Yes. Been keepin' an eye on the place since the Dalton family moved away."

"His land is not on the river or road. He uses the pier to take his crops to town. We shall be able to do that too." Rachel glanced between George and Nathan. "My pig is pregnant. We shall have little pigs running around here." She paused, cocked her head at George, and asked, "When, do you think?"

"Another month, ma'am." The large man snatched his hat off the table and plopped it on his head. "I best be going. I still have chores to do. Thank you for the tea and—bread."

"You are welcome. Please let me cut you a few slices, and you can take it with you."

George shook his head. "Ma'am, I don't wa—need any. I have a whole loaf at home." His face reddened, and he averted his gaze, looking straight at Maddy, which only deepened his color. Finally he whirled and hastened toward the door. "Good day."

He was out of the house so fast Nathan couldn't contain his laughter. "How did you get George to stay for tea?"

"I told him I missed having afternoon tea since coming to America."

"And that got him to say yes? Interesting." Nathan walked to the window that overlooked the area in front of the house. "My, he's already halfway across the field. I didn't know he could move so fast."

Rachel appeared at his side and whispered, "I think he has set his eyes on Maddy. I kept catching him glancing at her. I am not even sure he realized he was. She made quite an impression on him earlier today."

Nathan shifted toward Rachel. "How?"

"By threatening him with an ax."

"Maddy, the same woman who fled the room when you were going to give birth to Faith? The one who is scared of her own shadow?"

"Yes. She was defending me."

Nathan drew himself up, his arms stiff at his sides. "Why should she have to?"

"Shouldn't you see to the pig?"

"Not until you tell me what happened here today."

"It was nothing. I was going to chop some wood but had a"—Rachel held her forefinger and thumb apart about an inch—"tiny little problem. I lost my hold on the ax, and it almost hit Mr. Baker. I am thankful he was quick and caught it before it hit him in the chest."

"Why were you chopping wood? You know I do it when I come in from the field."

"I need to learn how, so I was practicing. You will not be here long." She dropped her gaze to the floor between them. "I thought it would be easier than it is."

"Now you see why it isn't wise for you to try things without me to supervise."

Her gaze pierced into him. "I am not a servant you need to supervise."

He knew when to escape, and this was one of those times. "I'm going to take care of the pig and chop some wood. Let me know when supper is ready."

He stormed from the house before she decided to follow and have him instruct her in how to chop wood. He skirted the stump where he split the logs and headed for the pig. *What was she thinking? She could have hurt herself or poor George.* Taking the rope, he escorted the animal to the barn.

As he entered the structure, he had to admit it was shrewd of her to barter a pig out of George—one that would have piglets she could raise and sell or slaughter for meat. And he had to give her credit for trying to learn to cook and keep house, although the thought of having the bread this evening didn't sit well with his stomach. He could always give her another lesson on kneading and letting the dough rise. The picture of him helping her the week before, his hands over hers while working the bread mixture, popped into his mind. Her fresh scent—nothing unpleasant about it—stirred a roiling sensation in the pit of his stomach.

No, there will be no more bread-making lessons. Too dangerous.

After securing the pig in the barn, Nathan made his way to the stump to work on chopping wood, at least enough for the next day.

As he struck the log over and over with the ax, he wondered what he was doing being a farmer—not something he had wanted to do with his life.

But what do I want?

No answers came as he brought the ax down onto the wood. Frustration churned his gut as he went through one log after another until pieces were scattered about the ground around the stump. The sun went down behind the trees in the swamp west of the house. As dusk settled over the landscape, Nathan finished his chore, scooped up an armful of logs, and pivoted toward the house, nearly bowling Rachel over. The wood tumbled to the ground onto his booted foot. Pain flashed up his leg, but he riveted his attention on Rachel's mouth, opened slightly in surprise.

She jumped back, brought her shawl closer around her shoulders, and crossed her arms over her chest. "I was coming to get you for supper. We are not having much. Just bread, the rest of the cheese your sister left for us, and mush."

"You should not ask strangers in for tea."

"But he wasn't a stranger. You know Mr. Baker."

"Did you?"

"Not till this morning, but once I knew he was my neighbor and actually quite sweet and shy, I saw no harm."

He itched to shake some sense into Rachel. "What if he had been lying?"

"He had an honest face. Is there any reason not to think otherwise about Mr. Baker?"

"No. He is honest and hardworking, but after you found that dead man in the house, did you not have second thoughts about allowing anyone too close? What if he had been the murderer returning for the body?"

"Whatever for?"

The knot in his gut had a stranglehold on him. "My point is that you need to be cautious. There are dangerous people in this world, and you need to have your guard up against them."

In the waning light, a smile slid across her mouth, a teasing gleam in her eyes. "Why? You seem to be doing such a good job for me."

He stepped closer until only inches separated them. "Because I will not always be around. Remember I'm only here until you can manage on your own." Which at the rate she was going would be never. More and more he was glad he had sent that letter to her family. He did not want to be responsible for her and Faith. He could do so little for the soldiers, for Papa, for Eliza and her baby. "I'm tired. I'm going to bed."

"But it is still early."

He moved back and turned to head to the barn.

Her hand on his arm stopped his progress. "What about supper? You must be hungry." She came around his side to face him.

Her nearness doubled his heart rate. For an awkward moment his mind went blank. All he could focus on were her lips turned down slightly, her forehead creased in question, and her eyes searching him for answers. But mostly the soft touch of her fingers on him enticing him to forget he did not want to care for another—to risk being hurt yet again.

"If you want, I can bring your supper to the barn."

Words flooded his mind. All the reasons he wished he could

leave and never look back demanded he do something to protect himself. But one thing came to the forefront of his mind and dominated his thoughts. He was responsible for her being here, and he had to stay until he could get her to see reason and leave the farm, the country, to go back to where she belonged.

"Nathan? Are you all right?"

He pulled his arm from her grasp and backed away. "I'm perfectly fine. I'm not hungry. Go in and bolt the door for the night."

"But—"

"Now, Rachel. 'Tis late."

"It is dusk."

"Do you like to argue about everything?"

Another smile graced her lips. "Only when I am right."

"We are looking at it from different perspectives."

Her grin grew. "So there is no right or wrong?"

"Exactly. This is not a contest."

She looked him directly in the eye. "I beg to differ. You want me to hightail it back to England and I want to stay." Whirling around, she flounced toward the open doorway and into the house.

When he heard the bolt being put in place, he trudged toward the barn, wondering who had been the victor in that skirmish.

* * * * *

People crowded the streets of Charleston four days later. After weeks in the countryside, the sights, sounds, and odors of the town bombarded Rachel from all sides. The stench of refuse assaulted her as they traveled through the part of Charleston where the poor lived. A woman dressed in a plain gown with mud caked on the hem threw the contents of a chamber pot into a ditch. People hawking their wares shouted above the din of voices.

Slowly the hovels and tenements gave way to the wider streets cluttered with chaises and carriages of the more wealthy citizens. Flowering bushes of unknown plants perfumed the air, chasing away the aromas of dirt and filth.

When Nathan drove the cart down a road with massive houses on both sides, Rachel spotted rose bushes. Thoughts of home drenched her in bittersweet memories. "I wish I could plant some roses at the farm."

"Why? You cannot eat them."

"You can make tea out of roses. Also nice-smelling rosewater."

Nathan harrumphed. "Not practical when money is tight."

He brought the two-wheeled wagon to a stop in front of a red-brick, three-story mansion with tall windows facing the street. A brick and black wrought iron fence skirted the property, and behind it Rachel saw many rose bushes, not blooming yet but fully leafed.

After Nathan helped both Rachel with Faith and Maddy down from the cart, he opened the wrought iron gate and escorted them to the large white door with a circular window above it. He used the knocker to announce them. A tall, thin man, dressed in black trouser and vest, white shirt and cravat, and a burgundy tailcoat, answered the door and stepped to the side to allow them inside.

"Mrs. McNeal is in the parlor, Dr. Stuart. Mrs. Bridges is here."

Rachel leaned close to him. "Is Sarah expecting us? I didn't know she was going to be in Charleston. I thought she was at Liberty Hall."

"She often stays in town from Sunday to Wednesday during the spring with so many social gatherings occurring at this time of year. I was counting on her following her usual schedule."

The trip into Charleston hadn't taken too long. Perhaps an hour and a half. Rachel could certainly understand Sarah going back and forth. Families often did in England. "We usually stayed in the country except for a couple of trips to London in the spring and fall."

"Being so close to town has its advantages. When you decide to sell, that would be helpful for you."

"Sell? Why would I do that?" Although she remembered her offer to Mr. Baker to sell the farm, that had come out of her mouth without her thinking it through. She didn't know if that was the wisest thing for her to do now. Even with the money from the sale, she would be left with a dilemma. What would she do to make a living in Charleston?

"Your circumstances might change. You might remarry or decide to leave the area."

"I am *not* remarrying." Hugging her daughter closer to her, Rachel shivered.

The butler opened the parlor doors and said, "Dr. Stuart is here to see you with two ladies, madam."

Sarah rose from the gold and royal-blue sofa and covered the distance to give her brother a kiss on the cheek then to embrace Rachel. "What a delightful surprise you all are in town today." She stepped back. "What brings you to Charleston?"

"We need some supplies, and I wanted to talk with the constable about the man we found." Nathan waited until Rachel and Maddy took a seat on two chairs across from the sofa before he folded his long length onto the sofa next to his sister.

"Mrs. Bridges, this is a friend, Mrs. Gordon, and her maid, Maddy. The adorable little baby she is holding is Faith. Mrs. Gordon recently arrived from England and is taking up residence at Dalton Farm." Sarah looked at Rachel. "Mrs. Bridges is my dressmaker. She has come to discuss with me some changes in my wardrobe now that I am with child again."

The scowl on Nathan's face drew Rachel's attention for a moment. Did something more than his sister having a difficult time when Sean was born bother him about Sarah expecting another baby? She couldn't shake the feeling there was more to it. She had seen the exchange of glances between brother and sister.

"Mrs. Gordon, I always love talking with ladies who have newly arrived from Europe. It takes awhile for the latest styles to make it here. Perhaps you would visit my shop today and take a look at some of my fashion plates."

"I would love to."

Nathan's frown deepened.

"I shall not be able to stay long, but a short visit should be fine," Rachel added to appease Nathan. She knew he wanted to get back to start planting the corn after he purchased the seeds today.

Mrs. Bridges clapped her white-gloved hands. "That would be perfect." She stood and turned toward Sarah. "I will leave you and begin on the gowns we talked about." She nodded to Rachel and to Nathan, who slowly rose, inclining his head in a bow. "It was nice meeting you."

When the plump dressmaker swept out of the room, Sarah turned to her brother. "What's that frown for? Have you forgotten your manners?"

"This is the very reason I stay in the country."

"You mean hide away." Sarah sent him a sharp look then turned her attention to Rachel. "I'm sorry my big brother can be so boorish. I hope you all will stay for dinner before you go shopping."

"I would love to. Is it possible Maddy can stay here with Faith while we are out? I don't want to expose Faith to the crowds."

"I would have it no other way. Come, Maddy, I will show you to the nursery then let Cook know you are staying for dinner. John should be home by then." Sarah headed for the door while Maddy took Faith and followed her from the parlor.

The moment Rachel was alone with Nathan she said, "When a woman is with child it is a happy time, but your sour expression puts a damper on the festive mood. What is the matter?"

Nathan prowled the room, glancing out the front window that overlooked the street. When he shifted around and peered at her, his expression revealed nothing of his inner thoughts. He was good at that, and Rachel wished she could do the same.

"Childbirth can be dangerous for a woman." He finally broke the silence, the flexing of his hands the only indication they were talking about a serious subject.

"Life is dangerous. Look at what happened to my husband on the voyage over here."

"There were complications with the birth of Sean."

"That does not mean there will be complications with this next one. If women lived in fear of giving birth, there would be no people to populate this world."

He rotated back toward the window, his posture rigid, his hand clutching the velvet draperies. "That does not mean someone I care about has to be the one to *populate* the world."

"So you never want children?" The moment she uttered the question she clamped her hand over her mouth. Where was this boldness coming from?

"Like you, I don't want to get married."

"You can marry and not have children. As I asked earlier, what is the matter? Sarah is fine now."

"How about what happened to you when Faith was coming?" He kept his back to her, his whitened knuckles clasping the drapery.

"I'm fine too. You were there to help me."

"What if I hadn't been?"

"The Lord was watching over me. It does no good to speculate over what could have happened. It does not matter because it didn't occur."

A heavy sigh sounded, and his shoulders slumped. Dropping his head, he murmured, "I could not help Eliza when her time came to deliver her child. Both died in the field."

Rachel came to her feet and cut the distance between them. "Died in the field? Why was she there? Who is Eliza?"

"A slave I grew up with. She was the housekeeper's child. We were close. Friends. I could tell her anything. Then one day my grandfather decided we were growing too close and sent Eliza to work in the cotton fields and live in the slave quarters. Nothing I said would change the old man's mind. Eliza married another slave, and I was happy for her. I begged Grandfather to let her come back to the house at least as long as she was with child, but he refused the request. Eliza went into labor early while she was working in the field farthest from her cabin. Patrick summoned me, but there was little I could do to save Eliza or her child. That was the final incident that caused the complete rift between Grandfather and me. I left Pinecrest later that day for good."

"I'm sorry about Eliza. Surely your grandfather understood you were upset."

"Don't you understand? I'm the reason Eliza went to the fields in the first place. He didn't like my friendship with Eliza. He didn't understand that Eliza and I were only friends, not lovers. She was like a little sister to me. I didn't recognize my grandfather after my father died. He changed. Before, he would have listened to reason. I never felt so helpless. So not in control."

She tugged him around and his face was contorted in pain. "Do you think we can control our lives?"

"No...yes. I will control my life because I will not accept the alternative."

"Then you are in for a disappointment. Any sense of control you think you might have is fleeting." She snapped her fingers. "Gone in an instant. Relying only on yourself will not work. Rely on the Lord. He is our strength."

"Is that why you think you can live on the farm and be successful? A woman alone in a new country?"

"Yes. I cannot do it without Him. That does not mean it will be easy. Anything worthwhile does not come easily."

He pivoted away, resuming his survey out the window. "That might work for you, but not me."

His pain became hers, as though a hand squeezed her heart. He had done so much for her, and yet he would not accept her help. She searched for the right words to soothe his anguish, but the sound of the door opening and Sarah returning snatched the opportunity from Rachel.

"I tell you, Rachel, you have such an adorable little daughter. I hope my next child is a girl. Why don't you all stay overnight or even a few days here with me?"

Afraid her voice wouldn't work right, Rachel cleared her throat. "Perhaps another time. There is so much to do at the farm, with spring planting and getting the place livable."

"I was afraid you would say that. But know the invitation is always open for you and Faith." Sarah stared at her brother, who remained with his back to them. "Did I interrupt something? Should I have another talk with the cook?"

Nathan turned and moved away from the window, an unreadable expression on his face. "No. It was nothing important."

His words burdened her heart. Nothing important? His welfare was important to her even if it wasn't to him. Just going through the motions of living wasn't living.

* * * * *

"I will meet you at the mercantile as soon as I talk with the constable." Nathan pointed to the building not far from the dress shop.

When Rachel entered Mrs. Bridges' establishment, Nathan drove the cart away. The moment he was gone, the tension melted away from Rachel. During dinner, he had said little to her or Sarah and had continued the moody silence on the ride to the shop.

Two ladies came from the back, said their farewells to Mrs. Bridges, and left.

The older woman smiled and headed straight for Rachel. "I'm so glad you are here, Mrs. Gordon." She swept her hand across her plump front. "Please have a look around. I have some new hats and gloves that came from abroad recently."

Rachel strolled around the large room with displays of Mrs. Bridges' merchandise. "Very nice. Your shop reminds me of the one I used to frequent in Devonshire. The proprietor always had the latest fashions from London."

"What are some of the trends you saw?"

"Rich colors. Outer garments that are transparent are not as popular. Gowns that fit to the bust then fall loosely are being worn. Paisley patterns for shawls are popular. A few women are wearing drawers."

"I like the dress you have on. I was admiring it at Mrs. McNeal's house. Did you buy it at that shop in Devonshire?"

Rachel fingered her dark green silk morning gown beneath her pelisse. This was one of the garments she had made herself because she couldn't afford to go to a dressmaker after she had married Tom. "I made this."

"The workmanship is beautiful. I love the lace and trim around the bottom. I didn't realize you sewed your own clothes."

"Only recently."

"Come, let us share a cup of tea." Mrs. Bridges gestured toward a sofa with a table nearby.

"I cannot stay long. I still need to shop for supplies."

"I have water heating in back. It will not take me long. I have a proposition I would like to make to you."

As Rachel eased onto the sofa, putting her reticule on her lap, the older woman scurried toward the back of the store. Rachel scanned the quaint shop and sighed. When she had lived at home in Devonshire, she had taken for granted that having beautiful gowns would always be part of her life. Not anymore. What she brought from England would have to do.

Mrs. Bridges came back into the front room, carrying a tray with a teapot and two china cups and saucers. After she poured the tea and passed Rachel hers, the older woman said, "Would you be interested in working for me?"

Rachel took a sip of her tea to give her time to come up with an answer. "What do you have in mind? As Sarah mentioned, I live at Dalton Farm, not here in Charleston."

"I heard a rumor about the demise of your husband on the voyage over here."

"You did?"

"Charleston is a big town, but whenever a lady of breeding arrives, the word spreads quickly. I understand your circumstances are less than ideal. I haven't been to Dalton Farm, but I have heard it is not a desirable place for a widow."

The thought she was the object of gossip coiled Rachel's stomach. She gripped the cup and drank some more tea. "But it is *my* place." She straightened her back, lifting her chin slightly.

"I understand, Mrs. Gordon. Ever since my husband passed away, I have been on my own and like it that way. It has not always been easy, so I know what you are going through. I only want to offer to help you."

"Why?"

"Because I was in the same place you are, so to speak, ten years ago when I came to America. My husband succumbed to consumption not long after our arrival." She offered Rachel a smile. "My business is thriving. I am in need of a good seamstress. While I was at Mrs. McNeal's house, I asked her about you. I heard that she as well as Dr. Stuart has befriended you. She mentioned you know how to sew and are making some clothes for your daughter."

"Yes, but I'm not leaving the farm." At the moment that was her only security. Land and a house were better than some people had. She had seen the tenements as they drove through parts of Charleston earlier.

"Is it possible for you to travel once a week to town? You can sew at your house and deliver the gowns to me when you finish them. If you do work as good as you did on that dress you are wearing, then we will have a profitable relationship. I will pay you for each gown you complete."

The farm and Faith required so much of her time. Rachel was going to decline the offer until Mrs. Bridges named her wage for each completed article of clothing. With the money she could purchase a cow for milk, cheese, and butter months before she could if she had to wait and see if her crops would bring in enough for one. "I accept."

Mrs. Bridges clapped her hands. "Wonderful. The first few dresses I will need you to sew are for Mrs. McNeal. Since you live near her, you will not have to come into town for any fittings that may be needed. Come, I will show you the material and sketch of the morning gown she wants done right away. Then there is a ball gown after that."

Rachel sipped some tea then placed her saucer and cup on the table and rose. "Thank you for this opportunity."

Twenty minutes later she had a bundle of cloth and accessories for both gowns that Sarah had ordered as well as some black crepe to make her a mourning dress for when she appeared in public, at least for a few more months. Rachel asked Mrs. Bridges if she could leave it at the shop until she had finished at the mercantile and had the cart to load the items she would use for the two dresses. Mrs. Bridges readily agreed, and Rachel set out for the general store to meet Nathan, a spring in her step. The Lord was providing well for her.

A commotion in the street caught Rachel's attention as she strolled toward her destination. A wagon nearly ran down an elderly gentleman, who then took his cane to the driver. Someone jostled her on the walkway, throwing her into a large man with blond hair tied back with a leather strap. The stranger reeked of alcohol, and he nearly toppled over. He latched onto her arm to steady himself.

She tried to yank herself free, but his fingers strengthened about her. "Sir, let me go."

He spat out the juice from his chewing tobacco. "Sir, is it? I like that, little lady. How about joining me?"

Disgusted at his improper behavior, she drew herself up as tall as she could and pinned him with a frosty look—at least she hoped so. "I have no intention of going anywhere with you."

Thunder descended on his features, and suddenly he seemed very sober as his gaze zeroed in on her. "You English are all alike. You think you are too good for us." He thrust his face into hers, his foul breath accosting her and arousing nausea in her stomach. "Well let me tell you, we defeated you twice in the past forty years." He stabbed his finger into her chest, his body trapping her against a post.

In the middle of a crowd transfixed by the older man railing at the driver of the wagon, fear seized Rachel as though she wore a corset pulled so tight she couldn't breathe properly.

* * * * *

"I was hoping you would find out who the dead man was at the Daltons' place. It might have helped us figure out why he was at the farm and who killed him." Nathan strode out of the courthouse with the constable, the warmth of the sun doing nothing to ward off the chill that had encased him ever since Rachel and he had talked at his sister's house.

"'Tis possible the man is part of that gang that has been plaguing travelers between here and Georgetown. I spoke to a man who had been robbed yesterday. They cover their faces and hold people up at gunpoint. There were two of them that stopped the family. They threatened to shoot the man's wife if he didn't hand over his money."

"I heard there were three of them."

"That's what I heard too. I know it is a ways from here. But if they are smart, they will not stay in one place for long. Which may mean trouble for me."

An elderly gentleman wearing a white powdered wig approached them. "Constable, Mr. Cochran is beating up Mr. Hawkins in the street. I think he is going to kill him." Then he strolled away.

"I had better go break up the fight." The constable started forward then stopped and looked back. "I will send you a message if I find out anything about the man. Keep your eye out for trouble. I feel it is coming."

That is what I was afraid of. Nathan stared at the constable until he disappeared into a crowd gathering at the end of the street near the mercantile. Rachel should be in the general store by now and out of harm's way.

Nathan closed the distance between the mercantile and the

courthouse quickly and entered to search for Rachel. She was nowhere to be seen. He stepped back outside and scanned the area, his gaze pausing a moment on the constable in the middle of the brawl that had broken out between Mr. Cochran and his two sons and Mr. Hawkins and a couple of his friends. Pulling his attention away from the latest form of entertainment for the townspeople, Nathan headed for the dressmaker, passing Rachel's cart where he had left it in the alley at the side of the general store.

Above the ruckus from the street, Nathan heard a scream— a woman's scream. He halted and tried to focus on where the sound had come from. Another scream pierced the air and several people nearby turned toward the sound. He looked behind him and saw Rachel scuffling with a large, heavyset man, who was dragging her down an alley. Heated anger replaced his earlier chill. He ran toward her, noticing as he got closer the long scar on the man's left cheek.

Halfway to her, Nathan shouted, "Let her go."

Her attacker glanced up at him. Their gazes locked across the expanse.

At that moment Rachel bit her assailant's hand that covered her mouth. He howled and struck her across the face then spun on his heel and raced away. Rachel crumpled to the dirt.

Nine

Rachel hit the ground, jarring her senses. Her eyes fluttered then closed. Suddenly arms trapped her against a muscular torso. No! She fisted her hands and started swinging. As she focused on the threat, Nathan's surprised face came into view. Gasping, she stopped pummeling him and threw herself against his chest, hugging him.

For a brief moment the feel of their embrace chased everything from her thoughts but Nathan. Then she realized he was hovering over her on the ground, clasped against her as though they were lovers. Heat scorched her cheeks, and she scrambled to the side. The warmth coursing through her turned to ice when she recalled what had happened in the alley.

"He—he wanted—wanted me to come with him. He told me an Englishwoman was only good for one thing." A shudder passed through Rachel's body, her gaze falling away from Nathan's darkening one. "I didn't. I was only trying to get—"

"Shh, Rachel. When I find that man, I will teach him some manners."

She looked up at him. "Don't. I don't want you to get hurt because of me."

A steel glint entered his eyes. "You need not worry about me." He pushed to his feet and offered her his hand.

She grasped it and relished the strong fingers as they wrapped around hers. What if he had not come when he did? She could have been... No, she would not think about it. *Thank You, Lord, for sending Nathan when You did.*

When she stood, she dusted off her coat and gown to keep her hands busy so Nathan wouldn't see how much she was shaking. If he did, he would start expounding on why she needed to return to England. But what had happened here could occur anywhere.

After she made herself as presentable as possible, she clutched her reticule and said, "We have some supplies to purchase, then I want to leave this town." The quiet of her farm beckoned to her as never before.

Nathan gave her his arm. "I agree. I still have some chores to do at home...at your farm before dark."

"At least the days are getting longer." She walked beside him toward the street and the mercantile. "Mrs. Bridges has hired me to sew gowns for her. I will be able to make some extra money."

Nathan paused and raised an eyebrow. "When do you propose to do that extra work?"

"At night. I need a cow. A supply of milk, cheese, and butter sounds wonderful."

"Do you know how to make butter and cheese?"

Studying his expression with a hint of amusement in it, she tilted her head and smiled. "No, but I am sure someone can teach me how."

"Like baking bread?"

"I'm getting better. At least the last loaves were edible."

He grumbled something under his breath that Rachel was sure was the word "barely," but she chose to ignore it and proceeded forward into the chaos that had erupted on the street—a brawl that must have encompassed half the people on the street in front of the mercantile.

Using his body, Nathan sheltered her from any contact with the fighters or onlookers and ushered her to the general store. "Stay close."

The owner stood at the door, and when he saw Nathan, he unlocked it and allowed them inside. "Good to see you, Dr. Stuart."

Nathan's mouth compressed, but all he did was nod and head deeper into the mercantile.

When Rachel saw a basket of eggs on the counter, she frowned. "I don't understand why the chickens are not producing eggs since that first day. Do you think they are ill?"

Nathan had started for the other side of the store but glanced back and said, "They don't look ill to me, but Patrick and John know more about animals than I do. Perhaps John will be at his house when we return to pick up Faith and Maddy. If so, I will see what he says."

"Good. I used to have eggs for breakfast and miss that." Like many things she had since she left her childhood home. Perhaps if she had read Mary Godwin's *Vindication of the Rights of Women* before she had met Tom, she would have been forewarned of the type of man he was.

* * * * *

Later that day Rachel carried her basket down to the barn. Hopefully, she would have some eggs today. John had thought the chickens would get used to their new environment and would begin laying eggs again soon. When she stepped into the dimly lit building, she let her eyes adjust after the bright sunlight outside, then she marched over to the area that Nathan had set up for the chickens to keep them safe from predators.

Why was the door open? It should be closed at all times.

She entered the stall-turned-henhouse and came to a halt. Not one chicken was sitting on her nest. The place was empty. The rooster crowed so loudly, she whirled around, expecting him to be behind her. He strutted into the barn and ran straight for her, with his wings flapping. She slammed the stall door closed and plastered herself against it to keep it shut.

The rooster made a ruckus outside the henhouse as though he were shouting at her to open up. She dared not. She had seen him attack the cat when it got too close to him or his hens. Surely he would tire of his squawking and leave her alone soon.

But ten minutes later he was still raging at her. Enough so that Maddy appeared in the barn's entrance and shouted she would go get Nathan in the field. Oh good, she would have to be rescued twice in one day.

No, she was not going to let that happen. She was much bigger than a rooster. She set her basket down, crept over to the door, and inched it open. The rooster charged her. She slammed the door closed, her chest rising and falling rapidly. She inhaled a deep breath. Then another one. *He is not going to best me.*

Another idea popped into her mind. She gripped the door handle and one side of her gown, then swung the door open so fast she hoped it made the rooster's head spin. This time she stormed out of the stall, flapping her gown as if it were her wings. Her screeches bounced off the walls of the barn.

The rooster froze for a moment then came at her. She didn't stop but grabbed the other side of her dress and waved it too. Not changing his speed, the rooster turned and made a beeline for the double doors that led outside.

At that moment, Nathan ran through the door and had to jump over the bird to avoid colliding with him. That movement sent Nathan stumbling forward and crashing into a post. He slid to his knees.

Rachel dropped the material of her dress and rushed toward him. "Nathan, are you all right?"

His dazed look greeted her question. She knelt down next to him and put her arm around him, intending to help him up.

He blinked, shook his head, and pulled away. "What's going on in here? I heard your screech and thought you were being attacked."

"Did Maddy tell you about the rooster?"

"No, only that you were in trouble in the barn."

"The hens are gone and the rooster didn't take a liking to me being in the empty henhouse, as if he thought I had something to do with his harem being gone."

Nathan's eyebrows slashed downward. "Where are the hens? When we left this morning for Charleston, I know the door to the stall was latched. I checked before I hitched up the cart."

"Nary an egg or hen in any of the nests."

"We have been robbed!" Maddy came running into the barn, bent over, and drew in gulps of air.

Rachel pivoted toward her at the same time as Nathan and said, "What do you mean?"

"The last of the salted beef you brought from your cabin is gone, Dr. Stuart."

Rachel's gaze locked with Nathan's. "Do you think that gang you told me about robbed us?"

"We need to check everything and see if any other items are missing. I cannot see a gang of thieves only taking a few hens, eggs, and salted beef."

"They would if they are hungry." Rachel went back into the stall and grabbed her basket.

"True, but an ox or pig is worth more than some chickens, and their meat would last a lot longer. I will look around here and outside while you and Maddy take stock of what is in the house."

As Rachel strode toward her home, she asked Maddy, "Where is Faith?"

"In her cradle sleeping."

"I don't want to leave her alone if there are robbers in the area."

"Yes ma'am."

"Nathan was telling me about a way the Indians carry their babies with them. It might be best if I have him show me how. Tomorrow we need to work in the garden planting the vegetables and herbs." Rachel pushed open the door and hurried toward the cradle near the fireplace to make sure Faith was still in it. The very thought of someone coming into her place while they had been gone made the hairs on her arms stand up.

"We need a gun," Maddy said.

"A gun! I don't know how to shoot. Do you?"

"No, but perhaps Dr. Stuart can show us."

"Us?"

Maddy nodded. "I want to be able to protect myself too."

"You did a mighty fine job with Mr. Baker."

Red patches colored the young woman's cheeks. "I really don't know what came over me that day. What if he took the hens and beef?"

"And left his pig?"

"If the pig went missing, we would immediately think it was him."

"Maddy, what is it about the man you don't fancy?"

"He is so…big."

"I think he is rather nice. Sweet. The other day, when he used the pier, he was a perfect gentleman. Didn't he even help you carry the water from the well to the house?"

"And sloshed some on my dress."

"Only because Cat ran across his path." Faith opened her eyes and looked right at Rachel. She stooped over and picked up her daughter. "Let's see if anything else is missing."

An hour later Nathan came in, carrying one of the hens. "I found her where the old nests were."

"How about the others?" Rachel asked as she put Faith back into her cradle.

"One was sitting on my cot and the other found its way back into the stall, or rather the rooster *escorted* her back."

"So no one stole the hens."

"It doesn't look like it, but I don't know how they got out."

"When I went to check if there were any eggs, the door was open."

"Hmm." Nathan rubbed his chin. "Was anything else missing in here?"

"Not that we could find. How about you?"

"Everything is accounted for."

"What about the salted beef?" Maddy walked back into the main room from the bedchamber.

"And the eggs? According to John my hens should be laying them, especially since they did that first day."

"I don't have an answer." Nathan started to leave with the chicken.

"Then that means we still might have a thief," Maddy said.

"Yes." Stepping outside, Nathan closed the door behind him.

The sound of it clicking into place echoed through the quiet. Rachel shivered. "We need to lay a trap for the thief."

"How?"

"Let me think on it. I cannot have someone stealing from us. We don't have that much."

* * * * *

A week later, Rachel paced in front of the fireplace. "Nothing we have done has caught the thief. I found a broken egg on the ground in the stall this morning. No matter when we stake out the hen-house, he comes when we are not watching. I think he is watching us. We need a dog."

Rising from the table, Nathan chuckled. "Where do you propose getting a dog?"

"Your brother has several hunting dogs. Do you think he would loan us one?"

"Actually, John has one that lives in the stable with the horses and can cause quite a ruckus if a stranger comes around. I am sure we can 'borrow' him. I probably will see him in town in a few days."

"A few days? Are they not at Liberty Hall right now?"

"Yes, but I still have the planting to finish up. I should be through in a few days."

Rachel stopped her pacing and swung around with her hand at her waist. "I didn't have the heart to tell you the rabbit you killed yesterday was missing this morning. At this rate we will starve."

"He took my rabbit?" Indignation sounded in his voice as his amused look evolved into a frown.

She nodded. "I was going to make a rabbit stew for dinner today. It is gone from the barn where you skinned it."

"Something needs to be done, but I cannot take the time right now away from planting."

"But I can. I can hitch your horse to the cart and go to Liberty Hall today. I shall leave Maddy here to do the washing, and I shall take Faith. I can set up something for her to lie on in the back of the cart."

"By yourself?"

The other hand went to her waist. "I have to do it sometime. You will not always be here. Besides, John and Sarah are neighbors. It is only three miles away. Not but thirty minutes. I thought I would take the gown I'm making for Sarah and make sure it is fitting properly. I understand this ball gown is for the big festival in May at Liberty Hall. I am not going by myself. Faith shall be with me."

"In that case, you have all the protection you need." His frown grew into a scowl.

She marched up to him, fury speeding through her blood as if it were lava pouring from a volcano. "I'm responsible for myself and my own protection. You will not be here for much longer, so you had better get used to my doing things for myself." As she had to get used to the idea she was totally on her own.

He halved the short distance between them, his own anger welling to the surface in a fierce expression. "How are you going to do that? Shake your finger at someone?"

"I have Tom's flintlock. I need to learn to hunt. You can teach me to fire a gun."

His mouth fell open, his eyes growing huge. "Shoot a gun? Hunt? What has gotten into you?"

"Reality. You are going hunting a couple of times a week to supplement our food supply. I am not so naïve that I don't think a stranger like the one who accosted me in Charleston could not do it again. Is there a problem with teaching me to shoot? Don't you want to leave me able to take care of myself?"

"No, I want you to go home to England and forget this foolishness."

"If you will not help me, I shall ask Mr. Baker. I think he would. I believe he is sweet on Maddy. She wants to learn too."

Nathan raked both hands through his hair. "Maddy! What has gotten into you women?"

"After that encounter in Charleston and this thief, I think my request makes perfect sense." She spun around and strode to the door, glancing back as she opened it to say, "I'm going to hitch your horse to the cart."

"What if I say no?"

"Then I shall walk. It is a beautiful day, and most likely Maddy will not get all the laundry done because she will have to watch Faith. So which way shall I go? In the cart or walking?"

He mumbled something she couldn't hear.

"I do declare you need to speak up. I cannot hear you."

"I was just wondering whatever possessed me to agree to help you in the first place."

"I don't know. What did?" She cocked her head to the side and sent him a grin.

"Use my horse." He closed the space between them. "I will be out in the field."

"I shall have Maddy prepare your dinner. She is becoming quite good at cooking." She was pleased at least one of them was, because she still had not mastered the art of making bread. Perhaps when she bought a cow, she would be better at butter and cheese making.

Nathan grumbled under his breath and left the house, his strides long and economical as he headed for the barn, his arms swinging stiffly at his sides. His body screamed anger.

At least she had made her point. She would take care of herself. The fact he had to rescue her a second time in Charleston did not set well with her. What would happen when he wasn't around? She had to learn to rely totally on herself.

* * * * *

Out in the middle of the half-planted field, Nathan glared at the plowed ground, the stench of manure mixed into the soil wafting up to him. *Rachel wants to learn to shoot a gun. She could kill herself. She could…*

The anger boiling inside of him churned his gut. She would ask Mr. Baker to teach her if he didn't. Since she had her husband's flintlock, the argument she would have to buy a gun would not work. At the moment he didn't see any way around it. He would have to teach her and ensure she learned the correct way. He didn't want to

FROM THIS DAY FORWARD

feel responsible for her shooting an innocent person—or herself—
by accident.

The memory of the man in the alley with his hands on her cur-
dled Nathan's blood, inflaming his anger even more. If he ever saw
that man, he would make him regret assaulting her. It should be safe
for a lady to walk the streets of Charleston—at least in that part of
town in broad daylight—without fear of being attacked. He would
have a word with the constable when they went back to town in a few
days after the planting was finished.

What if that man caught her on the road today going to his sister? Although the sun beat down warmly, coldness burrowed into
Nathan's bones. He would write another letter to her parents and
oldest brother just in case his first one didn't reach them. If they
came for her, his life could return to normal.

He knelt next to a small hill of dirt and poked a hole in it then
put two corn seeds in it and covered them with earth. Moving on to
the next spot, he continued the same procedure, glad it was mind-
less work, as his thoughts kept going back to the woman he felt obligated to watch over.

Her anger earlier at his attempt to get her to do what he wanted
in order to keep her safe still baffled him. Most women he knew
wanted to be coddled and taken care of. If Rachel discovered he
had asked Sarah to approach Mrs. Bridges about hiring her, she
would be furious. He had hoped the dressmaker could persuade
Rachel to move to Charleston and give up on this idea of running
a farm. Instead the lady had asked Rachel to sew for her at home,
giving Rachel a means to earn money for the farm. He had offered
to pay Mrs. Bridges for Rachel's wages, but the lady had declined,

especially when she saw the work Rachel was capable of. He had thought Rachel would welcome moving to town if she had a means to support herself.

Finishing one row, Nathan started another. Why didn't Rachel act like the other women he was acquainted with? But then his mother hadn't either, and she had been an Englishwoman. She had left them in Grandfather's care but had arranged a yearly income from her family for him so he didn't have to worry about money. Why? Because she had known about his desire to be a doctor, not a planter, and hadn't wanted Grandfather dictating what he did?

Overhead a seagull shrieked, gliding on a wind current. Nathan looked up at the bird as it disappeared from view then surveyed the field and surrounding woods. The hairs on his nape tingled. A sense of being watched heightened his alertness. Searching the dense undergrowth to the west where the swamp was, he rose, catching sight of movement about a hundred yards away.

Nathan charged forward, plunging into the thick brush.

* * * * *

The screech of a bird overhead jolted Rachel. She jumped on the wooden seat of the cart, gripping the reins in case the horse bolted at the loud noise. Nathan's gelding kept its steady pace on the road to Liberty Hall. She glanced back to see how Faith was doing. Her daughter was staring at the trees as though mesmerized as they passed them.

As much as Rachel didn't care for weapons of any kind, Maddy's suggestion made sense to her. They needed to know how to protect themselves, whether Nathan was with them or not. Their discussion—well, perhaps argument—firmed in her mind that she had to tell him she would split in half whatever the crops yielded this year. She would not allow him to do all the work he did for a small percentage. It was not right. And as much as she wished she could take over in the next month or so, she didn't know how she could. Perhaps after she understood what to do through the spring and summer months, until the harvest was complete in the fall. Would Nathan stay?

By the time Rachel reached Liberty Hall, she was resolved to approach Nathan about staying for six more months and being equal partners as far as the crops went.

Sarah greeted her with a hug. "You brought Faith. How is she doing?"

"Good. She's a happy baby."

"Has reading Moss's *Essay on the Management and Nursing of Children in the Earlier Periods of Infancy* helped you?"

"Yes. I especially like the part of not overfeeding Faith, and giving her room to move. She likes to kick her legs and wave her arms."

"I found Sean hated being confined by blankets and swaddling. Once I read Dr. Moss's thoughts on it, my son was much happier. Come into the parlor. We can have some tea and sweets Cook made yesterday, and you can tell me why you have come."

Settled on the sofa with Faith in her lap, Rachel waited until Sarah had returned with a tray and was sitting across from her before saying, "It is your brother. He can be most difficult at times."

Sarah poured the tea and gave Rachel a cup. "That is Nathan. I have tried everything to get him to be available when I go into labor, but he refuses, no matter how much I plead. After last time, I wanted a doctor in attendance rather than a midwife, but I don't care for Dr. Ellsworth." She fluttered her hand in the air. "Enough about that. What brings you to Liberty Hall?"

"We have a thief stealing food at the farm. I came to see if you all would loan me the use of a dog. Nathan told me you have one that is quite protective and lives in your stable."

"He is a most excellent watchdog. Sean loves him. I would be glad to lend him to you. You cannot have a thief. He will get bolder and bolder as he gets away with his stealing."

"I asked Nathan to teach me to shoot. I don't know if he will, but this thief has made it clear I need to know how."

"If he will not, I will show you what little I know from watching John."

After sipping her tea, Rachel placed the cup and saucer on the table and leaned back, cradling Faith, who was enthralled with her new environment. "I suggested seeing if Mr. Baker would teach me, which did not set well with your brother."

Sarah chuckled. "Men. They think we are so incapable of taking care of ourselves. During the war John was gone for several years, with infrequent trips home. I managed running the plantation and our affairs in Charleston quite well. Even John said so. Perhaps I need to remind my brother of that."

"I appreciate the offer, but I will convince him." Rachel picked up Faith and laid her against her shoulder and patted her. "I also brought the morning gown I made for you to try on. I want to make sure it fits, since I shall be working on the ball gown next."

"That would be wonderful. The one I would have worn will not do, since I am with child. I hope you will come to the ball in May. It will be here at Liberty Hall this year, and you can stay overnight with us. Some of our other guests will."

Thinking of the fine fabric and the dress she would make for Sarah, Rachel considered her limited wardrobe. She had sold her ball gowns before leaving England. If what Tom said had been true, she could have replenished her clothing when she reached America according to what needs she had. "I probably shouldn't—"

"I will not allow you to decline my invitation. We have become friends, and I want my friends to be at the festivities. I have a half-mourning gown I think would fit you perfectly. 'Tis lavender."

Rachel hadn't been to a ball in over a year. She loved to dance and had missed doing it. "If you are sure."

"Most definitely. Then it is settled. Besides, I have an ulterior motive for asking you. If you come, I am counting on Nathan coming too."

Rachel smiled. "I like how you think."

* * * * *

Knee-deep in water, Nathan spied a flash of blue to his left and plunged deeper into the swamp. He was sure whoever was watching him was the thief. If he caught him, perhaps Rachel would give up the notion of learning to shoot.

He sloshed up onto higher ground where his boots only sank a few inches into the muddy bog. Cypress trees closed in around him with vegetation thickening, making progress slow. But broken twigs and smashed-down greenery indicated he was on the right trail. A faint murmur of voices drifted to him. He halted and listened. To the left. He changed his direction and went through the thicket that clawed at his clothing and skin.

The voices grew louder. There were two thieves. This was Rachel's land, and no one would be here unless they were up to no good. What if it was the man who had attacked her in Charleston? Nathan's fingers clutched his flintlock while he peered down at his sheath that bore his knife. Well-armed, he would see this through and perhaps finally have some peace concerning Rachel.

A stick snapped behind him. He pivoted toward the sound, but halfway around, something hard crushed into his skull. Blackness fell over him.

Ten

Her visit with Sarah had been what Rachel needed to see Nathan in a calmer light. The past few years had not been easy for him with the war, his difficulties with his grandfather, and his mother's abandonment. Now that she was a mother, Rachel did not understand the woman's change of heart. From what Sarah had said, both her parents had loved their children and they had been a close family. What happened to change that?

Perhaps his mother didn't know what heartache her actions had cost her son. What if she wrote to her and let Nathan's mother know what her silence had caused her children? Perhaps she could help mend this family she had come to care about. She and Nathan would be going into Charleston when the planting was finished at the end of the week. She could post it then.

The laundry spread out on the bushes near the house as well as the line that Nathan had put up was the first thing Rachel saw when she came into view of her place in the early afternoon, the sun indicating it was perhaps two o'clock. Her servant was becoming indispensable to her. The sight of what Maddy had accomplished spread a smile across Rachel's face.

Until Maddy bolted from the house, running straight toward

her, alarm on her pert face. Her mobcap sat on her head askew, and mud caked the hem of her dress.

Breathless, she met Rachel a hundred feet from the front door. "Dr. Stuart is missing. I saw him going into the swamp earlier. He has not come back. I started to go search for him. I got stuck in the mud, and I screamed and screamed for him to come help. He never did, ma'am. Something is terribly wrong."

"How did you get out of the mud?" Rachel stopped the horse and twisted around to pick up Faith, who had fallen asleep.

The McNeal's dog stood up in the cart, staring at Maddy and growling low in his throat.

"Jasper, it is all right."

Maddy, wide-eyed, backed away. "What's that thing?"

"A dog."

"I never saw one like that. 'Tis huge."

"All the better to catch our thief. He is an Irish wolfhound, according to Sarah."

"Perhaps it has a horse somewhere in its lineage."

"He is really quite lovable. And big." Rachel motioned for Maddy to come closer and when she hesitantly did, Rachel passed Faith to her. After hopping down to the ground, she took her daughter again and started for the house, saying, "Jasper, come."

"He is!" Maddy's gaze grew even larger.

"You faced down Mr. Baker. Surely Jasper, who is smaller, is not a threat to you. Now who helped you out of the mud?"

"Mr. Baker. He heard me screaming and came and plucked me right out. You should have seen it. You would think I weighed no more than a feather."

Entering her house, Rachel looked around. "Where is Mr. Baker?"

"Searching for Dr. Stuart. He has been gone almost since you drove away. He left the field only partially planted. I know he was determined to finish that one today, so I don't know why he went into the swamp." Maddy wrapped her arms about herself.

"Help me strap Faith on and then you and I can continue planting until Mr. Baker comes back. It is probably nothing." She didn't really believe her words, but Maddy's agitation began to encompass Rachel with a sense of panic she dare not give into.

"Mr. Baker has been gone at least an hour. I turned the sand-glass over and the top is empty." Maddy pointed at the timekeeper, her hand trembling. "I am worried about…" She bit her teeth into her bottom lip.

I am worried too. But she would not voice that to Maddy. Rachel found the scraps of cloth she used to bind her daughter against her when she needed to work with her hands free. She gave them to Maddy and held Faith clasped to her chest while her servant crisscrossed the pieces of material and tied them in back, securing her child safely. *Now if only Nathan is safe. Please, Lord, bring him back here.*

She and Maddy walked out to the field, the one nearest to the house, where Nathan's sack of seed and a hoe lay on the plowed earth. She worked on one row while Maddy worked on another. Rachel's gaze kept straying toward the swamp. Although the temperature was seasonably warm, a chill encased her in fear.

What if Nathan is gone? Never returns? Is dead—like Tom?

Her fear mushroomed until she fumbled the seeds and a handful ended up in a hole. She returned the excess corn to the bag. Why couldn't she do it right? The way Nathan had shown her the other day. No wonder he was frustrated with her. No wonder he was worried about teaching her to shoot.

Finally, too upset with herself to continue, she knelt in the dirt and prayed for Nathan. If she had not wrecked on the road, he would right now be blissfully alone at his cabin, not feeling responsible for her.

Father, I need Your strength. I need Your guidance. Perhaps she could work something out with Mr. Baker—if he returned—and accept Mrs. Bridges' offer of a job at her dress shop.

"Ma'am, 'tis them. Mr. Baker is carrying Dr. Stuart."

Rachel swiveled around toward the swamp and saw Mr. Baker carrying Nathan over his shoulder, struggling in the calf-high water at the edge of the raised field. She leaped to her feet and raced toward the men with Maddy right behind her. The sudden motion awakened Faith, who began to fuss at the jarring pace.

"Shh, honey. I need to help Nathan." She circled her arms around her daughter as she ran.

Mr. Baker trudged to high ground as Rachel reached his side. "About halfway to my land, I found him wanderin' around. We started back toward your place and he passed out. He has a lump on his head."

Rachel positioned herself so she could see Nathan's pale face, his hair matted with blood, the nasty wound. "Did he say anything?"

"'Twas only babblin'." Mr. Baker continued his steady pace toward the house.

Inside, Rachel directed her neighbor to take Nathan into her bedchamber and lay him on her bed, wishing her straw mattress had his feather tick—soft, comfortable—on top. "Maddy, help me unwrap Faith and take care of her while I see to Nathan. I shall need you to bring me water and clean rags."

Mr. Baker removed Nathan's wet, muddy boots then stood back while Rachel examined the injury. "Is there anything ya want me to do?"

"Yes, please get a shirt and trousers. He stays in the barn. We need to get him out of these dirty clothes."

Mr. Baker nodded then left the room. Kneeling next to the bed, Rachel probed Nathan's scalp to see if there were any other lumps. "What happened to you?" she whispered. When her fingertips grazed his wound, he jerked, his eyes flying open then sliding closed.

At least there was only one bump. Did he get it falling and hitting his head? Or did someone do this to him? The thief plaguing them?

Maddy rushed into the room with a bowl of water and some pieces of cloth. "I washed them this morning, so they are clean. What else can I do?"

"Make willow bark tea. When I had a head injury it helped me some." Inadequacy drenched her in a cold sweat. This was Nathan's expertise, not hers. All she could think of was to clean the wound and make him comfortable. *And pray.*

As gently as she could she cleansed the injury and the scalp around it, praying the whole time that he would wake soon and continue his argument with her. Then she would know he was going to be all right. Her plea to the Lord calmed some of her fears, but a little voice kept whispering in her mind, "What will you do if he dies?"

Mr. Baker came back into the bedchamber with Nathan's garments as she finished doing what little she could. She dropped the bloody cloth into the bloody water, her gaze riveted on them. Her body quaked. Nathan was hurt because he was helping her.

She pushed herself to her feet and turned toward Mr. Baker. "We need to get him out of those dirty, wet clothes and into some dry ones."

"Not we, ma'am. Me. I will take care of him."

"The bed linen needs to be changed too. All I have until it is washed is a blanket for him to lie on."

"Git me the blanket. I will do it. Not a job for you."

The expression on Mr. Baker's face shouted that he would not be persuaded to do anything but what he said. Since he was twice her size, she decided not to argue with him. "Very well." She strode to the trunk along the wall and withdrew a blanket then put it at the bottom of the bed and left the room, closing the door.

"What happened to Dr. Stuart?" Maddy held Faith and paced in front of the fireplace, worry tingeing every feature.

"I don't know, but we need to find out. It cannot happen again."

"Send for the constable?"

"I will need to go into Charleston in a few days to deliver my work to Mrs. Bridges. I can report this to the constable then."

"Alone?"

"If I have to. Because if Nathan is not better by then, a doctor needs to see him."

Loud voices sounded from her bedchamber. One angry. One appeasing. The door flew open and Mr. Baker came out into the main room. "I'm thinkin' he will be all right. He ordered me out. Told me he was capable of dressin' hisself."

Through the entrance into the bedchamber Rachel glimpsed

MARGARET DALEY

Nathan, bare-chested as he shrugged on a muslin shirt then tried to stand. He collapsed back on the bed, wincing, a moan escaping his lips.

Rachel scurried into the room and planted herself in front of him with her hand on her hip. "What do you think you are doing?"

His gaze remained downcast. "Going back to work. There is still a lot to do."

"Not for you."

His attention fastened onto her face, intense, heated, and pain filled. "If the seeds are not planted, then there is no crop. Which means no money."

"Maddy and I will finish the field."

He snorted and tried to rise again. He swayed and nearly toppled into her.

She caught him and helped him back onto the bed. "You are staying right here if I have to get Mr. Baker to tie you down. I doubt you are in any condition to fight him."

His eyes slid closed, and he sighed. "Fine. I will rest for a little bit then go out and complete the field. Will that satisfy you?"

"Yes. What happened to you?"

"Someone hit me over the head."

"Who? The thieves?"

"I don't know." He moved his head and winced.

"I will get you a cup of willow bark tea. That should help you."

He didn't say anything. Rachel walked from the room and went to the kettle in the fireplace, poured hot water into a cup, retrieved some willow bark to steep in the liquid, and took it to him.

When she returned to the main room, Maddy frowned. "You are going to let him go back and work? He can barely stand."

165

"No." Rachel lowered her voice so only her servant and Mr. Baker heard. "I'm going to shut the door to let him rest. Then, Maddy, you and I shall go out in the field and plant the rest of the seed. Mr. Baker, will you stay and keep him from getting up?"

"How do I do that?"

"Any way you can. It is for his own good."

"All right. I can do that. Thank goodness he is not known to be a violent man." Mr. Baker marched toward the door. "I saw somethin' in the barn I can use. Be back."

Maddy peered at Rachel. "What?"

"Don't know. Don't care so long as it keeps him from doing too much." Rachel picked up the strips of cloth she had used earlier to strap her daughter to her chest. "I cannot ask a bachelor like Mr. Baker to watch over Faith while we are in the field."

After Maddy secured Faith to Rachel again, Mr. Baker returned to the house with a fist full of rope. Rachel chuckled. "I don't think I want to know what you are going to do with that."

"Only what is necessary. I hope that Dr. Stuart is a forgivin' man." He eased the bedchamber door open and peeked inside the room and then back at Rachel. "He is asleep. I think I will take the opportunity to tie him up. Then I can go nose around that area where I found him. I will feel a lot better knowin' what's goin' on out there."

"So will I. Thank you for your help, Mr. Baker. I hope you will come to dinner next Sunday."

He beamed. "I ain't goin' t' turn down a home-cooked meal I don't have to cook, ma'am."

* * * * *

"'Tis getting dark, Mrs. Gordon."

Rachel put a couple of seeds in the last hole of the last row. "There. Finished. Only one more field to be planted, then everything is in the Lord's hands." Rising, she stretched and arched her back to ease her tight muscles. "Let's go check on Dr. Stuart. Perhaps we can get the ropes off him before he wakes up." So far Nathan had not awakened when Maddy or she had gone back to check on him through the rest of the afternoon. She would just as soon not have to deal with an angry, trapped Nathan.

Maddy helped take the strips of cloth off Rachel then took Faith. "She's such a sweet baby."

Rachel started for the house, allowing Maddy to hold her daughter. The young woman was becoming more attached to Faith each day. *She* was becoming more attached to Faith. Having her changed everything in Rachel's life. She pictured what her child would look like when she was four. Or eighteen, when the beaus would come around.

Ferocious barking coming from the barn blasted the air. Rachel dropped the sack and hoe and without thinking raced across the short distance, swinging open the double doors at the same moment a four-foot-tall girl plowed right into her with a small basket in her hand, knocking Rachel to the ground with the child on top of her. Before the young girl could hop up, Rachel locked her arms about her and pinned the little thief against her.

"Let me go!" The child rocked back and forth.

But Rachel gripped her hands together to reinforce her hold. "You are not going anywhere. What were you doing in there? Stealing my eggs?"

The wild-looking girl, her brown hair tangled, her face dirty, drilled her stare into Rachel as though it could harm her. The child pressed her mouth together so tightly her lips disappeared into a hard, thin line. With her arms plastered to her sides, she tried one more time to wrestle herself free by kicking her legs.

"Ouch! You want to make the situation even worse. I wonder what the constable will say about stealing and hurting people."

"I ain't hurtin' ya. Let me go and I git."

"So you can steal from me again. No." Rachel suddenly flipped the girl onto her back. Rachel was now on top and she asked, "Where are your parents?"

The girl averted her head and glared at Maddy standing a few feet from them, while Jasper stood alert, growling.

"I shall go put Faith in her cradle and come back and help you, ma'am."

"Please do. This wildcat needs to be tamed."

The child returned her attention to Rachel. "Ya can beat me. I ain't sayin' a thing."

"Beat you? Who beats you?"

Again the girl's lips locked together, her green eyes becoming slits.

Maddy rushed across the yard toward Rachel with some rope in her hand. "Mr. Baker didn't use it all. We can tie her up until the constable comes."

"I don't think we have to do that. We are two women, and she is only a child. You take one arm, and I will the other." When Maddy neared them, Rachel rolled to the side, letting go partially so her servant could grab their little thief.

Rachel rose and she and Maddy tried to pull the child up. As they tugged harder, the girl leaped to her feet, sending both of the women sprawling backwards into the dirt. The thief whirled and made a dash toward the swamp. Jasper gave chase, barking. The child increased her speed.

"Jasper, stop."

As the Irish wolfhound obeyed, Rachel jumped up, and from some well of energy deep inside her, she ran after the girl and tackled her to the ground. Maddy snatched one arm while Rachel took the other, and they yanked the child to her feet. She continued to twist and kick at both of them.

"Let me go!" the girl yelled.

Jasper began barking again.

"Jasper, go inside." Rachel pointed at the barn. The dog walked to the doors, glancing back every few paces.

Rachel started for her house, dodging the flailing limbs as much as possible. But the child got in a couple of well-placed hits. Rachel ground her teeth and increased her pace. When they reached the house, the little thief let out a bellow of rage followed by a screech like the owl that nested in a live oak by the barn. The moment she was inside, as Rachel angled around to lock the door, the girl jerked free and frantically looked around for a way to escape.

"There is only one way in and out of here." Rachel motioned to Maddy to stand by the cradle where Faith was while Rachel leaned back against the door with her arms crossed.

The wildcat ran toward Rachel's bedchamber and pushed the door open, its crashing sound bringing Nathan fully awake. He tried to bolt upright and discovered the ropes that bound him.

"Rachel!" He swung his head toward Rachel, who could see him clearly on her bed through the open doorway. "What have you done?" Then his gaze latched onto the young girl standing a few feet inside the room, frozen in place. "Who are you?"

The child swept around and raced back into the main room, scanning for another place to go. She saw the second bedchamber and frowned, a glimpse of fear in her eyes, before pivoting away from the closed door. She spied the stairs that led up to the loft and clambered up them. After she poked her head through the opening and glanced back, she sank down on the top step.

"Rachel, what is going on? Untie me."

"Ya ain't goin' t' tie me up. I will kick and hit and scream and..." The fury in the child petered out.

Rachel considered the girl perched on the stairs and Nathan struggling to free himself on her bed. At the moment she would rather face the child than Nathan. His howl of rage prompted her to move fast.

"Maddy, don't let her leave. Call me if you need me."

"Yes ma'am." Her servant took Rachel's post at the door and glared at the wildcat, her look daring her to move.

Rachel trod toward her bedchamber, feeling as if all her energy had been siphoned from her. Perhaps she should not have let Mr. Baker tie up Nathan, since he hadn't awakened the whole afternoon. Then she wouldn't be in the situation where she had to explain why he was bound to her bed.

"If the thief hadn't struck again, you would have never known you were tied up." Rachel paused a few feet from him in case he somehow had loosened the ropes and could escape his confines.

He opened his mouth to say something but instead snapped it closed. The steely expression in his eyes said it all.

She was sure if he could get his hands on her right now, it would not bode well for her. Anger slashed his face. When Tom had been upset with her, he usually hit her at least once. It seemed to make him feel better to hurt her. In those cases she had rarely done anything to Tom, but when he started drinking, he imagined all kinds of offenses.

Now, though, she was partially responsible for Nathan's latest predicament.

"I was afraid you would try to work when you should rest. You were being unreasonable earlier, and I didn't want anything else to happen to you. Your wound was quite nasty. I know how much a head injury can hurt." When his expression remained cold and furious, she continued. "You are stubborn, and I know if Mr. Baker hadn't tied you up, you would be out trying to plant the rest of the corn." She drew herself up tall. "Maddy and I finished the job. You don't have to." Her rambling came to a breathless halt, no other words material-izing in her mind.

"Undo these ropes." Each word was distinctly pronounced with a fierce undertone.

"Promise me you will not hurt me."

Nathan's eyes widened. "Hurt you?"

She nodded. "You are angry with me."

"Yes, I am, but that does not mean I will hurt you. I cannot make the same guarantee concerning Mr. Baker, though."

"He was only trying to help me."

Nathan snagged her gaze, some of the hardness in his eyes soft-ening. "I promise I will not hurt you. Ever."

The tense set of her shoulders sagged, and she covered the distance to the bed. Kneeling next to it, she worked on the ropes until the first set slipped away, and Nathan could sit up and finish the job. Then he swung his feet to the floor and rose halfway before sinking back onto the mattress.

"Let me help you." She laid her hand on his arm.

He shook it off. "I can do this myself."

Rachel backed away, giving him plenty of room. She still didn't know he would not come after her. She didn't think so. Nathan's word meant a lot to him. He had not wanted to bring her to the farm, and yet he had promised her, so he had brought her in the end against his better judgment.

He sat for a few minutes, clutching the side of the bed. "Who's that girl?"

"Our thief. I caught her coming out of the barn when John's dog began to bark."

"What's her name? Where does she live?"

"She refuses to say."

Nathan frowned and slowly pushed himself to his feet. Closing his eyes, he stood for a couple of minutes.

"I can help you."

His eyes snapped open. "No!"

"You helped me. Why can I not help you?"

"Because I am fine."

"You are a doctor. I think you know what it means to be fine, and you are not that."

He peered at her and rubbed his forehead.

"Can I get you more willow bark tea?"

His gaze zeroed in on her face, and for a long moment he didn't say anything, then he sighed. "All right. Yes, I could use some."

She whirled around and hurried from the room to prepare his drink. She had the water poured into a cup when Nathan came to the doorway and leaned against it, taking in the young girl still on the stairs, glaring at him.

"Who are you?" he asked the child.

She folded her arms across her chest and averted her head.

He slowly walked farther into the main room and stopped near the stairs. "From the looks of you, does your family live in the swamps?"

Rachel finished making the tea and came to Nathan to give it to him. Now that she could study the child, she saw that she appeared to be about eight or nine, wearing a dress that was badly torn, almost as if she had managed to gather a bunch of rags to wear about herself. Her feet were bare and mud caked. On the part of the legs Rachel could see, the child had sores and cuts.

Suddenly all Rachel's anger at the wildcat drained away. She needed the eggs more than they did.

"Maddy, prepare supper while I go get the eggs that are hopefully in the nests." She peered at the girl. "I am bringing the dog up here to make sure you don't go anywhere tonight. We need answers from you."

"Ya can beat me. I ain't talkin'." The child lifted her chin and wouldn't meet Rachel's look.

Nathan turned toward the door. "I will go get the eggs and dog." But he swayed from the movement and fell back against the staircase, gripping the wood to steady himself.

"No. Between Maddy and me I think we could tie you up again.

If you will not lie down, then at least sit. You can keep an eye on our little thief."

He grumbled and made his way slowly to the chair in front of the fire, near the cradle and the entrance to the house. Rachel doubted he could do anything if the girl tried to run away. He was wobbly on his feet, but she would not say anything to Nathan to disillusion him about protecting them.

Taking her basket, she left the house. The light from the two windows in front and the lantern she held were the only illumination in the darkness. Surveying the black curtain surrounding the house and barn, she sensed eyes on her. Was the girl alone or with someone else? She would feel better with Jasper in the house.

Inside the barn the soft glow from the lantern shone on the path to the stall where the hens were. The huge dog came up, sniffing her hand and waggling his tail. "You did good, Jasper. I wish I could keep you. When Nathan leaves, I would feel better having a watchdog."

After checking the nests and gathering half a dozen eggs, Rachel closed the stall door and made sure it was latched shut. At the entrance to the barn, she said, "Come, Jasper."

The dog trotted toward her and out into the night. Halfway to the house, Jasper stopped, a low growl coming from his throat. Rachel halted too and swept around in a full circle, trying to penetrate the darkness that bathed the landscape. She saw nothing but the faint lines of the barn and several large trees. Was someone behind one of them?

Chills snaked up her spine and prodded her forward toward the safety of the house. "Come on, Jasper." The dog followed but kept looking about him.

Inside, the first thing she did was lock the door, throwing the bolt. She turned away to find Nathan watching her. One eyebrow rose in question. "Clouds are covering the moon," she said, as though that would reassure her and the others. "I have six eggs and one was broken on the ground." She threw a look toward the child still sitting on the top step. "We can use them tomorrow when we break our fast."

Maddy set the food on the table while Nathan covered the short distance and sat to eat. Rachel tore off some bread and passed it to Maddy. The child remained where she was.

After saying the blessing, Rachel peered at the girl. "You can join us if you are hungry."

The girl angled away and stared at the fire as if the flames were the most fascinating sight she had seen. But Rachel caught her glancing at the food with longing in her eyes before she masked it and returned to her study of the blaze.

* * * * *

"I had better go to the barn." A smile touched Nathan's lips as he watched Faith in the cradle in front of the fire.

"No, you should stay here tonight." Rachel worked on Sarah's ball gown, using the light from the blaze. "I would feel better in case you have problems with your injury."

Nathan shot a look at the child, perched now at the bottom of the staircase. "Then I will make a pallet to sleep on out here."

"When I was hurt, you gave me your bed. I will return the favor. You should sleep in my bedchamber while we girls stay out here."

As expected, he scowled. "I cannot allow that."

"Why not?"

He rose to his feet, his hand going to the back of the chair. "Because…" He closed his eyes for a moment then, when he opened them, murmured, "Very well. But if you have any trouble"—he slid his glance toward the young girl—"call me."

"I doubt we will." She, too, peered pointedly at the child. "Jasper is capable of taking care of any intruder. Don't you think?"

The girl snorted. "He tooks me by surprise."

Rachel put her sewing down in the large basket she kept it in and stood. "Don't worry about us. Maddy and I caught her with Jasper's help. We are not going to let her go until we get answers."

Nathan gave her a nod then headed for the bedchamber. His slow pace and occasional hand on a piece of furniture attested to how he felt, but what really emphasized the toll his injury had on him was the fact he had not argued much at all about staying in her bedchamber.

After Nathan shut the door, Rachel shifted toward the child. "I have left some bread and cheese out for you if you decide you are hungry after all."

"I would rather—"

"You have a choice. You can sleep in here with us or in the other bedchamber by yourself."

The girl's wide gaze swung to the closed door of that room. Fear flittered in and out of her expression so quickly that Rachel wasn't sure that was the emotion the child experienced. But it was the second time she had reacted to the bedchamber. Did she have something to do with the man who was killed?

"What is the matter? Scared to be by yourself?" Rachel hoped

MARGARET DALEY

the taunt would produce some kind of reaction that would tell her something about the child.

"Me?" The girl bolted to her feet and glared at her. "I ain't scared of nobody. Certainly not you or being alone."

"Well then, Maddy, why don't you give her a blanket?" Rachel changed Faith's nappy then scooped up her daughter to nurse her before putting her in her cradle.

Maddy handed the child a blanket from the trunk, and she trudged toward the bedchamber. At the entrance she inched the door open and glanced back before moving into the room. With Faith in her arms, Rachel crossed to the chamber and peered inside. The child stood only a foot inside, clutching the blanket to her, staring at the place where the man had been.

"Is there something you need to tell me? Have you been in this room before?"

The girl whirled around, anger welling to the surface, her eyes slits, her body rigid. "No! I likes to sleep outside."

"See you tomorrow morning then." Rachel gave her a smile that did nothing to thaw the fierce expression on the child's face.

She waited a moment to allow her to find a place to sleep while the light from the fire illuminated the room. The girl went to the opposite side from where the man had been and curled up on the floor, pulling the blanket over her. Since the small bedchamber was windowless, Rachel didn't fear the child would escape. Rachel quietly shut the door then resumed sitting in her chair by the fireplace to nurse Faith.

* * * * *

177

A whimper penetrated Rachel's dreamless sleep. As exhausted as she was, she couldn't surrender to the black void when a sob followed the first sound. She came awake and stared at the ceiling for a moment to get her bearings in the faint glow of the fire. In the main room. Maddy sleeping by the door near Jasper. Faith in her cradle.

Another cry echoed through the quiet. Coming from the other end of the room. Nathan? No. It was coming from the bedchamber the girl was in. Rachel sat up on her pallet and scanned the area to make sure all was well, then she clambered to her feet as yet another sob drifted to her. A sound of such sorrow that her heart twisted.

At the door she listened, wondering if the child was laying a trap for her. But as the cries continued, cries that tightened a grip about her chest, cutting off her next breath, Rachel pushed into the bedchamber. The light from the fire barely touched the room, and it took her a moment to locate the girl in the far corner, curled in a ball. Rachel rushed to her and knelt next to her.

"What's wrong?" She laid a hand on the child's back.

The sounds coming from the girl wrenched Rachel. The same sounds of agony had come from herself only months before. Remembering the time on the ship when Tom had beaten her so badly she thought she might have lost her baby, she stroked the girl, trying to impart as much comfort as she could. When Tom had left her, she had poured her sorrow out to the Lord. The next night Tom had fallen overboard in a drunken stupor. Was she the reason Tom was dead? She never wanted to feel responsible for someone dying. For nights after that, she had not been able to sleep.

"You are safe here," Rachel whispered, wanting to take away whatever hurt enveloped the girl.

"No, I ain't." The child threw herself against Rachel, clutching her as though she were a safe harbor after a long, perilous journey.

When Rachel embraced her, the girl wept even more, her tears soaking the front of Rachel's gown. "Nothing is so bad the Lord cannot help. You are not alone." She did not even know if the child heard her.

"Ma'am, are you all right?" In the doorway, Maddy stood framed in the glow of the blaze.

"Yes, add a few logs to the fire and go back to bed."

"Are you sure?"

"Very." When the girl was through, she would be emotionally exhausted and would seek sleep. Rachel knew this from experience.

Minutes ticked away and slowly the child calmed down. By the increased illumination Rachel saw that she had fallen asleep. She laid the girl down and covered her with a blanket, smoothing the hair away from her dirty face, streaked with her sorrow. What had caused those tears in the girl?

When Rachel left the bedchamber, she kept the door wide open. From her pallet she could see into the room where the child slept. After checking on Faith, Rachel stretched out on the pallet and tried to sleep. But images of her own anguish taunted her peace of mind. She was twenty-one. This child could only be eight or nine. What had she gone through?

Her eyelids drifted closed finally, the crackling noise of the fire comforting in the silence. As Rachel felt herself sink toward sleep, she sensed someone standing over her.

Rachel's eyes eased open, taking in the dirty bare feet not far from her. She rolled over and stared up at the child, who held the blanket against her chest, fear in her gaze. Rachel threw back her cover and patted the pallet next to her. The child hesitated, glanced toward the door to the house, then back at Rachel.

"It is all right. You are safe."

Her teeth biting into her lower lip, the girl sank down onto the pallet near its edge. Rachel spread the blanket over the child, who lay stiff, staring at the ceiling. Slowly her eyes closed and the tension in her relaxed. Even through the dirt, Rachel glimpsed the youthful innocence in the little girl. At least at her age, Rachel had felt loved and protected. Until she had thrown it all away because a man had spoken lies that she had believed.

In that moment Rachel realized she would care for this child— at least until she found her family. No one should live in fear.

Eleven

A warm body plastered next to her awakened Rachel with a jolt. She started to bolt upright when she realized it was the little girl curled against her. Not Tom returning to demand his rights.

Rachel heard Faith fussing in the cradle. She eased away from the child and crept toward her daughter. After changing Faith's nappy, she picked her up and held her for a few minutes. *Thank You, Lord, for giving me Faith. She is the reason I hold on when things seem impossible.*

While the house was quiet, Rachel sat in the chair and nursed Faith. Sunlight streamed through the two windows, announcing the start of a new day. Rachel relished the quiet serenity, purposely not thinking about what needed to be done that day. What were they going to do about the child?

Jasper growled and sprang to his feet, facing the door.

Rachel placed Faith in the cradle and snuck up to the window closest to the door to peek outside. Nothing, not even the leaves on the trees stirring from a breeze. The dog snarled, the rumbling continuing deep in his throat.

Maddy came awake with a start. "What's going on?"

"I don't know. I think someone is outside, but I don't see anyone."

Rachel scanned the empty yard in front of her house then angled to look toward the barn. The door was slightly open. "Stay here and make sure she does not leave."

Rachel hurried to the trunk and retrieved Tom's gun. As she rushed into the yard, she realized it was not even loaded. At the barn door she squeezed through the opening, letting her eyes adjust to the dimness inside. The hens clucked. She tiptoed closer to the stall where they were kept.

Five feet away, she saw the henhouse door open, then arms locked around her from behind.

*****

"Dr. Stuart, wake up."

Maddy's frantic voice reached into the fog that captured Nathan's mind. "What's wrong?" He opened his eyes but did not move.

Maddy hovered over him, worry darkening her plain features. "Mrs. Gordon went to the barn with a gun."

Nathan sat up straight, the movement causing the bedchamber to swirl. "Why?" he bit out between gritted teeth while he tried to right his world.

"Jasper starting growling and snarling. I think someone is in the barn."

Nathan whipped back the blanket and swung his legs to the floor. "Where is the girl?"

"She's asleep by..." Maddy glanced over her shoulder. "She's gone." She whirled about and raced out to the main room.

Nathan clenched his jaw. The pounding in his head made even thinking difficult. With his hands on either side of him he struggled to stand. When the room stopped spinning, he strode forward as quickly as he could.

Maddy started for the door.

"You stay here with Faith."

When he emerged from the house, the sunlight blinded him momentarily. He looked toward the barn, the brightness obscuring most of his surroundings. As he headed toward the structure, the sight of the barn door completely opened riveted him to what he had to do: save Rachel. With every step he took the hammering against his skull increased. He gritted his teeth and kept going.

At the barn, he reached out to balance himself before he fell. Raised voices coming from inside demanded his full attention.

"Ben, let her go," the young girl shouted.

"You ain't hurt?" A male voice cracked.

"I am fine. They gaves me food last night to eat."

"They did?"

Nathan stepped into the barn, assessing the situation. A boy, perhaps twelve or thirteen, grasped Rachel, pinning her arms to her sides, the gun lying on the dirt near her feet. He saw Nathan and pulled her back with him toward the stall, bringing one arm up across her neck.

"Get back or I will hurt her," Ben yelled, scouring the area for a way to escape. "Emma, get out o' here."

The boy nearly had the voice and body of a man, but his face still revealed a youth, although hardened from life. But what persuaded Nathan to speak was the expression of fright in the boy's green eyes. "Emma is not going anywhere and neither are you."

"Go, Emma. Now."

"I ain't goin' without ya." The little girl swung her attention between Ben and Nathan. "Don't hurt her," she finally said to the boy. "Papa is dead. I'm tired o' runnin'."

"I can help you two." Rachel's gentle gaze honed in on the girl's and held it. "If you are hungry, I have food I can share with you both. You don't have to steal it."

"There is bread and cheese." Emma started toward Ben.

When he saw that the boy ease his tight hold around Rachel, Nathan relaxed his tense muscles. Then all of a sudden a large gray wolfhound sprinted past Nathan and launched himself at Ben, who had released Rachel.

Rachel stepped in front of the boy. "Jasper, sit."

The dog came to a halt, alert, his eyes fixed on the boy.

Rachel rubbed Jasper behind his ears. "Good boy."

Nathan strode to Rachel and positioned himself between her and Jasper, with his hand resting on the wolfhound's back. "'Tis time we all talked. Come up to the house and break the fast with us."

Rachel slipped her arm around him, and he didn't refuse the help. The brief adventure had taxed his strength.

"You ain't sendin' for the constable?" Emma asked, placing herself next to Ben in a protective gesture.

"I would have to take you in, and frankly I don't have the time to do that. Unless you want to hang around until I can." Nathan leaned into Rachel.

Ben blinked then grinned. "No, sir. But I'm right hungry and wouldn't mind breaking the fast with you all."

"Good." Rachel turned to the dog. "Jasper, stay here." Then she walked to the stall door and secured it. "Are there any more of you?"

Emma shook her head. "We are on our own."

The hint of desperation in the girl's voice and expression reminded Nathan he was dealing with children, even if they stole from Rachel. "Not any longer."

* * * * *

Breakfast of eggs, bread, mush, and cheese on the table, Rachel poured tea for everyone and passed them their cups. After setting the pot down, she bowed her head and said, "Bless this food and our guests, Lord. Help us to figure out what is going on around here. Amen." When she lifted her head, all eyes were on her. "In order for us to do that, I need you both to tell me how you ended up here at my farm."

Ben and Emma exchanged glances. The young girl hung her head while the boy looked directly at Rachel and said, "We are brother and sister. Our ma died a couple of years ago. We lost our farm during the war. None of our neighbors could help. They had nothing."

Rachel fingered her cup. "What happened after that?"

The boy shrugged while wolfing down a slice of bread. "We traveled 'round. Pa worked when he could."

"How much was that?" Nathan cut off some cheese and wrapped his bread around it.

Ben studied his almost empty plate. "Not much."

"So you resorted to stealing?" Rachel asked.

With their heads still down, they both nodded.

"Where is your pa?" Nathan took a bite of his cheese and bread.

Ben fixed his gaze on Nathan then Rachel. "Dead. A few weeks ago. He was the man you found in this house."

Nathan straightened. "How did he die?"

"Someone shot him." Ben frowned, his brow wrinkled.

"Who? Where were you?" Nathan rubbed his fingertips into his temple.

"Don't know. Hidin' in the swamp." Ben's gaze narrowed on Nathan.

"Did you hit me over the head yesterday while I was in the swamp?"

Ben's direct expression did not waver. "No."

"Do you know who did?"

The boy slid his attention away, centering it on Emma. "No. And I don't know who killed our pa. Knowin' wouldn't change nothin'. Emma and me would still be alone."

"What was your pa's name?" Nathan grimaced and wiped his hand across his eyes.

"Ben, like me. Ben Adams."

"Who were you hiding from in the swamp?" Rachel cut Nathan off before he could say anything. The pain on his face emphasized the difficulty he was having remaining focused on the conversation.

Another shared glance passed between brother and sister. "We don't know. Pa told us to lay low while he came heres to meet someone. Never said who."

"That's the truth," Emma said right after her brother spoke. "We don't have no one now."

Although Rachel felt there was more to their story, she would not turn them away. What if Nathan had ridden right past her on the road after the wreck? What would have happened to her and especially to Faith? "You are not alone any longer. You can stay here. I don't have a goodly amount, but what I have I will share with you, if you will help around the farm."

"No constable?" Ben asked, taking his sister's hand.

"No. But if you two didn't hit Dr. Stuart, then who did? If you know anything, you should share it with us. If someone means us harm, we need to be prepared."

"There are bad men everywhere. That is why Pa kept us hidden in the swamp." Ben tore off a bite of his bread.

"But there are good men too." Rachel touched Nathan's arm. "Are you all right?"

"Nothing a little work will not make better."

"You should not work today in the field."

"I will be fine."

"If it was me hurting, you would insist I take it easy. The same should go for you."

He furrowed his brow. "I am a doctor. I know how hard I can push myself. The last field needs to be planted."

"Then I will help you. Maddy and I finished planting the corn yesterday."

"Don't you and Maddy have to work on the vegetable garden?"

"I can help ya," Ben said while chewing his last piece of bread. "I ain't afraid of hard work."

Nathan shot him a long, assessing look. "Fine."

"I can help in the garden." Emma rose from the stool she shared with her brother and started clearing the empty plates.

As the children assisted Maddy with cleaning up, Nathan motioned for Rachel to follow him outside. A few yards from the house, he shifted toward her and said, "When we go into town, I will talk to the constable and see if he knows of a Ben Adams."

"Are you going to tell him about the children?"

"Yes, but not the stealing. If they have family somewhere, they should be with them."

"But in the meantime they can stay here."

"If you are sure."

"Yes. I don't think they have any family, or else why are they not with them? Their pa has been dead for several weeks."

"Perhaps they live too far away for them to make their way to them. You know taking on the responsibility of these two children will not be easy. There is something going on here. I don't know what yet, but I will be keeping my eye on them. They are not telling us everything. I don't even know if they are telling us the truth."

"They don't know if they can trust us. They will tell us when they feel they can."

"And what if whomever attacked me decides to do something else? Come after you?"

"Teach me to use my husband's gun."

Thunder descended over his features as fast as the storm that first day she was in South Carolina. "I should tell you no. But after this morning, when you took a weapon you did not know how to use to the barn, I know I cannot. I will give you lessons, and I will ask John if we can keep Jasper for a while. At least until we know what is going on here."

"I'm glad. I am becoming quite fond of that dog."

"Do not get too attached. Jasper is John's favorite dog. I know he bred him and has a litter of his pups. Perhaps we can get one of those."

The use of the word *we*, as though they were in this together, accelerated Rachel's heartbeat. It had been a long time since she felt really connected to another—since she had left her home. For a moment she let herself give into the feelings he generated in her—ones she had no business having. He was only here because he felt responsible for her and Faith, and ultimately she wanted to learn the skills she needed to be able to stand alone and not have to depend on others. That was all she needed from him.

* * * * *

Sitting next to Nathan as he drove the cart, Rachel peered behind her at Emma and Ben, dressed in the new clothes she had made them. Their grins warmed her heart and reconfirmed her decision to spend some of her money for shoes for the children. She had burned the rags they wore the minute she finished a simple dress for Emma and a shirt and trousers for Ben. After she completed another gown for Mrs. Bridges, she would have scraps she could fashion into more outfits for the two of them.

"I cannot believe we are goin' t' a party," Emma whispered to her brother so loud everyone in the cart heard.

"And stayin' overnight at a fancy place." Ben's eyes grew round as Nathan neared the front of his sister's house.

"There will be other children at the celebration." Rachel angled around and faced forward, her arm brushing up against Nathan. "Do you think they will be all right at your sister's?"

"Do you want me to turn around and take them back to the farm?"

"Oh no. I am just worried about how they will get along with the others. I have been working with them on their speech. They are a little better."

He slanted a look at her. "You are becoming too attached to them."

"The constable didn't know a Ben Adams. We have heard nothing from him about any family."

"'Tis only three weeks since you took them in."

"Nothing else has happened. Perhaps you surprised a poacher or someone passing through."

"Perhaps." His tone conveyed his doubts.

Whereas with her, she had hope for the first time in a long while. The hens were producing eggs, enough to keep up with their needs. The pig would give birth soon. She was earning extra money with her sewing. All the vegetables in the garden were coming up, although the children had to spend much time chasing away the crows and other pests. Mr. Baker had become a good friend and suitor for Maddy. Faith was gaining weight and becoming more alert each day.

Nathan brought the cart around to the stable at Liberty Hall then dismounted to assist Rachel down from the seat. The children leaped from the back. Emma took Faith from Maddy, and Ben helped the maid down. For a brief moment Rachel wondered if this was what a real family could be like. An attentive, loving husband. Adorable children.

Then thoughts of Tom and his brutality invaded her mind, putting a pall on her musing. She knew the Lord wanted her to forgive Tom, but she could not do it. He had caused her so much pain.

"Where are the puppies?" Emma came around to the front of the cart.

"In there." Nathan pointed toward the stable.

"We can pick any one out to take back to the farm?" Ben's green eyes clouded with uncertainty.

Rachel put her hand on the boy's shoulder, and for the first time he did not flinch away. "That is what Mr. McNeal said."

"Can we do that now?" Emma nibbled on her bottom lip.

John came out of the stable. "Yes, you can. I want you to be sure before you take it home tomorrow. The litter is in the last stall."

Emma and Ben scurried into the building.

"I will go and make sure there is not a problem." Maddy went after the two children.

"Leave this. I will have a servant take care of your bags and horse." John gestured toward the cart then started toward the house. "How is Jasper? Has he caught any more thieves?"

"No. Finding Emma and Ben took care of our missing food." Nathan glanced back at the stable as if he were not sure if he should leave the children there.

"But nothing else about whom might have attacked you in the swamp?"

"It has been quiet for the past three weeks." Rachel fell into step next to Nathan.

"Quiet. I am not sure you and I define quiet in the same way. The children are constantly talking and asking questions. Ben wants to know everything about the crops. He is a quick learner."

"Has he had any schooling?" John opened the back door into his house.

Rachel stepped inside. "I don't think so. He mentioned his mother teaching him some before she died. I am thinking of working with him on reading. Emma too. I have a few books I brought from England I can use."

Nathan frowned. "When are you going to find time for that, between keeping house, tending to the animals and garden, sewing for Mrs. Bridges, and taking care of Faith?"

John chuckled. "I will leave you two to talk. I'm sure Sarah is in the parlor. A few of our neighbors have already arrived."

The moment John left, Rachel rounded on Nathan. "You don't need to worry about me. Everything has been fine lately. I have managed to keep up, and I am learning every day more of what I need to do so you will be able to leave with a clear conscience. If Emma and Ben stay, I will have a lot of people around me. A lot of help. You cannot deny they are doing their share of the work without us even asking half the time."

"They are still not telling us everything, and it has been over three weeks. We have given them no reason not to trust us. I'm just not ready to accept them with no reservations like you."

"They are children, eight and twelve. I don't agree with stealing, but they needed food." She moved closer and lowered her voice. "Have you ever thought perhaps they sense you don't accept them totally? If we want them to trust us, we must trust them."

"You have not lost any of your naïvety."

She settled her hand on her waist. "At least I don't try to hide from life."

"If I were hiding from life, I would be at my cabin right now. Not here for my sister's party." He turned on his heel and strode toward the front hall.

Rachel stomped after him, intending to continue the conversation.

Nathan came to an abrupt halt, the sound of male voices—familiar ones—drifting to Rachel. She stopped at his side and stared at Sarah hugging their brother then their grandfather. Rachel backed away a few feet. The last she had heard from Sarah only Patrick Stuart was attending the party.

The old man peered across the foyer, his sharp gaze skimming over Nathan and landing on her. His mouth compressed into a scowl, and he stepped toward his granddaughter and said something to her that Rachel could not hear. Then he put his top hat back on his head and stormed out the front door.

"I will talk to him, Sarah," Mr. Stuart said then hurried after his grandfather.

Nathan closed the space to his sister. "We have decided to leave."

"*We* have not decided that," Rachel said, giving Sarah a hug.

Nathan glared at her. "I don't want to ruin my sister's party."

"I know you will not do that." Sarah walked to a window that afforded a view of the front lawn. "'Tis about time you two mend this rift between you. Patrick and I are tired of this feud. We want our family back."

"Then you tell *him* that."

"I will."

"You think Patrick can talk him into staying?" Nathan shook his head. "He will not stay."

"Don't be too sure of that. Patrick and Grandfather are coming back to the house." Sarah shifted away from the window.

Rachel glanced around for a place to disappear. But then the front door swung open again, and both men entered the house.

FROM THIS DAY FORWARD

Anger carved hard planes into the older man's face. Who was he more upset with, her or Nathan?

"The only reason I am staying is because my grandson refuses to leave and take me home. I would walk, but my gout has been acting up lately."

"Then 'tis good that Nathan is here. He can give you something for it." Sarah smiled and slipped her arm through her grandfather's. "Mr. Baker is here and so are Mr. and Mrs. Grayson, as well as Mr. and Mrs. Calhoun. We will have a merry time."

Although Sarah's voice was full of gaiety, the corners of her mouth twitched as if it were hard to maintain her grin. Rachel couldn't even muster a smile. Her heart thudded in her chest. The constriction about her torso made breathing difficult.

As the trio entered the parlor, Nathan rotated toward her. "We can leave if you want."

"This might be the time you and your grandfather can make amends. You certainly will not go to Pinecrest. I see your sister and brother's reasoning behind getting you two here together for the celebration."

"That is not what I asked you. Do *you* want to stay?"

"Being born English is not a crime. I have been looking forward to this party for weeks. I want to stay."

"Then we will, but after my last visit to Pinecrest, I have come to realize my grandfather does not want to make amends, so I have no illusions it will ever happen."

"That does not stop you from telling him you forgive him for what happened five years ago—whatever led to your fight with him."

"But I don't. I thought I had, but I'm discovering I really haven't. He is responsible for Eliza and her child's death as much as I am."

Another group of people arrived in the foyer. Rachel pulled Nathan toward the library and closed the door. "You did what you could. I know you. There was nothing else you could have done under the circumstances. Forgive yourself then your grandfather. Have you ever considered he is a hurting man? He lost people he cared about because of the war with England. That doesn't mean I condone his hating every Englishman or woman, but that hatred has been eating at him for years. Perhaps you should make the first move. Free yourself. Hatred and anger are poisons." She listened to her own words and wondered if she would ever be able to do the same with Tom.

"So I'm supposed to march in there and tell him I forgive him. Then all will be well."

"No. First you have to mean it. If you do, then at least you have done what you can. You are not responsible for his feelings. Only yours."

A tic twitched in his jaw. "Have you forgiven your husband?"

The question iced her veins. "We are not talking about me. My husband is dead. I don't have to spend time with him anymore."

"How convenient for you. Because he is no longer around, you don't have to follow your own advice."

The sarcasm in his voice hit its mark, piercing through her heart and bringing forth all the pain that Tom had caused in their short marriage. And the guilt because she could not forgive him.

"If he were standing right here in front of you instead of me, would you be able to tell him you forgive him for his abuse, for leaving you stranded in a strange country with little means of support?"

She opened her mouth to reply, but no words came to mind. All she could focus on was the palpable fury emitting from Nathan.

"That's what I thought. You cannot, any more than I can. I tried several times and had it thrown back in my face. I will not try again. I did everything my grandfather wanted and that was not enough for him. In a short time after my father's death, he pulled the family apart. We should have come closer together in our sorrow."

"I know what it is like to have a rift in the family. I wish my circumstances were different, but I forgave my father on the voyage over to America. That doesn't mean I am not hurt by his actions and pride, but I do not hate him."

"Then sell the farm and go back to England."

"I cannot. When I left, Papa said that my husband and I would not amount to anything. That I would come back begging for help, and he would not give it. I needed to make the choice, family or Tom. I could not have both."

"That doesn't sound like you forgave him."

"I have forgiven him, but I have not forgotten what he said. Going back, begging for help, is not the way I will return to England. I will make something of this situation given to me. Then I will consider returning to England."

"So this is temporary."

"South Carolina is not my home. England is."

"I see." Nathan strode toward the door and opened it.

Rachel shivered at the sight of the coldness in his expression. "Where are you going?"

"To join this little celebration. Is that not why we came today?" He left Rachel alone. The click of the door closing resounded through the room with finality.

Rachel eased onto a chair, holding herself rigid for a moment before the effort was too much, and she sank against its back. In spite of what her father had done, she still loved him and hoped one day to return to Mansfield Manor, to visit at least. She wanted Faith to get to know her family. The economy in South Carolina was finally starting to improve after the recent war. If she could make the farm successful, she could sell it for enough money to allow her to return to England and establish herself without depending on her family. But what would happen to that plan if Nathan walked away right now? She still had much to learn. She wished she didn't have to depend on him, but she did. She was realistic enough to know she couldn't run the farm without Nathan, at least not yet.

* * * * *

"The Nathan I know loves to dance. Why are you over here holding up the wall? Have you not seen all the ladies eyeing you?" Grinning, Patrick raised his glass. "Here is to you and Grandfather. You have not killed each other yet."

"Should you not be dancing with all those ladies? Or have you given up finding a wife as Grandfather wishes?" Nathan peered at Rachel laughing at something Mr. Baker said. And then there was Mr. Chester hanging on her every word.

Patrick's expression became serious. "She will not approach you. You will have to approach her."

"Who is 'she'?" Nathan asked while his gaze stayed glued to Rachel, now going out on the floor with Mr. Peterson.

"You know who I am referring to." Patrick glanced over his shoulder at Rachel. "Ask her to dance. You have barely said two words to each other since your arrival."

"It looks like she has enough partners to keep her busy for a while."

Patrick studied him for a long moment. "You are jealous."

"No, I am not."

His brother waved his hand. "You can protest all you want, but I don't believe it."

Nathan needed the subject of their conversation to change. He didn't intend to discuss Rachel with anyone. They all assumed the reason he was helping her was because he was interested in her. They were wrong. He cared for her, of course, but he felt obligated to see her settled. That was all. Then he would go about his life as he had before she disrupted it.

"What did you and Sarah think you were going to accomplish with this little reunion between me and Grandfather?"

"Just that, a reunion. We want our family back together."

"We cannot go back to the way things were. Too much has happened for that to ever occur."

"He will not be around much longer. Since you were at the plantation last, he recovered, but he has yet to get his former strength back. Lately his gout has been giving him a lot of problems too. So much so, he has turned over most of the running of the plantation to me."

"He must not be doing well. Why didn't you come get me?"

Patrick's eyebrows rose. "You would have come to Pinecrest after what Grandfather did the last time you were there? Demanding Rachel and her maid leave?"

"I would have tried. You know I would have."

"Yes, you would have, and he probably would have thrown you off the plantation again. He cannot throw you off *this* plantation. Try to see him before he leaves tomorrow."

"I do not expect it to work, but I will see him."

"Thank you." Patrick inclined his head.

"In spite of what has happened in the past, I still love him. He is the one I followed around on the plantation. I wanted to grow up to be like him until I realized I did not love the same things he did. But I tried. I was willing to run Pinecrest and still be a doctor. There are other planters who are doctors."

"What is stopping you from being a doctor now?"

Memories I cannot shake. Screams of men in pain. Sounds of cannon fire, which only signaled more wounded who would be brought to me. The sight of desperation in the men's faces, wanting to live but knowing they were not going to make it through the night. And worse, the look on the English soldier's face when I killed him. "I am tired of losing my patients." *Tired of being haunted by the memories.*

"How about the ones you have helped? Rachel. Grandfather. And that has only been recently."

"When I trained to be a doctor, I had visions of helping others. Curing them. Easing their pain. I know that it was not realistic, but during the yellow fever epidemic, I thought I could do something to keep everyone from dying just because I wanted to." Nathan laughed, but there was no merriment in the sound. "I have accused Rachel of being naïve, but I am as bad as she is."

"You two have a lot in common."

"Patrick," Nathan said with a frown.

"I know. She is not to be discussed. I will leave you to contemplate your future. I see Anne is free, finally. At least this Stuart is going to dance."

As his brother slipped through the people on the dance floor to approach the daughter of a neighbor, Nathan scanned the room for Rachel and found her participating in a reel with a son of a prominent merchant in Charleston. For a moment her gaze zeroed in on him, holding his full attention, until she swung away and was lost in the crowd.

Nathan then searched the large parlor, which had been cleared of some of its furniture to make an area for dancing. When he glimpsed his grandfather by the entrance alone, a grimace on his face, Nathan sighed. Perhaps it was the right time to approach him and see how he was. The ashen tint to his face worried him. From his pallor it appeared he was not spending any time outdoors, which was not like him whatsoever.

Nathan started toward his grandfather and saw him twist about and, using his cane, limp out into the foyer. Nathan followed him down the hallway to the library. As his grandfather entered the room and shut the door, Nathan hung back, not sure of the wisdom of bothering him when it was obvious he wanted to be alone. He and his grandfather had always liked their solitude, not like Patrick or Sarah. He could respect that. Perhaps he should talk with him tomorrow, before he returned to the farm.

Nathan hesitated. A niggling in the back of his mind prompted him to make his way to the library. Grandfather had not looked good. He had noticed his hair was damp. Had a fever returned? He had not been coughing, but still…

"Nathan, is your grandfather all right?" Rachel asked behind him.

Pivoting toward her, he noted the flush to her cheeks, the concern in her eyes. Sarah's lavender gown fit Rachel perfectly after a few alterations, which she had done the evening before. The color heightened her beauty even more, and the short sleeves and scooped neckline emphasized her femininity. This was his opportunity to ask her to dance.

"I am not sure. He didn't look well. I was going to check on him. For the past half hour he has been standing off by himself. That is most unusual for him at a party like this."

"Then I will not keep you. I hope he is fine."

"You can say that after he threw you off his land?"

She tilted her head. "Yes. I don't want any harm to come to him. He is your grandfather. I don't agree with his blanket hatred of anyone English, but I can see his side. He lost two very important people in the Revolutionary War. Losing a child would be the worst tragedy. I know that since I have had Faith."

"After I check to see if he is all right, would you dance with me?"

She smiled, a smile that brightened her eyes and gave her a radiant glow. "I would love to. I will wait out here. I don't want your grandfather to get angry because he sees me."

Nathan stepped close—so near that her scent of roses, from a special soap she had brought all the way from England—surrounded him. "I am sorry about our argument earlier. I don't want us—"

She pressed her gloved fingers against his lips. "We have to be able to express our feelings and concerns. The fight was just as much my fault as yours. Seeing your grandfather did not make matters better."

He clasped her hand and turned it so he could raise her palm and kiss it. "My grandfather does not deserve your compassion. Wait here and I will be back in a few minutes after I satisfy myself that he is fine."

Nathan crossed to the door of the library and pushed it open a few inches. Peering inside, he saw his grandfather standing in the middle of the room, his back to Nathan, his cane moving back and forth as though he had tremors.

Nathan went into the library, leaving the door ajar. "Grandfather?"

His grandfather shifted around partway, his dilated eyes fixing on Nathan. Sweat rolled down his face. He wobbled then crumpled to the floor. Nathan surged forward and caught him before his head hit the wooden planks.

Nathan eased the old man down and brushed his hand across his forehead. Heat burned his fingertips.

"Rachel," Nathan called out.

She hurried into the library. "What is wrong?"

"Get John and Patrick. Grandfather has had a relapse."

As she left, Nathan turned back to his grandfather, who started shivering, curling up and clutching himself. Nathan had seen this many times before. This wasn't the same ailment he'd had six weeks ago. This was malaria.

Twelve

"George has agreed to take you all home to the farm. I should be along in a day or so. Until then he will stay there. I wish you would stay here. Sarah would love your company." Nathan stood in the upstairs hallway at Liberty Hall outside the room his grandfather was in.

"There's so much that needs to be done at home. Besides, for the past two days your sister has had company. I am sure she would appreciate some quiet."

"True. 'Tis hard enough all the work she normally has to do to be the mistress of a plantation, but now that she is with child she needs to rest."

"She told me she feels fine, better than with Sean."

"She would tell you that to keep me from worrying about her."

"How did you talk Mr. Baker into staying with us?"

"It was not hard. He fancies himself in love with Maddy."

"I thought that. I think she returns his affection."

"Grandfather has had malaria before. Hopefully, he will recover as he did last time. I have given him cinchona bark and I am trying to keep his fever down. Otherwise 'tis out of my hands."

"And in the Lord's. We shall be all right. Nothing else has happened in the past three weeks. Whoever was in the swamp has moved on. I cannot see anyone wanting to live in such a vile place." Rachel shivered, remembering the few times she had gone a short distance into the bog around her farm.

"You could cultivate the low-lying areas with rice and indigo. That would produce more money."

"We can talk when you come back to the farm. Right now, concentrate on your grandfather." Because if he didn't, he would blame himself if his grandfather died. Rachel did not want that for Nathan. He carried enough guilt because of the soldiers he could not save and Eliza and her baby. Impulsively she reached up and brushed her lips across his cheek. "This may be your opportunity to repair your relationship with him. I shall not be around to distract your grandfather."

She pulled back, but Nathan grasped her upper arms and hauled her against him. He angled his head and slowly lowered it until their mouths met in a deep kiss. He wrapped her in an embrace that plastered her to him.

Leaning back, he seized her gaze, a smoldering look in his eyes. "I have wanted to do that for weeks. I know 'tis not wise…" He swallowed hard, averting his glance. "I shouldn't have done that. I'm sorry. It will not happen again."

He separated himself from her and stepped away then pivoted and wrenched open the door of his grandfather's bedchamber.

Rachel wilted back against the wall, her chest rising and falling rapidly as she gulped in air to fill her lungs. The sensations his kiss created caused her heartbeat to race. Finally she made her way downstairs on trembling legs. She clutched the banister to keep herself upright. Only the sight of Mr. Baker, Maddy, Faith, Ben, and Emma waiting for her at the door reinforced the need not to give in to the feelings Nathan aroused in her.

Emma ran to the staircase and took her hand. "Liberty is in the cart ready to go home."

Home. The word came so easily to the child's lips. "Is that what you are going to call the puppy?" Rachel slipped her arm around the little girl, dressed in another gown she had sewn for her.

"Ben cames up with the name. I like it. He is goin' t' be as big as Jasper."

Where was she going to come up with enough money to get the necessary supplies to make the farm profitable and still feed all the people and animals? The last trip into Charleston had taken the rest of her money she brought from England. Now all she had was what she got from sewing. In a couple of months, if all went well, she would have cash from the crops. She stared at all the people she was responsible for and a heaviness weighed on her.

Somehow, Lord, You will provide. Worrying does no good.

Although common sense dictated the wisdom in those words, she could not totally rid herself of worry. She had four mouths to feed. She could not let them down.

* * * * *

Nathan's grandfather's eyelids fluttered open. He drew in a shallow breath and centered his attention on Nathan. "Where am I?"

"At Liberty Hall. You collapsed in the library. I had you brought upstairs to your bedchamber."

"When?"

"Two days ago. You have been going back and forth between shivering and burning up with fever. But you are better today." Nathan dipped a cloth into cool water and wiped his grandfather's face, half-expecting him to push his hand away. He didn't.

"Malaria?"

"Yes."

"It will beat me one day."

"No, you are too tough for that. You will be back on your feet soon and…" Nathan couldn't keep the pretense up any longer. "Your fever was high."

"I knew I should not have come to the celebration. I felt tired, more so than usual for this old body."

"Why did you?"

His grandfather pinched his mouth together, his eyelids veiling the expression in his eyes. "I figured you would be here."

"But that day you arrived here, you acted so upset."

"I know. I saw you with *her* and couldn't stop myself."

"You mean Rachel Gordon?" Nathan again soaked the cloth in the water then squeezed the excess out and cooled his grandfather's face with the linen.

"Yes. I have to tell you she will be no good for you. I know you are helping her at Dalton Farm. She will use her charms on you to get you to do what she needs then discard you."

Nathan fisted his hand around the cloth and rose. "You don't know her. You have no right to say that."

"She is just like your mother. A user."

Lord, how am I supposed to forgive this man who continues to do harm? "How can you say that? Because she is English? You are petty." Nathan backed away from the bed.

"On your father's deathbed, he told me how much he loved your mother, and she never returned those feelings. He had given her everything, and she had given him nothing. He died a broken-hearted man."

"She gave him three children. Two sons to carry on his name."

"Get out. You will never understand. She fooled you too." His grandfather shut his eyes and averted his head.

Fury rampaged through Nathan like a wild stallion escaping his corral. He strode out of the bedchamber and leaned against the closed door. He could not draw in enough air to fill his lungs. His chest felt as though it were squeezing his heart. He had always thought his parents had a loving marriage. Why did his grandfather want to destroy even his good memories?

* * * * *

"Moses, you are gifted with carpentry." Rachel panned the bedchamber at her house that no one used because the children's father had died in it. Now taking up a good part of the room was a bed that Moses had constructed. She and Maddy had made a mattress for it.

Being a man of few words, Moses beamed.

"When you go back to Liberty Hall, please thank Mr. McNeal for sending you to help while Nathan was tending his grandfather."

Maddy paused in the doorway. "Emma agreed to try sharing this room with me. Ben wants to remain in the loft."

"Good. It is about time we use all the space we have. Has Mr. Baker returned yet from his farm?"

"No, but he should be here shortly." Maddy adjusted her mob-cap and smoothed her apron.

Rachel left Moses to complete his work and headed into the main room. "I saw you two dancing the other evening at the party. On more than one occasion. Did you have a good time?"

Maddy's face glowed, as though she were recalling a joyful memory. "Yes. Very much. I had never been to a fancy party before. I was surprised Mrs. McNeal wanted me there."

"It is because we have become friends. You have been invaluable to me. Besides, we all needed time away from the farm. I know the children had fun. Where are they?"

"Ben is outside with Jasper and Liberty. Emma went to see if there are any eggs."

"Those hens have become hers, the way she watches over them."

Ben burst through the door with his sister right behind him. "The pig is having her babies. Now. What do we do?"

"Nothing. She will take care of it." Rachel hoped she could sell several of the piglets to purchase a cow. "In the meantime, we need to see to the garden. It has been neglected long enough." When they had returned home two days before, they had worked in the fields and hadn't been able to do much of anything else.

Fifteen minutes later, with Faith strapped to her chest, Rachel, along with Maddy, Ben, and Emma, marched out to the plot of land where various vegetables from beans to carrots to onions were planted, only to find a whole row of newly sprouted leaves were gone.

Rachel's mouth fell open and her shoulders sagged. "What happened?"

Ben dropped his head. "'Twas not us. Probably some kind of animal."

Rachel put her hands on his shoulders. "I know that. You have no need to take food. I gladly share with you."

Ben raised his gaze to hers. "Why are you being so nice?"

"Because that is what the Lord expects us to do. Love one another."

"Love?"

Emma tugged on Rachel's arm. "Will you read us another story about Jesus tonight?"

"I will. I want to start teaching you both how to read so you can read those stories any time you want. We can work an hour at night on learning to read and write. Also to cipher."

Emma's forehead wrinkled. "Cipher? What is that?"

"Working with numbers. Learning to add."

"Why?" Ben asked, his eyes dark green.

"I don't want anyone to cheat you. If you know how to add and subtract, you can make sure you are being charged the correct amount."

"Pa taught me some of that." Ben thrust out his chest. "I ain't dumb."

"I know."

The sound of a single gunshot in the distance brought Rachel around in a half circle, facing the way to Mr. Baker's farm. She frowned.

"George said something about going hunting since we are getting low on meat." Maddy knelt at the edge of the garden to begin weeding.

"I bet a raccoon did this." Ben waved his arm at the missing row of plants. "Maybe Mr. Baker will bring us a raccoon to eat."

The thought of eating a raccoon rumbled Rachel's stomach. But people did. Raccoons were plentiful and could cause quite a bit of mischief.

"Can I check on the pig? See if the babies are here?" Ben looked toward the barn.

"Yes." Rachel knelt on the ground, patting Faith, who was nodding off. "Emma, you know where the seeds are in the house. Please get them for me. We will replant this row."

"What if the animal comes back?"

"Perhaps I will have Jasper guard the garden. I don't think many animals would come near the vegetables with him here."

As Rachel and Maddy weeded the garden, Emma ran to the house. In the distance Jasper barked. Rachel peered toward the barn, but the house blocked most of the structure from her view. Jasper didn't care for the pig. Perhaps the addition of piglets set him off.

Emma raced back, fear on her face. "A man has Ben."

"Where?"

"I saw him git Ben when he came out of the barn." Emma pointed toward the swamp on the other side of the building. "Went thataway. We have to go git him. He is a bad man."

"Who?" Rachel motioned for Maddy to come over as she struggled to loosen the straps about Faith and her.

"Bad man. I seen him 'fore."

"Maddy, have Moses go to Liberty Hall and bring Nathan back here. Then you and the children go to Mr. Baker's. Jasper will go with you to protect you. I am going after Ben."

"In the swamp?" Maddy's eyes grew huge. "You cannot."

"I have to. I am taking Tom's gun. Get help." Rachel kissed Faith on the cheek then passed her to Maddy. "Emma, stay with Maddy and help her with Faith."

"Yes'm."

Rachel rushed into the house, grabbed the flintlock pistol, and loaded it. Wearing her half boots, she made her way to the edge of the swamp. She inhaled a deep breath of the musky scented air and plunged into the bog.

The cold water lapped at the top of her boots. With her hand clasping the gun, she scoured her surroundings for any sign of Ben and the man. She had no idea what she was doing, but she wouldn't let someone take Ben from her. If she waited for Nathan or Mr. Baker, he could be long gone. Her target practice had gone all right, especially the last time. She had actually hit the tree she shot at.

Then the thought of pulling the trigger and firing at a person—even a "bad man," as Emma had called him—terrified Rachel. Tentacles of fear in her stomach snarled into a big ball.

Through the thick foliage, evidence of snapped branches confirmed she was going in the right direction—deeper into the swamp. A sound to the left, a deep bellow, caused her to jump then stumble, going down on to her hands and knees in the water. Mud oozed up between her fingers, and she lifted her head to look at a snake curled around a limb hanging down low. A scream welled up in her.

* * * * *

Nathan rode toward the farm with John and Patrick right behind him. His horse's hooves pounded against the road as his heart did against his chest. What had gotten into the woman to go into the swamp after the person who had taken Ben? With the pistol on top of that? She had only hit her target once in all the times they had practiced. But worse, she did not realize how dangerous the swamp could be.

The house came into view. Nathan didn't let up until he arrived at the barn. Jumping to the ground, he checked out the barn, noticed the pig had five piglets, and the hens and rooster were all accounted for. Liberty was in his place on Nathan's cot, but Jasper was gone. Who with? Maddy or Rachel? Knowing Rachel, she had sent the dog with Maddy and the children.

When John and Patrick strode in, his brother said, "Maddy must still be getting Mr. Baker. No one is up at the house."

"Moses said Rachel went into the swamp by the large live oak." Nathan searched the area. "There, I think."

"I am coming with you." John stepped forward.

"Fine. Patrick, please stay here in case Rachel comes back and we missed her. When Mr. Baker arrives, let him know what is happening and where we went. He knows this area better than anyone."

"Nathan. Nathan." Emma sprinted toward them with Jasper at her heels. Tears coursed down her cheeks. She skidded to a stop. "Mr. Baker has been shot on the path to his house. Maddy wanted me to get you."

Nathan glanced behind him toward the swamp and then at Emma, torn between going after Rachel and helping Mr. Baker.

* * * * *

Rachel choked back her scream, not daring to alert the man who had taken Ben. The green snake unfurled and dropped in the water.

Rachel shot to her feet and pointed the pistol at the serpent. Her unsteady hand held the gun, wavering in the air. When the snake slithered into the brush away from Rachel, relief swooshed out between her lips. She brought her arm close to her body, her fingers still quavering, and pointed the weapon downward.

She stared at the way she had come. Or at least she thought that was the direction her house was. What if it wasn't? Everywhere she looked myriad shades of green greeted her inspection with splashes of brown mixed in. The odor of rotting vegetation overpowered her the deeper she plodded into the bog—nothing like what she had seen in England. This was wild, full of plants, dense and raw in its primitiveness. Like the country she now lived in.

Which way should I go? She studied the wall of green surrounding her and saw a trampled patch. She headed that way. Again a bellow echoed through the trees. *An alligator, not a beast I want to encounter.*

She began reciting Psalm 23, the words giving her the courage she needed. *Yea, though I walk through the valley of the shadow of death, I will fear no evil; for thou art with me; thy rod and thy staff they comfort me.*

Diving through thick bushes that clawed at her wet clothes, Rachel listened. Voices up ahead? As she drew closer, she discerned a man's voice and Ben's. Nearing them, she crept forward, her pulse speeding, her breath coming in shallow gasps. When she peeked through the dense foliage, she spied a wiry, medium-built man gripping the back of Ben's shirt as he held the boy up in front of him.

"Where is it?"

Ben's eyes were so large they overwhelmed his face.

"If'n you don't tell, I will snatch your sister and wring her neck in front of you."

Ben opened his mouth to say something, but no words came out, as though fear had robbed him of his voice. Rachel knew that kind of fear from when Tom had gone into his drunken rages.

She prepared the flintlock to shoot, ramming the ball and wad into the barrel and priming the pin. Then inhaling a fortifying breath, Rachel parted the branches and stepped out into the glade in the middle of nowhere—at least that was the way it seemed to her. She raised her pistol and shouted in the toughest voice she could muster, "Let him go. Now." It was a shame it came out in a squeak barely heard across the feet separating her and the pair.

"What are you goin' t' do if'n I don't?" The man tossed Ben to the ground and stalked toward her. "I seen you shootin'. You cain't hit the side o' the barn."

With each word he came a step closer. The sight of his fierce expression, his dark eyes boring into her, seized her breaths and locked them away. The tremors in her body increased and she backed up, her hand shaking so badly she was afraid she would drop the gun.

"I shall use this if I have to." This time her voice toughened to a steel thread.

He laughed and kept coming toward her.

Her lungs burning, she pulled the trigger.

* * * * *

"You need to take care of Mr. Baker," Patrick said.

"But what about Rachel? I cannot let anything happen to her."

Nathan swiveled his attention from the swamp toward where Mr. Baker was. *What should I do, Lord?*

"John and I can find Rachel. Go."

I promised her I would look after her until she was settled. I cannot—I took an oath to help anyone in need when I could. How can I turn my back on that? Nathan nodded. "I am going to Mr. Baker. Get Ben and Rachel out of there. Take Jasper."

John called his dog then both men headed into the bog near the large live oak while Nathan jogged to the house, got medicines and supplies, then hastened to the path between George Baker's and Dalton Farm.

Nathan glimpsed George on the ground with Maddy next to him, pressing a cloth into his shoulder, her gown covered in the man's blood. As he approached the pair several hundred feet away, a gunshot reverberated through the air.

Nathan came to a halt. Rachel! No! He peered behind him. A knot lodged in his throat. *What if she is shot? What if I have lost her?*

"Dr. Stuart, hurry. He needs you," Maddy shouted, prodding Nathan into action.

He had to do what he could for George. *Lord, Rachel is in Your hands. Please protect her.*

* * * * *

The flintlock pistol went off, momentarily stopping the kidnapper in his tracks, as the shot struck a tree to the left—a wide left from the man. Surprise flitted across his face, immediately to be replaced with fury. He charged Rachel, covering the few remaining feet quickly.

His hands gripped her upper arms, the pistol falling from her nerveless fingers. "A big mistake."

No words came to mind as Rachel stared into the pockmarked face with the deadliest eyes she had ever seen. Suddenly Ben launched himself at the kidnapper and clung to his back, his hands digging into the man's face. A finger found an eye and the man howled with rage. His grasp on Rachel loosened. She jerked free then flew at him while Ben rode his back. She scratched and kicked him wherever she could.

Finally the kidnapper shook Ben off him, the child landing in a heap at their feet. Rachel glanced at the boy to make sure he was all right, then brought her fist back and swung it at the man's stomach. He doubled over.

Ben struggled to his feet and jumped on his back again while Rachel's booted foot connected with the man's shin. A guttural groan echoed through the glade, followed by barking and Jasper loping out of the thick vegetation, straight at the kidnapper. The wolfhound latched onto the man's arm, sending him to the ground.

"Git him off," the kidnapper yelled.

John appeared with Patrick next to him. John whistled, and Jasper released the man's arm and backed away a few feet, growling, his whole body alert.

Rachel rushed to Ben and hugged the boy to her. "Are you all right? Did he hurt you?"

He pressed himself against her for a moment. "I am all right." Then he moved away, darting his glance to John and Patrick.

John yanked the kidnapper to his feet. "You have some explaining to do before we take you to the constable."

Patrick positioned himself within inches of the man. "Starting with why you took the boy?"

* * * * *

Hours later, Rachel sat in the chair before the fireplace, staring at the blaze, seeing the orange and yellow flames dancing about the logs as though they were drawing her toward them. Numbness still clung to her body, briefly overriding the deep ache from the bruises and cuts of her encounter with the kidnapper—still nameless because the man refused to say a word, even when Patrick and John threatened bodily harm. She was never so glad to see a person leave as that man, escorted to Charleston by the two men.

Rachel finally tore her gaze away from the fire and scanned the main room for Ben, who had planted himself on the staircase to the loft and not moved in hours. A war of emotions had played across his face since his rescue, with a pensive look finally settling into place.

A niggling in the back of her mind grew, demanding her attention. Ben knew the man. She had seen it on both of their faces before she had spoken in the glade. So why hadn't the child told them who the kidnapper was? Ben had said few words, other than he had been leaving the barn when the man grabbed him. He insisted he did not know why.

Nathan and Maddy left the second bedchamber. The expression on their faces offered Rachel hope that Mr. Baker would make it. She rose. "Is he still doing all right?"

"He is hanging on. I removed the ball, so now we have to

pray no infection sets in." Nathan walked to a bowl and poured water into it to wash his hands.

"It will not if I have anything to do about it," Maddy said and then used the liquid in the pitcher to rinse the blood from her own hands.

Maddy hadn't left Mr. Baker's side from the beginning. She had insisted on helping Nathan any way she could while Rachel was left to deal with the children and seeing John and Patrick off with the kidnapper in tow and Jasper trotting next to them. Emma had finally fallen asleep on Rachel's bed about an hour ago, with Faith in the cradle next to her.

"Mr. Baker ain't goin' t' die, is he?" Ben asked in the quiet that had descended.

"Don't know yet. Time will tell," Nathan said in a serious tone.

"I heard him yell." Ben's eyes swam with tears.

"It hurts to remove a ball. But he is sleeping now." Nathan rose. "I am going to check the barn and animals. I noticed the pig had her babies in the middle of all this commotion."

"Oh, I forgot about that." Rachel moved toward the food. "Maddy, you sit with Mr. Baker. I shall take care of preparing something for supper. Tomorrow I think we should make a soup. Mr. Baker may want something to eat by then." She doubted he would wake before morning. His body had been through a trauma and still had a long battle ahead.

At the door, Nathan glanced at Ben. "Come help me. You can bring back any eggs we collect."

Ben trudged toward Nathan. "I am going to miss Jasper. Liberty probably is lonely out there by hisself. Can I sleep in the barn too?"

Nathan stepped outside. "I think it would be better to let Liberty sleep up at the house. We need to teach him how to be a guard dog."

"Can he sleep in the loft with me?"

With the door closing behind Ben, Rachel did not hear Nathan's reply, but she suspected the dog would be in the loft with Ben tonight. She would not be surprised if they became inseparable. Ben needed something like that, because he still had not fully accepted her and Nathan or trusted them. *What is he keeping from us?*

Emma appeared in the entrance of Rachel's bedchamber, rubbing her eyes. "Where is Ben?"

"He went to the barn with Nathan. How do you feel?"

"Scared."

Rachel spanned the distance between them and drew Emma toward the staircase, where Rachel sat so they were on the same eye level. "Why, honey? The bad man is gone. You saw him leave with Mr. McNeal and Mr. Stuart for Charleston. He will not be bothering Ben or you again."

"Promise?"

"Yes. He is in serious trouble and will spend a long time in jail."

"Very bad man."

"Do you know him?"

Emma dropped her head and didn't say anything for a long moment. "He took my brother. He killed my pa."

"He did? Did you see it?"

The child looked up at Rachel. "No, Ben tolded me."

"When?"

"After y'all came back from the swamp."

"How did he know?"

Emma shrugged. "The man tolded him?"

"That was probably it." *Or was it?* "I could use some help. I hear Faith making noises. Can you play with her while I fix supper?"

The girl's eyes brightened with the first smile Rachel had seen in hours from her. "Yes."

As Emma went into the bedchamber to pick up Faith from the cradle, Rachel remained seated on the stairs, watching the girl hold her daughter and hug her, whispering words to her that Rachel could not hear. Her heart swelled at the sight. The constable had told Nathan if no relatives could be found she could keep Ben and Emma. She wanted that. They needed someone to love them and care for them. She had a feeling there had been little of that in their lives.

* * * * *

"Do you want to talk about what happened today?" Nathan asked after picking up the last piglet and checking it over.

"Nothin' to say." Ben scuffed his shoe into the dirt in the stall where the pig and her babies were staying.

"'Tis all right if you were scared. I was."

"You were?"

"Sure. I was scared something would happen to you or Rachel. I was afraid Mr. Baker would not make it back to the house for me to remove the ball from his shoulder."

"So was I." Ben stared at the ground. "Especially in the swamp with that man."

"He didn't say anything about why he took you?"

Ben shook his head.

"That is strange."

"Could have wanted me to work for him?"

"You think that was it?"

Ben nodded. "Yes, that has got to be it."

"I wonder what kind of work."

"Farm work. I have been doin' a good job here. He has been watchin', so he would know that."

"He said he has been watching?"

"Yes. Or what if he's a pirate and wanted me to work on a ship?"

"There haven't been any rumors of pirates in these parts, but that could be a possibility." Nathan stood and left the stall to move to the henhouse. He gave Ben the basket and let him go in to get the eggs. "You know that Rachel and I want to help you and your sister any way we can. If there is anything that is bothering you, you can come to us."

Ben collected three eggs. "Not many this evening."

"Perhaps the commotion disturbed the hens."

"You think so?"

"Animals are sensitive to people's emotions. That is what makes Jasper such a good guard dog. He senses when someone is in trouble."

"He could have gotten killed today."

"Yes, he could have."

"I miss him."

"John will make sure he is taken care of. We have Liberty now to care for. I thought that could be one of your jobs."

Ben searched the barn and saw the puppy stretched out on the ground, sound asleep. "Rachel tolded me the constable was looking for a relative to take me and Emma in. We don't have none. What will that mean? Will he take us away?"

Nathan walked to Ben and clasped him on the shoulder. "No. I will not let that happen. Neither will Rachel. She went into the swamp by herself because you were in trouble. A person does not do that unless she cares."

Ben quickly veiled the shiny gleam in his eyes. "We work hard to pay for our keep."

The child kept a barrier between him and others—afraid to care. Nathan could understand that. He felt the same way. He had lost enough people in his life. When a person cared for another, he risked getting hurt. "You do work hard and what you do is appreciated, but that is not why Rachel wants to keep you."

"Then why?"

"Why don't you ask her?"

Ben's mouth puckered into a thoughtful expression. "Maybe."

"Let's go up to the house. I don't know about you, but I am starved."

Ben handed Nathan the basket and then ran to Liberty and scooped the large puppy into his arms. Together the two left the barn and headed toward the house, the firelight pouring out of the windows, coupled with the almost full moon, illuminating their path.

As Nathan strolled with the child, he thought back to earlier when he had seen Rachel coming toward him to see how Mr. Baker was. Wet, mud-covered, she was the best thing he could have seen in that moment while he was fighting to keep George alive.

She was safe. For now. He could not shake the feeling it was temporary. She had been in this country only a short time and in danger on a number of occasions. The farm was doing well and might even be a success. But it only took one of those perils going totally wrong to change everything. Today he had to make a choice between saving George or searching for Rachel. Yes, Patrick and John had been here and the decision had been easier because of their presence.

What will happen next time when the choice is not as easy?

Thirteen

A pounding on the door awakened Rachel from a deep sleep, but before she could don a wrapper, the sound stopped and she heard Maddy's voice. Hurrying, she tied the sash to her dressing gown and left her bedchamber. The look on both Maddy's and Nathan's faces alarmed her.

"What is wrong?" Rachel peered out the window and noticed that night was giving way to dawn, but the light was all wrong—too bright for the time of day.

"The field closest to the house is on fire. Get everyone up and out of here in case I cannot do anything to stop it." Nathan pivoted and hurried out the doorway.

"Get Emma and I will get B—"

"I'm here." Ben stood at the bottom of the staircase. "Nathan said there's a fire?"

"Yes, we need to get out. The fire is heading toward the house. Grab what you can and then go help Nathan."

Rachel rushed into her room and stuffed some clothes into a bag then scooped up Faith. When she returned to the main room, the front door was open. The scent of smoke permeated the air, a haze snaking through the trees like a serpent wanting to devour them. Maddy and Emma came out of their bedchamber with their arms full of clothing and linens.

"We need to help Nathan fight the fire." Once they were outside, Rachel handed Faith to Emma. "I want you to stay with Faith, away from the fire. Protect her."

The little girl nodded and cuddled Faith against her.

Leading the others, Rachel started for the road, away from the fire that raged about five hundred feet behind the house. The wind blew, catching the clothes and dancing about her. At the edge of the flames, Nathan used a shovel and threw dirt on what he could. The battle seemed impossible.

Lord, help. I don't want to lose the farm. I have too many depending on me. Please, You are the only One who can help.

At a safe distance, Rachel knelt in front of Emma. "If you need me, yell. I will come. Maddy, Ben, and I are going to work with Nathan to stop the fire."

In the dim light of dawn Emma's eyes grew huge. "You might get hurt. Don't."

"This is my home. Your home. I shall do what I need to do to keep it safe. I shall be all right." Rachel hugged the girl and Faith to her then rose. "Let's go. We only have one shovel, but we have buckets and can draw water from the well."

Ben raced ahead of Maddy and Rachel and retrieved some buckets from the house. Each of them filled a container with water from the well in the yard and walked as fast as they could toward the burning field, the wind whipping up the blaze.

Nathan glanced toward Rachel. "Stop. Don't come too close. If a spark hits your clothes, you could catch fire quickly. The same for Maddy. Have Ben throw the water on the fire."

A flaming piece of debris landed a few feet away from Rachel. She lifted her dressing gown and stamped on the tiny fire then took an empty bucket from Ben and hastened to the well to refill it.

Back and forth she and Maddy went with the water for Ben to toss on the fire. After multiple trips to and from the well, Rachel paused long enough to notice the wind had died down some. Perhaps they had a chance after all. Nathan continued to shovel dirt onto the blaze. He had actually made a little progress.

Renewed with hope, Rachel worked as fast as she could. The sun peeked over the trees to the east, painting the sky a fiery color to match the flames consuming her corn stalks. The ache in her arms protested every bucket of water she lugged to Ben, but she did not relent. This was her home now—all she had.

Mr. Baker arrived, out of breath, his arm still in the sling Nathan had fashioned for him. When he had gone back to his cabin two weeks ago, Maddy had not wanted him to leave. She thought he needed a few more days being nursed by her. But Mr. Baker had not been comfortable with her waiting on him nor with being idle.

Because of his arm, Mr. Baker could only help with transporting the buckets back and forth from the well to the fire. On one of his stops he asked Maddy, "What happened? There hasn't been any lightning."

"We don't know. Nathan woke up to Liberty yelping in the barn. He got up and smelled the smoke then saw the fire."

Mr. Baker turned his attention to Rachel, who handed him a pail. "Do you think this has anything to do with the man in the swamp? 'Tis been three weeks. He is in jail, but the constable does not know much more than you all did that first day."

"Your guess is as good as mine. I have no idea. I hadn't thought about there being another person associated with the man in the swamp. But what if the person who shot you was not the one the constable has in jail?" Rachel peered toward the bog. The sight that filled her vision brought more hope to the surface. "The wind has shifted." She swung her gaze to the nearly destroyed field to find the line of flames had turned back toward the singed part of the ground.

"In that case it will die if it does not have anything to burn." Mr. Baker grabbed the bucket and rushed toward the area still ignited with fire.

"The wind is blowing toward the swamp. If it burns anything it will be that." Maddy met Mr. Baker halfway and passed him another pail.

He leaned down and kissed her cheek. "Thank you. Be back."

Maddy returned to the well with a rosy hue to her cheeks that had nothing to do with the blaze and a gleam in her eyes. "Even hurt, he comes to help us."

"Yes, Mr. Baker is a good neighbor." Rachel lifted the bucket out of the well and transferred it to Maddy then looked over where Emma was with Faith.

A couple of bags on the ground met her perusal and sparked panic. Where were the girls? Rachel dropped the pail she was holding and raced toward where she had left the two girls. Her heartbeat accelerated with each step she took. She heard Maddy shout behind her, but she did not stop to answer.

"Emma! Where are you?" Rachel yelled over and over.

Close to the pile of their possessions they had taken from the house, she spied the girl running out of the barrier of trees between the river and the house. Emma clasped Faith to her, her screams piercing the air. Fright stamped its mark on her features. She kept glancing back over her shoulder.

"Help. It is after me." Emma's foot caught on a root, and she fell to the ground, rolling to keep from squashing Faith.

It? Rachel searched the woods as she neared Emma struggling to her feet. "What is after you?"

"Alligator." Emma tossed a glance over her shoulder and pointed.

Rachel saw a large, ugly beast—with the biggest mouth— charging out of the brush right toward them. "Run. Get help."

She could not let the alligator go after Emma, which meant she had to stay between Emma and the reptile. Scouring the area for some kind of weapon, she spied the bags and snatched up the top one. Throwing it at the alligator, then the one below it, she continued to look for something to stop the animal.

A thick branch lay on the ground near a tree. She raced toward it, yelling at the beast, "I am over here." With a quick peek toward Emma, she latched onto the "weapon" and spun about to face the animal. It slowed and bellowed, eyeing her. Opening and closing its massive jaws, its sharp teeth gleamed in the light. Rachel swung the branch to keep the alligator focused on her but still at a distance.

A glance to the right found Emma at the house. Another glance behind her centered on a tree with limbs low enough for her to hoist herself out of reach of the beast. She stomped her foot and shouted, "Get out of here."

It wasn't afraid of her. Instead it sprinted forward on its short stubby legs—amazingly fast for such a large creature. Rachel screeched and dropped the branch then vaulted onto the first limb of the elm tree. The alligator leaped up, and its jaws snapped onto her dressing gown, nearly pulling her to the ground. She clamped her arms around the limb above her and yanked on her clothing. A rip reverberated through the air. But she was free to climb higher. She did without looking down.

Because she suddenly discovered she did not like heights. Three branches off the ground, Rachel clamped herself to the trunk and squeezed her eyes closed. The pounding of her heartbeat knocked against the wood of the tree. The thundering of her pulse nearly drowned the bellows of the beast below her.

Alligators cannot climb trees, can they?

She knew so little about this American animal. Now she wished she knew more.

Lord, help.

A ruckus below her riveted her attention to Nathan wrestling the alligator on the ground under the tree. Mr. Baker held out his hand clenching Tom's pistol but couldn't take a shot because the animal and Nathan were entwined together. Her gaze fastened onto the knife in Nathan's grasp as he sat on the creature's back and locked his hands on the jaws to keep them closed. Then, releasing his grip on one side, he slit the alligator's throat. The beast went limp in his hold, and Nathan rose.

Nathan had often supplemented their food supply with fresh meat from the animals around the area, but Rachel had never seen him kill one—and he certainly had not brought home an alligator before. Her stomach roiled. Bile rose into her throat. This country was too primitive for her. She was used to an estate not far from London or staying in their townhouse there. How in the world did she think she could make a life for herself and Faith in this place?

"You can come down now, Rachel."

Nathan's deep, gruff voice floated up to her in the midst of the panic seizing her. She gasped for a decent breath. The rapid beating of her heart threatened to overtake her whole body. One damp hand slipped on the bark, the wood scraping her palm. She could not move. Her muscles were frozen in place.

"Everything is all right, Rachel."

Again his soothing words reached her ears, and she heard them, but when her gaze fell on the large alligator, bigger than Nathan, who was at least six feet tall, the enormity of what she had done with a puny little club-like weapon hit her as though someone had punched her in the stomach.

"I don't know if I can."

"You are not too high up. I will help you. Step on the branch lower than you."

She tried to move her foot down to that limb. She couldn't. "I—I…" She panned the view from the tree. Her vision blurred, her surroundings whirling.

"I am coming up," she vaguely heard in the distance—the far distance.

Black rushed toward her, and she went limp.

* * * * *

Nathan caught Rachel as she wilted on the branch. Her eyes fluttered and closed. He cradled her, pinned between the limb and him, as he tried to figure out how he was going to get her down.

"Ben, George, can you help me lower her to the ground?"

"Yes," they answered at the same time. Then George added, "I can get rid of this sling."

"No," Maddy said. "You might open your wound."

"I'm fine, woman. I have been telling you that for days." He flung off the cloth that had held his arm then positioned himself beneath the tree with Ben next to him. "We are ready. Pass her to us. I wonder what made her pass out. Do you think she is ill?"

Nathan chuckled, staring at the soft, beautiful features of Rachel's face. "No, I think she finally realized how dangerous it is to fight an alligator."

George joined in with laughter.

Maddy punched him in his good arm, half playfully, half seriously. "Nothing better stand in the way of a mama protecting her own. That includes monsters, whether it is two- or four-legged. Do you hear me?" She shouted the last two sentences for the neighbors to hear.

As Nathan handed off Rachel to George and Ben, he couldn't shake the image of the alligator caging Rachel against the tree. The beast had opened its jaw as though showing her she did not have a chance against him. Rage had zipped through every part of Nathan, and somehow he ended up on top of the alligator. It happened so fast he was not even sure how it came about.

Hopping down to the ground, he knelt next to Rachel and felt for a pulse. Steady beneath his fingertips. Good. "I'm taking her to the house. I need you all to keep an eye on the burnt field. If a fire reoccurs, come get me. We will have to stop it before it gets out of hand. We were lucky this time. The wind changed directions away from the house and barn."

Rachel stirred and murmured, "Not luck. The Lord." She swallowed and moistened her lips as her eyes slowly opened. "I asked the Lord to save the house, and He did."

"Sure He did," Nathan muttered, but when he thought back to the desperation he had felt at battling a fire that was consuming everything in its path and spreading quickly, what other explanation was there?

Nathan scooped Rachel up into his arms. The feeling that she belonged in his embrace stunned him. It had to be a reaction to the fact she could have been killed today. That was all. He cared about Rachel and Faith—felt responsible for them even, but he would not let himself feel anything beyond that. She didn't belong here, and hopefully her family would come and take her back to England.

He looked down at her and found her staring at him. His throat constricted.

"I can walk. I am fine. You can put me down."

He clenched his teeth, drawing in deep breaths through his nostrils. "No."

"What do you mean no?"

"No means I will not put you down." He mounted the step into her house. "Besides, we are here."

"Good. Now you can."

He kept striding toward her bedchamber. Her brows furrowed, and her mouth tightened into a thin line.

After he shouldered his way into the room, he crossed to the bed and placed her on it. "There. I have put you down." When she started to get up, he laid his hand on her shoulder. "You are not going anywhere until you have rested."

"I told you I am fine." She propped herself up on her elbows and stabbed him with a narrow-eyed look.

"Yes, you did. I don't believe you. You have dark circles under your eyes. Your arms are trembling with exhaustion. You have spent the past hour fighting first a fire and then an alligator. Rest, at least for a while."

The tension in her face relaxed, and she sank back onto the bed. "There is so much to do. What am I going to do about the field? This is really going to hurt me. I only have the money now that I make from Mrs. Bridges." Rachel's gaze shifted, and she smiled. "Come in, honey. As you can see, I'm all right."

Emma shuffled into the room. "I brought Faith back to sleep in her cradle."

"Thank you. You were so brave today." Rachel pushed herself up into a sitting position while the girl put Faith down. "Are you all right? You gave me a fright today."

"I went into the woods to go to…" The child slanted a glance at Nathan. "I didn't want to leave Faith alone. I took her with me. The alligator surprised me. I was so scared."

Rachel held out her arms and Emma went into her embrace. "You were brave. Now that it is warm we are going to have to keep a watch out for alligators."

"At least we will have some fresh meat for a while. Alligator meat is good." Nathan knew that fact would not make up for the loss of a field of corn. He did not have an answer for Rachel. This would hurt her. They could replant, but that did not help the immediate money problems.

"We need to share with Mr. Baker. He has been a big help." Rachel squeezed Emma then kissed the top of her head. "Honey, you saved Faith. I cannot thank you enough. We shall make a cake later and celebrate that we are alive and did not lose our home."

"A party?" The child stepped back, her eyes sparkling.

"Yes. We have a lot to celebrate."

Emma darted forward and gave Rachel a kiss on her cheek then scurried out of the bedchamber.

Tears shone in Rachel's eyes. "What if she had not been able to get away from the alligator?"

"But she did. Don't worry about something that did not happen."

"Can I worry about what the loss of the corn will mean?"

"I will prepare the field and replant when I can. I also thought about using some of the swampland for rice and indigo. There are parts that don't flood very much that might be able to support those crops."

"We do have the piglets. You are right. I need to look at my blessings. There are many. One is you. I cannot pretend that I would have made it this far by myself. You are the reason the farm is doing as well as it is."

"We still have a problem. How did the fire start? It was not lightning, so what was it?"

"Why would someone try to burn me out?"

"Why was that man in the swamp? Why did he kidnap Ben?"

"Do you think it has anything to do with Ben's father being killed here?"

Rachel's question made Nathan pause. Did their troubles all go back to the murdered man? "When we go into Charleston, I will talk with the constable and the kidnapper. We need some answers."

"Also, we need seed if we are going to replant. Perhaps Mrs. Bridges can give me more work. We need to go soon to town."

"Only if Mr. Baker will stay here with Maddy and the children. From the way he is here a lot of the time, I don't think he will mind."

Rachel swung her legs over the side of the bed and rose. "There is a lot to do before we go."

Nathan grinned, moving to block her path to the door. "Do you not understand what it means to rest?"

Rachel peered down at her torn, dirty dressing gown. "Look at me. I am a mess."

He stepped closer and clasped her upper arms. "You look beautiful," slipped out of his mouth before he could censor himself.

She blushed and lowered her head.

He lifted her chin with the tip of his finger. The sight of her full lips stirred a need in him that he had buried. She made him feel needed. She made him feel as if he could make a difference.

He leaned toward her and whispered his mouth across hers. The taste of her on his lips heightened his need to hold her close, their hearts beating as one. He tugged her near and wound his arms about her as he kissed her properly—deep and long. She melted into him as though her legs gave way and he needed to support her. Which he gladly did. For now he would enjoy the kiss. Later reality would set in.

* * * * *

Later that night after supper, Rachel served the cake she had baked—a little lopsided, but she hoped edible. She set it on the table in front of Nathan. He took his knife and sliced the sweet then passed the pieces to each one. Ben licked his lips. Mr. Baker beamed with a huge grin.

When Nathan gave her the plate with her dessert on it, their gazes connected and the sensations she had experienced when he kissed her earlier that day bubbled to the surface along with the heat of a flush. He winked and resumed cutting the cake. Her heart fluttered and beads of perspiration covered her upper lip and forehead.

Today she had finally admitted out loud that she would not have made it without his help. When the words had come out, at first she had been surprised at herself, but the more she acknowledged Nathan's role in her life, the more it felt right. From the very first, when she had gone into labor with Faith in a storm, all the way to today, when she was chased by an alligator, he had been there. She tried to picture Tom being there for her like Nathan. She couldn't.

Emma kept her head down and picked at her cake.

"I thought you wanted to celebrate tonight, Emma." Was the cake that bad? Rachel took a bite. The taste was a little too sweet. She should not have put in that extra honey, but she had thought more of a good thing would make it even better.

"I am tired." She raised her chin, her eyes half veiled with sleepiness. "Can I save it till tomorrow?"

"Yes. I can do that for you if you want to go to bed."

The child rose, her movements slow, her steps labored as she bridged the distance to the bedchamber.

As Rachel watched Emma, concern mushroomed in her. Something was wrong. Was she ill?

After a few minutes to give Emma a chance to get ready for bed, Rachel pushed back her stool and stood. "I am going to check on Emma. Make sure everything is all right."

When she entered the room, Emma sat on the side of the bed in her nightgown, staring at the floor. She did not even look up as Rachel approached her.

"What is wrong? I know today set us back, but we could have lost so much more. We were fortunate. We have a place to live and the other two fields are still all right."

Emma raised glistening eyes to Rachel. "But what if he burns them too?"

"Who is 'he'?" Rachel settled on the bed next to the girl.

"The bad man."

"He's in jail. Remember? He didn't do this."

"But he has a friend."

"Friend? How do you know?"

Emma averted her face, her hands twisting together in her lap. "You said it might be the bad man's friend."

"You listened to everything Nathan and I talked about this morning?"

Her shoulders hunched even more, and she mumbled, "Yes." A tear fell from her eye. "I am sorry. Don't be mad."

Rachel slid her arm around the child's shoulders and pulled her close. "I am not mad. But you should not eavesdrop on people's conversations."

"I know. But there's something I need to tell ya." Emma sniffled and inhaled a deep breath. "I know the bad man that took Ben."

Fourteen

"You know the man? How? Who is it?" Rachel's stomach plummeted.

Emma nodded. "Pa worked with him. He was mean."

"What is his name?"

"Pa called him Geoffrey. Pa kept us away from him."

Rachel could understand that. "What did your pa do for him?"

Emma hung her head, her clasp so tight her knuckles were white. "Bad things. That is why Pa ran away."

"Where did he go?"

"Here. We were living here. No one else was," she mumbled into her lap.

"Do you know why Geoffrey kidnapped Ben?"

"He wants Ben to tell him something."

"Do you know what?"

Emma nodded. "Ben don't know I tolded you." She peered up. "I don't want you to lose the farm. Ben and me don't want to be sent away. I want to live here…with you."

"I am not going to send you two away. You don't have to worry about that."

Tears glistened in the child's eyes. "What if we do somethin' wrong?"

"That will not change how I feel about you and your brother."

"What if you lose the farm 'cause of the fire?"

"Then I will figure something out."

Emma brushed a tear away from her cheek. "The money can help you keep it."

"The money?" Dread knotted Rachel's abdomen. What was going on? What had the children been involved in?

"Pa tolded Ben where he hid it."

"I thought you two did not have any money."

"Not ours. Bad man's." Covering her mouth, Emma yawned.

Rachel would not get to the bottom of this until she had a conversation with Ben. "Don't worry about it. You get some sleep and we will talk tomorrow."

Emma scooted back until she could pull the covers up over her.

Rachel leaned down and kissed her goodnight. "Honey, you have a home with me. I don't intend to lose this farm." *I cannot. Where would we all go?* She had more than herself and Faith to look out for now.

Rachel left the bedchamber with the door slightly open. Until Maddy went to bed, Emma did not feel comfortable staying by herself without the light coming from the main room. When she returned to the table, Maddy had already cleared the dishes away. Rachel sat across from Ben.

Rachel directed her full attention to the boy. "Who is Geoffrey?"

His mouth dropped open. His pupils dilated. "What did Emma tell you?"

"That you know the man who took you. What was he after?" Rachel felt Nathan's look on her, but she focused totally on Ben. She needed answers. Today they could have all died if Liberty had not barked and Nathan was not quick to act.

"Pa stole some money from him." His gaze cut into her with defiance.

"He wanted his money back?"

"'Tis not his money."

"Whose money is it?" Nathan asked.

Finally Rachel peered at him. The hard edge to his words carried over into his expression. A muscle in his jaw jerked.

Ben shrugged. "I don't know. Different people. Pa tried hidin' us from Geoffrey and the other man."

"What other man?" Nathan rose and towered at the end of the table.

"Don't know his name. He's one reason Pa stopped workin' for Geoffrey." Ben shifted his attention from Rachel to Nathan then back to Rachel. "No one stops workin' for him. 'Tis why Pa was hidin' here."

"That and the fact your pa took some money that did not belong to him." Nathan paced a few feet then swung around and came back.

Ben shot to his feet, his hands balled at his sides. "The money didn't belong to Geoffrey. They stole it," he shouted then raced up the staircase to the loft.

From the pounding sound he made, he must have thrown himself on his pallet.

"We have a problem," Rachel said, spying Emma peeking into the main room.

"Yes. There is another cutthroat thief out there bent on getting back the money stolen from him, and he thinks we have it."

"Yes, that is a problem, but that was not what I was referring to. Emma and Ben are afraid we…I shall leave them."

Nathan pivoted toward Rachel and caught sight of Emma in the doorway. His expression softened. "Ben, come down here. Emma, come out of the room."

A long moment passed with not a sound coming from the loft. Then Ben poked his head out of the opening. He clambered down the steps and slunk toward the table, his gaze trained on the floor. Emma crossed to her brother and sat next to him.

Nathan positioned himself behind Rachel and said, "You will always have a home here."

Ben peered at Rachel. "Promise?"

Rachel nodded, her throat clogged with emotions that made talking difficult.

"When Pa lost the farm, we got nowhere to go. He met up with Geoffrey. He talked Pa into robbin' people. When Geoffrey killed a man, Pa got mad. He never wanted to do that. Pa ain't like that. All he wanted was to git food for us."

Desperation made a person sometimes do things he would not ordinarily do. Rachel had been close to that place. She was thankful the Lord had sent Nathan to help her.

"Pa took Geoffrey's stash and we ran. He found this farm. Ain't nobody here so we stayed. He was sure Geoffrey and the new man would be watchin' in the towns and on the roads."

Nathan placed his hand on Rachel's shoulder. "Where's the money?"

For a moment Ben's eyes darkened, his forehead creased.

Emma nudged him. "Tell 'em. That money is bad."

"'Tis in a hollow of an oak tree. In the swamp."

"First thing tomorrow morning I need you to show me. We need to give the money to the constable."

"But Rachel needs it to save the farm," Emma said, tears welling into her eyes. "We won't have a place to live."

"Do you believe me when I tell you something?" Rachel asked. The child nodded.

"You will always have a place with me."

"If you lose the farm like Pa, where will you go?" Ben put his arm around his sister.

"All of you will have a home with me. That is a promise I can keep." Nathan squeezed Rachel's shoulder.

She appreciated his words, but she could never live with him without marriage, and she'd vowed after Tom's death she would not become subject to another man like she had. She would find a way to keep the children by herself, if need be.

"The money does not belong to you, us, or the bad men. The constable will be able to get it back to the proper folks who were robbed."

Ben dropped his arm from around Emma and straightened. "Pa died so we could have it. Those two men tried to get him to tell 'em where it was, but he wouldn't."

"What happened that day?"

"They found Pa at the house. Emma and me were at the barn. We caught a couple of chickens. The men didn't know about us and didn't see us. When they took Pa into the house, I snuck up to the window." Ben's voice thickened, and he swallowed hard. "I saw 'em beat him then shoot him when all he tolded 'em the money was hidden in the swamp." He closed his eyes, but a tear leaked out. "I didn't know what to do. I didn't have no gun. Nothin'."

Rachel couldn't remain seated any longer at the anguish pouring from the child. She came around the table to both of the children and drew them into her embrace. "Your father would not have wanted you to try. They would have killed you too. Money can make men do evil things. Your pa would have wanted you to protect your little sister."

Ben swiped his hand across his cheek. "I know. But…"

Emma hugged Ben and would not let go.

"When they left Pa and the farm and went into the swamp, I dragged Pa into the room where we were sleepin'. He was barely alive, but I thought I could help him. If he rested and I stopped the bleedin'…" Ben cleared his throat and tried to say something, but no sound came out.

"You did what you could." His pain tore Rachel's heart.

"Pa's last words to me was to take care of Emma." Ben looked at Nathan. "I didn't know what to do. The money is in a tree a little ways into the swamp. The men were looking all around. Then you all came to the farm."

"Why did you not tell me about the men?" Nathan sat on the stool Rachel had been using.

"They left. I thought for good." Ben glanced at his sister. "I wanted to leave, git the money, but Emma didn't. I couldn't leave without her."

"How did the man know who you were when he kidnapped you?"

"He saw Pa with me. Pa didn't know, but Geoffrey followed Pa and saw where he went every night."

"Did he also know about Emma?" Nathan settled his elbows on the table.

"I don't think so. At least not till he saw her here."

"Why would his partner burn the cornfield?" Rachel asked as the little girl shifted toward her and wound her arms around Rachel. The child quaked. Rachel stroked her back, conveying as much comfort as she could.

Ben shrugged. "To run you all off or kill you."

"Can you describe this second man?" Nathan asked.

"I ain't goin' to forget him. He is huge, strong. Has blond hair, long, and a scar on his left cheek. He's got a big knife he carries."

The description brought to Rachel's mind her assailant in Charleston. He had targeted her. Her legs weakened, and if she hadn't been holding Emma, she would have sunk to the floor. Her gaze riveted to Nathan's. He realized who the man was too. His mouth twisted into a frown, his expression hard, fierce.

Nathan rose. "We will get the money then go to Charleston tomorrow. Once we don't have the money, we should be out of danger. I will be staying in the main room tonight in case the man decides to pay us a visit. I am going to get Liberty. He may be a puppy, but he is taking after his sire. Bolt the door after I leave and don't open to anyone but me."

Rachel straightened to follow him to the door. Her heartbeat accelerated so much the room spun. She grasped the edge of the table and waited a moment for the dizziness to pass.

Before leaving, Nathan moved close to her. "Don't open the door unless I say all is quiet."

"Fine. Do you think he is out there watching?"

"Perhaps. We have to think he is."

FROM THIS DAY FORWARD

"Don't go."

"Maddy is outside telling Mr. Baker good-bye. They both need to know what is going on and get inside."

"If Mr. Baker wants to stay tonight, he's welcome to."

"That's a good idea, especially since we now know what is going on. We all will come back together." Nathan left the house, the sound of the door closing propelling Rachel into action.

She threw the bolt in place, closing her eyes and sending up a quick prayer that nothing would happen to Nathan, Maddy, and Mr. Baker. Facing the children, she inhaled several breaths to bolster herself for their sakes. Their expression prompted her to say, "We are going to be all right. Nathan and Mr. Baker know what they are doing."

"But the man is mean. When he saw Pa, he was…" Ben slid his glance to Emma, who chewed her lower lip then pressed his lips together.

Rachel bridged the gap between them and held their hands. "Let us say a prayer for the Lord to watch out for them. Emma, would you like to?"

The little girl nodded.

Rachel bowed her head, noticing both children following suit.

"Please stop the bad man. Amen."

"Perfect."

"Will God listen to us? We been bad too." Ben pulled his hand from Rachel's.

"He always listens. We all make mistakes. The important thing is being sorry we did. If you ask the Lord's forgiveness and mean it, He will give it to you."

Suspicion clouded Ben's eyes. "How do you know He does?"

"The Bible tells us He does."

"Even if I lie? Hurt someone?" Ben fired back.

"Yes."

Emma yawned, her eyes closing then popping open.

"I think you both need to go to bed. Tomorrow will be a long day. I shall be heading for bed as soon as Nathan comes back with Maddy and Mr. Baker."

"And Liberty," Emma said, trying to stifle another yawn.

"Can I stay up to make sure Liberty is all right?" Ben asked, walking to the window and looking out at the dark landscape.

"Me too?"

"Yes, but then to bed."

Ben stood watch at the window while Rachel paced in front of the fireplace and Emma sat in the chair nearby, falling asleep. The minutes seemed to crawl by. With each moment the danger they were in multiplied in Rachel's mind until the throb of her pulse beat increased to a maddening speed.

"They are comin'." Ben moved to the door.

"Wait!" As much as she wanted to swing wide the door, she would follow Nathan's instruction in case the man was hiding and Ben had not seen him. She scurried to the bolt and placed her hand on it. When the knock came, she asked, "Who is it?"

"All is quiet out here."

Nathan's deep, gruff voice sent relief through her. She threw the door open and resisted the urge to fling herself into his arms. "Did you see anything suspicious?"

"No, and neither did Maddy or Mr. Baker." Nathan held Liberty in his arms.

All three entered the house, then Rachel locked up again and faced the group. "What took you all so long?"

"We checked the area around the house." Nathan put the puppy on the floor and Liberty immediately loped to the children, licking them and wagging his tail.

In the distance thunder rumbled with a flash of lightning illuminating the darkness outside the window.

"As you can hear and see, the good news is a storm is moving in. The moon has clouded over just in the time I was outside. If it rains, it will be hard to set more fires."

"That is good. But what if it continues tomorrow? Will that make it hard to retrieve the money?" Rachel asked while Ben patted Liberty then headed up to the loft.

Liberty yelped and lumbered toward the staircase to follow Ben. The boy stopped halfway up and had to go back down. He rubbed the wolfhound and said, "Stay here." Then he started up the stairs again. The puppy tried to go after him but couldn't quite make the big step. He whined while Ben disappeared through the opening into the loft.

Emma padded to Rachel and hugged her. "Good night," she said, yawning between the two words. Then she made her way to her bedchamber.

"The children have the right idea. See you all in the morning." Maddy trailed after Emma into the room.

Rachel withdrew from the trunk what extra blankets she had and passed them to Mr. Baker and Nathan. "Good-night."

Her gaze latched onto Nathan's and warmth suffused her body at his intense look. The kiss they had shared earlier stayed in her thoughts as she prepared for bed and fell asleep. The image of Nathan accompanied her into the world of dreams.

* * * * *

Before dawn broke over the landscape the next day, Rachel finished nursing Faith, who had awakened early then fallen back to sleep. Rachel tried to go back to bed, but thoughts swirled around in her mind. Finally she got up again and rummaged in her trunk until she found her sketchpad and pencil. The picture of the man who accosted her in Charleston had haunted her dreams. She needed to draw him and see if it was the same person Ben referred to.

Half an hour later, in the dim light from her candle, her attacker stared back at her from the paper. A shudder shivered down her spine. She did not want to meet him again. The thought of his whiskey-laced breath, coupled with the stench of tobacco, nauseated her even now. The smell reminded her of Tom. The remembered feel of her attacker's hands on her iced her blood, and she crossed her arms over her chest to warm herself.

A noise from the main room drew her attention. She quickly dressed in a plain gown she had made since living at the farm. The muslin and simple lines fit the work she did here, not a parlor in Charleston or London. But this was her life now and there was something satisfying in knowing she was carving out a life for herself and her daughter.

While sitting on the bed, she put her boots on and wondered if she had not met Tom, what she would have been doing in England. Probably married to the man her father had chosen for her. Practically a stranger but from a good family, with plenty of money to support her, according to Papa. As though that was the only thing important to a woman.

Do I want to go home to England, if given the chance?

Not too long ago, she would have immediately said yes. She was not so sure now. She could not leave Emma and Ben.

How can I expect Nathan to stay much longer? Maybe through the harvest, but after that he had his own life. *Can I make it by myself without him?*

She didn't have any answers to the questions that floated through her mind, taunting her with her precarious situation.

A knock at her bedchamber door aroused her from her thoughts. She rose, saying, "Yes?"

"Ben and I are leaving."

She rushed to open the door and found Nathan standing in the entrance, a serious expression on his face.

"It stopped raining," he said, his look skimming over her features. "If Ben and I are not back in three hours, you go to my sister's then Charleston and let the constable know what's going on. Mr. Baker is staying to look out for you all. Promise me you will not come looking for us in the swamp."

"I cannot do that."

He grasped her upper arms. "You have to promise me. I cannot go if you don't. Get the constable, and he can go into the swamp. Mr. Baker knows the location of the oak tree where the money is hidden. He can show the constable."

"But it could be too late."

He rubbed his hands up and down her arms. "I don't intend to get caught."

"But what if you—"

His sudden kiss cut off her next words. His lips claimed to hers, and she shuddered, melting against him, not caring who saw her and Nathan kissing.

"I don't want to worry about you. Don't go outside. Stay indoors until Ben and I return. We will return with the money and this will be all over soon."

"Oh, I almost forgot. I drew a picture of the man who attacked me. I want Ben to see it. I think it is the same person." Rachel hastened to her bed, picked up the sketchpad, and then went into the main room, where Ben was wolfing down some bread and cheese.

"I have a picture I want to show you of a man who bothered me in Charleston." Rachel placed it on the table for Ben to look at. "Is he the other man working for Geoffrey?"

The boy studied it for a moment then nodded.

"Then when we go to Charleston, I shall show this to the constable." On impulse she kissed Ben's cheek and whispered, "Stay safe."

He snatched up the last piece of bread and cheese and marched to the door where Nathan waited. When they left, she glanced from Maddy to Mr. Baker, desperately wanting to call Nathan and Ben back to the house. What if this were the last time she saw either one? Her heart plummeted to her stomach.

Rachel paced the main room, trying to squash the uneasiness that gripped her. Stopping, she swept around. "Mr. Baker, you need to follow Nathan and Ben. We are not in danger here. They are. If the thief is watching the place, he will go after them because Ben is with Nathan."

"I cannot do that. Nathan wanted me to protect you all."

"If you don't, I shall." Rachel planted her fists on her waist and pulled herself up tall. "I have my husband's gun. I shall keep the door bolted. We shall be safe. They are not." When Mr. Baker's expression remained frozen in indecision, she added, "Please. As soon as they find the money, that man will attack them."

"Nathan knows that."

"Yes, but Nathan is not ruthless like that man is. Look what he did burning the field."

Mr. Baker peered at Maddy, an appeal for help in his eyes.

"You need to go after them. You know the swamp and can track them." Maddy came to stand beside Rachel, united in their request. "We will be all right. If you don't, I will help her go after them." Her face set in a determined look.

Mr. Baker swung his attention between Rachel and Maddy. "Nathan will not like this."

"But he and Ben will be alive. I have a bad feeling about this. Please. I am begging you." Rachel's panic mushroomed with each word she spoke. Nathan was here because of her. He could not die because of her. Ben was a child who should never have been exposed to a situation like this.

"Very well. Neither one of you will come after me?"

Maddy shook her head. "I promise I will keep Mrs. Gordon here. We have the girls to protect."

Rachel's servant had come a long way since they had landed in America. For that matter, Rachel had too. In England she would never have envisioned going into a swamp alone after a kidnapper and Ben.

Mr. Baker picked up his musket, looked back at Maddy, and opened the door.

"Wait." Maddy scurried toward him and kissed him on the cheek. "Take care of yourself."

A smile transformed his solemn expression. "I will. There is unfinished business between you and me." Then he left.

Maddy went to the window to watch his progress away from the house.

Rachel came to her and stood next to her in silent support. They were both waiting. Praying. If the men and Ben did not come back, she did not know how she would overcome the guilt. She was the reason this was happening. If she had returned to England and thrown herself on the mercy of her family, perhaps they would have taken her back. Instead, she had let her stubborn pride take over. She had been determined to make it on her own, to show her father she did not need his support or money.

Pride goeth before destruction, and a haughty spirit before a fall.

Lord, I am so sorry. Whatever You want, I shall do. Just bring them back safely.

Fifteen

If Nathan could have looked for the money without Ben, he would have, but he was not as familiar with this area as George. And he would not send George out to do what was his responsibility. If the man who set fire to the cornfield was still near, he would follow them into the swamp. That was why he and Ben pretended to go to the barn and then snuck out through a loose board on its side closest to the bog.

But still, even with those precautions, he sensed the man out there watching Ben and him slosh their way through the murky swamp in the dim light of dawn. Armed with his musket and knife, Nathan tried to avoid places where footprints would show. Which meant he and Ben stayed in the water most of the time. Its cool temperature numbed his feet and lower legs.

"'Tis not far. Do ya think he is out there?" Ben stared behind him.

"We have to assume he is. We will get the money and go back a different way."

The silence of the marsh kept Nathan's nerves on alert. Too quiet. As though the animals were waiting for a confrontation. *Lord, please keep Ben safe. I know You have no reason to answer my prayer, but Ben is a child. He needs Your protection.*

"We are here." The boy gestured toward a piece of land in the middle of a waterlogged area with one large oak standing sentinel.

Nathan locked his gaze on the hollow in the tree about eight or nine feet off the ground.

"I will have to hoist you up to get the money."

"Pa had to."

Emerging from the couple of feet of water surrounding the small island, Nathan scanned the shadows. The hair on his nape tingled. He tensed. At the base of the oak, he lifted Ben up to reach into the hole in the trunk.

"Got it."

Nathan lowered Ben to the ground, and the boy handed him a sack, filled with coins as well as jewelry—two necklaces and four rings. "Let's get out of here."

Again Nathan scouted the terrain. Not seeing anything unusual, he started toward the water to the right of the path they had used to come to the island. His chest constricted, and he forced a deep breath into his lungs. He couldn't relax until he had given the money and jewels to the constable. Then perhaps Rachel and the children would be safe.

This time he led the way, with Ben slightly behind him. Careful to make as little noise as possible, Nathan chose his steps with caution. Off to the side, about twenty feet away, he saw an alligator scurry into the water and sink below its surface. He paused and watched for any signs of the animal.

In a low voice Nathan said, "We need to hurry." He pointed to a spot where there was some dry land, indicating Ben was to go first while Nathan backed away to guard their escape.

The sloshing sound of their footsteps echoed through the quiet. The alligator surfaced a few yards away. The only part of him visible was his eyes and snout. Nathan kept moving backward, but he brought his musket around and loaded it then aimed it at the beast. He did not want to fire his gun if he did not have to.

He made his way toward the small rise in the swampland, his gaze trained on the alligator. "Ben, all right?" he asked in a whisper since he had not heard him for a moment.

No answer.

A chill skimmed down Nathan's length. He chanced a look behind him at the small dry spot of land. His heart plummeted. The man who had accosted Rachel in Charleston had his arm locked around Ben and a knife at his throat.

"Drop that musket or…" The man let his threat trail off into the silence.

The wild-eyed look on Ben's face held Nathan's attention. He evened his expression into a calm one, trying to convey a composed bearing to the boy. Nathan stepped out of the water and leaned over to lay the weapon on the ground.

"Move away from your gun to the left."

Nathan did as the assailant ordered. As he sidled toward higher ground, the man, still gripping Ben to him with the knife pressed into his neck, sidestepped toward the musket.

"I want the money. Toss it to me." His dark eyes bore into Nathan with lethal intent. When Nathan hesitated, the man grinned, revealing tobacco-stained teeth. "Now. You don't want me getting impatient."

Having stuffed the sack into his shirt so his hands could be free,

Nathan reached inside and withdrew it. The assailant's eyes flared. Nathan only had one chance. He threw the bag off to the man's side into the water. The assailant followed the bag as it made a splash and began to sink below the surface. He loosened his grasp on Ben.

"Run, Ben!" Nathan leaped toward the large man as he went after the money.

Nathan tackled him in midair, and they sailed into the swamp. The man still had his knife clasped in his hand and brought it up between them. The blade caught the sunlight filtering through the trees and gleamed. It nicked Nathan's neck before he got a good grip around the thief's wrist. Nathan poured all his strength into his hand about the man's and managed to push the knife away, a few inches from his throat. Squeezing, Nathan grappled for control, the blade hovering between them. The thief's fierce expression slowly evolved into one of pain, but he did not relent.

Ben screamed. "The alligator, Nathan!"

Nathan glanced up and spotted the beast making straight for them. He continued to struggle for the knife, but when the animal was a few feet away, Nathan lunged back toward his musket, releasing the man's hand. Nearest to the alligator, with his body mostly submerged in the water, the assailant could not move fast enough. The beast opened its jaws and clamped down on the man's right arm. As Nathan scrambled for the gun, the alligator shook his head and grasped more of the man, biting into his shoulder.

The thief's screams pierced the damp air. He thrashed about, but the alligator dragged him farther out into the swamp. Nathan clasped the musket and lifted it to shoot the beast, but the animal pulled his prey below the murkiness and disappeared.

Nathan hurried to the place where the sack went into the water and felt around for it, his gaze fixed on the spot he had last seen the alligator. Finally he clutched the bag, brought it up, and clambered out of the swamp.

The sound of Ben crying behind him swung him toward the boy. "We will be all right. He will not bother us."

"The alligator?"

"Both. Let's get out of here."

"Are there more?"

"The weather is warm. There might be. Keep an eye out for any. I still have my knife and musket."

Ben panned the dense vegetation then nodded.

Nathan clasped the boy's shoulder. "I am not letting anything hurt you."

Ben gave him another nod, but doubt darkened his eyes.

A sound behind Nathan stiffened him. Was there more than one thief? He whirled around, bringing up his musket.

* * * * *

Rachel paced back and forth in front of the window, giving her a view of anyone who would approach the house. "Where are they? They should be back by now."

Maddy sat on a stool at the table, biting her nails. A frown marred her features.

Father, I need Your help again. Please bring them all home unharmed.

"Rachel, what's wrong?" Emma asked from the doorway into the bedchamber. She rubbed her eyes and looked away. "Where's Nathan and Ben? They leave already?"

"Yes, honey." Rachel cut the distance between them and hugged her. "They should be back soon. They left at first light."

"I wanted to say good-bye."

"Then you can tell them hello when they return. I hate good-byes."

Emma peered up at her. "Me too."

"Are you hungry?" Rachel cradled the child to her as they walked toward the table where the bread was.

Emma shook her head. "Can we go outside and wait for 'em?"

"We should stay in here until they return."

Maddy hopped up and took Rachel's position at the window.

Rachel sat next to Emma. "Try to eat something. It might be a long day." She slid the plate with bread close to the child. Rachel's stomach knotted in a tangle of nerves. Here she was telling the little girl to eat and she couldn't. The very thought nauseated her.

"Was Pa a bad man?" Emma asked, fingering one slice but not eating it.

"It is wrong to steal, but I leave the judging to the Lord." *Or do I? Have not I judged Tom and his behavior? I have not been able to forgive him. I determined he deserved what happened to him.*

"Pa was scared. That's why we ran away."

"When you are scared, you sometimes do things that are not smart."

"Like stealin'?"

Rachel nodded. "The Lord tells us not to covet what others have. When we do, it can lead to unhappiness and trouble."

"Like now. I'm scared for Ben and Nathan."

So am I. Rachel forced a smile to her lips. "The Lord is with them."

"They are coming. They are safe." Maddy rushed toward the door.

"Hold it," Rachel shouted and hurried to the window to look out. "What if it is a trap?" But when she saw Ben smiling, even running ahead of Nathan and Mr. Baker, she relaxed. "Go ahead."

Maddy threw open the door and ran out of the house with Rachel and Emma right behind her. Rachel's gaze fixed on Nathan, and the gleam in his eyes warmed the coldness that had encased her since he left. Her pace picked up, and before she realized it, she was only a few steps behind Maddy.

Her servant launched herself into Mr. Baker's outstretched arms. He gave Maddy a kiss, laughter dancing in his eyes.

Rachel slowed some, but when Nathan's focus centered on her, as though she were the only one around, she threw her arms around him and kissed him—on the cheek until he shifted slightly and claimed her mouth. His embrace welded her to him, and she didn't want to be any other place.

When she finally leaned back, tears obscured her vision. "I was so afraid something would go wrong. That..." Her words jammed her throat as thoughts of what could have happened tumbled through her mind.

He cupped her face within his large hands and gave her a quick kiss. "We don't have to worry about the man who attacked you in Charleston anymore."

"What happened?"

His eyebrows slashed downward. "An alligator got him. The man had Ben and wanted me to toss him the money. I threw the bag. Not to him but into the water. He went after it, and I went after him. I think the alligator was attracted by our splashing."

Mr. Baker, his arm around Maddy's shoulders, joined them.

"That was when I found them. I will not forget that man." He rubbed his shoulder where he had been shot. "He was most likely the one who shot me."

"Is that the money?" Rachel pointed to the bag clutched in Ben's hand.

The boy nodded and opened the sack to show her.

Rachel peered inside at the massive amount of coins and jewelry. "That is a lot of money."

"Yes, and I cannot wait until it is in the constable's hands. It has caused enough trouble." Nathan took the bag.

"Then I think we should leave right away." Rachel started for the barn.

"We?"

Nathan's one-word question halted her. She swept around. "Yes. You are not going by yourself. I have business in town with Mrs. Bridges as well as seed to buy to replant that field." Which would take the last of her money.

"I will stay with Maddy and the children." Mr. Baker swung his attention to Maddy. "Just in case."

"Then it is settled. We leave now," Rachel said.

Nathan glanced down at his dirty, wet clothing. "Not like this."

Maddy took Mr. Baker's hand and led him toward the door. "Come in and I will fix a proper breakfast."

Rachel waited until everyone went into her house before turning to Nathan. "Are you really all right?" She touched a nick on his neck. "You are bleeding."

Nathan pressed his fingers into the cut then pulled them away and stared at the small amount of blood on their tips. "We fought over the knife until that alligator"—he swallowed hard—"took hold of him and dragged him into the deeper water. I would not want anyone to die that way. His screams reminded me of what I heard on the battlefield." A shudder rippled down his length.

His distress reached out and drew her close to him. She cupped his jaw. "If that man had not come after you and Ben, he would be alive. He chose his fate. You have done so much good for others. Even for your grandfather, in spite of him throwing you off the plantation. You said it. You were defending someone. You cannot save everyone."

"In the war I killed an English soldier because he surprised me while I was tending one of our wounded. I did not stop to think. I picked up a musket and used the bayonet to defend my patient. I killed a man who was no more than twenty. I—"

"Again, you were defending a patient in your care. That soldier would have killed you and the wounded man."

"I know, but when I looked into his eyes as he died, all I saw was how frightened and young he was. I was to save lives, not take them."

"Then you need to be a doctor again. You will have patients who die but also many who will not. All you can do is your best."

"Sometimes that isn't good enough."

"No, it isn't. But that doesn't mean you don't try."

His expression unreadable, he stared at her long and hard. "I will change and then we will go." He pivoted and strode toward the barn.

* * * * *

"This is for you, Mrs. Gordon." The constable palmed a small sack. "A reward."

Stunned, Rachel tried to make sense of the constable's words. Three weeks before, she had accompanied Nathan to Charleston to turn over the money to the authorities, and the constable wanted to give them a reward for returning the money and jewelry to its rightful owners.

He placed the small bag of coins into her hand. "A token of the victims' appreciation. A couple of pieces of jewelry were heirlooms."

"Come inside." Rachel stood in the middle of her vegetable garden, her basket filled with carrots, spinach, and turnips. "I can fix you some tea after your long ride out here."

"I have business at Pinecrest and must be leaving."

Pinecrest? "Is there a problem there?"

"Not anything that cannot be settled peacefully between two neighbors. Good day, Mrs. Gordon. The area is safer since that gang has been taken care of." He bowed his head then vaulted into his saddle and rode toward the road.

"Rachel, is something wrong?" Maddy scurried toward her, carrying Faith.

All servant/mistress boundaries had fallen over the past month with what Maddy and she had endured. Maddy had become an invaluable friend. "No. Actually everything is wonderful." She hoisted the small bag of coins. "The constable gave me a reward. With my share perhaps I can finally buy a cow."

"Your share?"

"We all were involved with the capture of the gang and the return of the stolen money and jewels."

Maddy shook her head. "That is yours to use for the farm."

Rachel took Faith from her friend and passed the basket and bag to her. "Things are starting to look up. Let's plan a party for tonight. Where is Emma?"

"At the barn collecting the eggs and I think playing with the piglets."

"She does have a soft heart." Rachel kissed the top of her daughter's head. "She is so good with Faith." They started walking toward the house. "We better get dinner on the table. I reckon it will not be long before Nathan and Ben come in from the field and want something to eat."

"I will go get Emma."

While Maddy headed for the barn, Rachel entered her house and took stock of her surroundings. A rocker along with two chairs sat in front of the fireplace, not used as much because of the beastly hot July temperatures. Her gaze shifted to the heart of the main room, the table with six stools around it. Mr. Baker joined them so often that he had made a stool for himself.

This was her home now. A sense of accomplishment flowed through her as she crossed to the cradle where she placed Faith. "I love you." She smiled at her daughter and was overjoyed to see Faith return it. She was three months old and already trying to roll over. Before she knew it, Faith would be walking, then talking. The thought of Faith growing up faster than she wanted swept over her.

"I wish you could meet your grandparents. Mama would love holding you. Papa…" She did not know what her father would think of Faith. Would he let his feelings toward Rachel color how he felt about Faith? She probably would never know. She glanced at the trunk along the far wall. Inside was a piece of paper with a letter partially written to him. She had not been able to finish it yet. Also in there was a completed one to her mother.

She went to the trunk and lifted its lid. Retrieving the incomplete letter, she stared at what she had written. *Faith has your eyes. Every time I look at her, I think of you.*

Tears welled up in Rachel's eyes, blurring the words together. The sound of the door opening swept her around to face Nathan coming inside, his strong, tan features tugging at her heart. What would she have done if she had not met him that first day? A tear slid down her cheek.

He covered the distance between them in long strides, concern puckering his brow. "Why are you crying?"

"Oh, it is nothing."

"I have learned from my sister that it is never nothing if she is crying."

"I was reading an unfinished letter I had written to my father."

"Why is it unfinished?" He moved closer.

"I wanted him and Mama to know about Faith. I described her, but I didn't know what else to say after that. I said it all when he disowned me for marrying Tom."

"Cross words?"

"No, actually. Amazement at his actions. And hurt. Anger came later."

"If he walked into this house, how would you feel?"

"Amazed again." She tilted her head. "I love my family. I miss them. I think a lot like how you feel concerning your grandfather. If he welcomed you back to Pinecrest, would you go?"

"Pinecrest will always be my home."

"That is the way I feel about Mansfield Manor. I lived there for twenty years. It was my whole world for so long."

"Until now." One corner of his mouth lifted.

She wanted to touch the cleft in his chin, the dimple in his cheek that appeared when he smiled, but she kept her arms at her sides. "Yes, but I shall always miss England. You know what I mean. Is that not why you came back here after the war? You missed Pinecrest, South Carolina."

"Yes. I have realized from my encounters with my grandfather since I have come back that I will do what I can to amend our differences. He can be a hard man, set in his ways, but at one time our bond was strong, more so than the one I had with my father."

Remembering the connection she had with her parents before Tom brought the tears back, several rolling down her cheeks. "I know what you mean."

Nathan brushed his thumbs across her cheeks, erasing any evidence of her sorrow. "I saw Maddy at the barn. She said the constable gave you a reward."

"Gave us. It is everyone's, including Mr. Baker."

"No, 'tis yours. Put the money into the farm. That way you won't have to work as much sewing into the late night hours for Mrs. Bridges."

"I like to sew. It is all the other work I have to do that is menial and boring. I don't think I shall ever be a good cook. I hate washing day."

Laughing, he tweaked her nose. "You were raised to be a mistress of a manor."

"That was my papa's dream for me."

"Was it yours?"

"According to Papa, I was to marry to strengthen our family with connections and money. There were times I felt like I was being bartered. That is why I responded so strongly to Tom's attention. Most men would not come near me because of Papa's influence. People just did what he said."

"He would get along great with my grandfather."

"You are probably right except that Papa is an Englishman."

"And my family is Scottish, who often do not get along with the English."

"There has been a volatile history between Scotland and England."

"But also a shared one."

Someone pounded on the door. Nathan pivoted, strode to it, and opened it. Moses stood in the entrance, trouble shadowing his eyes.

"'Tis Miz Sarah. She's havin' her baby. I was told to come git ya."

Color drained from Nathan's face. "Where is the midwife?"

"Charleston. No time."

Rachel hurried to Nathan's side. "I want to come too. She might need me."

Nathan remained in the doorway, his expression shutting down to a bland one, his body frozen in place.

Rachel placed her hand on his shoulder and shook him. "Nathan, you need to get your bag. The baby is early. Sarah will need you."

"Give me a moment, Moses." Then Nathan turned away from the man. "What if I cannot do anything to help her? What if..."

She waited until he looked at her. "She needs you. All she wants is for you to do your best. That is all you can do."

A haunted look invaded his eyes. "But Eliza died. Sarah almost did with Sean. I…" He inhaled a deep breath and nodded. "I have to go." He made his way to his bag.

"I want to come too," she repeated.

He made his way outside. "Moses, I will take this horse to Liberty Hall. I need you to bring Mrs. Gordon in the cart."

"Yes sir."

Before mounting Moses's horse, Nathan faced Rachel, clasping her hand and tugging her close. "Don't be long. Sarah may need you."

"I shall only take the time to tell Maddy and the children where I am going and then come." He began to mount, but she stopped him. "Faith is here because of you. Remember that. I know you have seen a lot of death in the past few years. But I would not be here if it were not for you." She reached up on tiptoes and kissed him, a quick mating of lips before stepping back and allowing him to vault onto the horse.

The look he sent her—full of caring warmth—laid claim to her heart. In that moment she knew she loved him. But would he ever be free of his past?

* * * * *

As Nathan neared Liberty Hall, it became harder for him to drag enough air into his lungs. The heat of the day bore down on him, sweat coating him. The thundering beat of his heart sounded in his head. If anything happened to his sister, he would not be able to forgive himself.

The baby was almost a month early. That did not bode well. Was he going to deliver another dead child?

Faith is here because of you.

Rachel's words resounded in his mind. For someone who had not thought he would continue to be a doctor, he had done quite a bit in the past few months. Could he ever turn his back on his training? Rachel didn't think he should. Now all he needed to do was figure out what he wanted to do.

The sight of Sarah's house in the distance spurred his pace. He had known becoming a doctor would not be easy, that there were times he would not be able to help as he wanted. He had known that being a surgeon during the war would be demanding and disheartening. Often the option was limited to an amputation, surgery that had to be done quickly, with nothing to ease the intense pain for the patient.

Lord, if this is what You want me to do, I need a sign. If it is not what You want me to do, then what? But whatever Your decision is, please protect Sarah and her child. Allow me to help both of them.

As he galloped up to the house, he saw John standing on the porch waiting for him. A grim expression on his face seared the gravity of the situation into Nathan.

* * * * *

Rachel entered the bedchamber while Sarah was in the middle of a contraction. Nathan's soothing voice talked his sister through it while Bella, Sean's nanny, held her up to push. Rachel rushed to the bed and positioned herself behind Sarah to help the older black woman with Nathan's sister.

"I cannot push anymore," Sarah said as the pain subsided and she collapsed back against Rachel and Bella.

"Yes, you can. I see the head. The baby wants to be here." For a moment, Nathan's expression showed his concern before he masked it.

"Like you did, Miz Sarah. Your ma hardly had time to make it to her bedchamber," Bella said.

Nathan roped Rachel's gaze to him. His damp hair curled on his forehead. "Sarah, only a few more, then you will be able to hold your new baby."

Sarah gritted her teeth and stiffened then groaned and pushed. Ten minutes later a baby girl slid into Nathan's hands, and he held her up for Sarah to see. Exhausted, she sank back as her child let out a howl.

"She's small but beautiful. She is going to break men's hearts like her mama." Nathan laid the child on Sarah and cut the cord.

"She has got a good set of lungs like her mama." The black woman helped Rachel settle Sarah back against the headboard.

Sarah gently ran her hand over her little girl. "Thank you, Nathan."

As he finished up, Nathan looked at Rachel and said, "Why don't you take the baby to see her papa?"

Something was wrong. Rachel could see it in Nathan's eyes, the tensing of his body. She rose and took a blanket from the servant and wrapped the squalling child in it. As she moved toward the door, she glimpsed the blood—too much of it. Nathan was trying to stem the flow. The black woman came around to help Nathan, handing him a linen.

* * * * *

Nathan stood a few feet from the bed, watching his sister sleeping from exhaustion and so much blood loss. He had finally stopped the bleeding, but was it too late? He pivoted away and strode to the window overlooking the front of the house. The sun sank below the tree line to the west. The darkness blanketing the landscape mirrored his emotions. If he couldn't save his sister...

He would not allow the thought to develop in his mind. *Please, Lord, save Sarah. She has two children who need her.*

He had checked over her baby daughter, and she was small but seemed healthy. Eliza's mother, Bella, had found a wet nurse for the baby. Seeing Bella at the birth had thrown him for a moment. Her appearance brought forward all the emotions he had experienced when he had delivered Eliza's dead baby and then could not do anything to save his childhood companion and friend. But Bella was the perfect one to help with the birthing, because she had been at all of their births—his, Patrick's, and Sarah's. Would it have made any difference if Bella had been available to help Eliza in the cotton field?

Observing the last rays of the sun disappearing, Nathan shut down his remembrances. He stared at the gray of dusk evolving into the black of night. The sound of the bedchamber door opening brought him around to face Bella. She smiled, such kindness in her eyes. He had known she had come with Sarah to Liberty Hall but had avoided her when he had visited, even though she was Sean's nanny. Although she had never said a word about Eliza, he had always wondered if she blamed him. He was the reason his grandfather had sent Eliza to work in the fields rather than staying in the house as a servant.

Bella shuffled toward him, her movements slower than he recalled when she was at Pinecrest. Her black skin was still smooth, showing few age lines, but gray was sprinkled throughout her dark hair.

"'Tis good to see you." Bella glanced at Sarah, still asleep. "She will be all right. De Lord will see to it."

"I hope so. How have you been?"

"A few aches here and dere."

"Taking anything for those aches?"

"I have my herbs. Dey work most times."

He had learned a lot from her about herbs and plants that helped ease pain.

"Some dings ya just cannot outrun. Old age is one."

Nathan chuckled. "I have missed you."

"You know where I have been." Her sharp eyes assessed him.

"Yes, but since Eliza's death—"

"Hush, child. You did what you could. Dere was no one else. Miz Sarah told me dat you and Master Stuart fought 'cause of Eliza. Is dat why you two don't talk?"

The compassion in her voice unraveled what was left of his composure. He sank back on the windowsill. "It started when Papa died. Grandfather changed. Papa's death was hard on him. You were living with Sarah and John, but you would not have recognized Grandfather after that. He sent Mama away. Nothing I did satisfied him. He did not want me to be a doctor at all. I did not know him anymore."

"I didn't get a chance to say good-bye to your mama."

"Why did he send her away? I don't understand his anger toward her just because she had been born an Englishwoman. She lived over half her life in America. She was an American citizen."

"She never told you why she was leaving?"

"She did not say much of anything. It was so rushed. When I

came back from the war last year, I tried to approach Grandfather and settle our differences. He threw me off the plantation. He is not an easy man, but I loved him. Still do."

Bella wound her arms around him and hugged him as she often did while he was growing up. She had raised him and his siblings even more than his own mother. "Child, I am sorry for your pain. I suspect I know why."

Nathan leaned back and peered at Bella. "Why?"

"Have you written your mama and asked her?"

"Yes, on several occasions. I received a letter back once. She was happy in England and hoped we would be happy at Pinecrest. She had stayed in America because of Papa, but now that Papa was gone she wanted to return to her homeland." *Like Rachel.* His heart thudded with that realization, adding a new pain on top of all the rest.

"I was with your mama when you were born, seven months after your parents married. You were a little small, but not two months early small. You don't look like your papa. In her pain she called out another man's name. She never told me you were not your papa's son, but I have always wondered."

Nathan stiffened, his hands curling into fists. Her revelation explained so much—his grandfather's reaction after his son died, the fact his father had always been a little standoffish to him, his mother giving him money from her side of the family but not Sarah or Patrick. But he still had a lot of questions that needed answers. There were only two people who could tell him—his grandfather and his mother, who lived thousands of miles away. Which meant he would have to demand answers from the one man who did not want to see him.

Nathan clasped Bella's upper arms and pressed her to him. "Thank you for telling me."

When she stepped back, she scrutinized him for a long moment. "What are ya goin' t' do?"

"See my grandfather. This time I will not allow him to kick me off the plantation until I get answers."

Sixteen

"What will you call her?" Rachel asked John, who continued to prowl around the parlor.

"Sarah wanted to name a girl after her mother, Louise Anne, so that will be her name." John held his new baby, staring down at her. "She is going to look like Sarah." A grin leaked through the serious expression that had been on his face since he had seen Sarah after Nathan stopped the bleeding a couple of hours ago.

Rachel had been able to lay the child next to Sarah for a few minutes before the exhausted woman drifted off to sleep. Then Nathan had asked everyone to leave and let the mother rest. That was what she needed the most. John sat with his wife for a while longer then came down to the parlor to cradle his baby against him as if that would calm his worry. But deep lines of concern grooved his face since he appeared in the room.

"I like that name. Nathan will do all he can for Sarah."

"I know. I watched him work in the war. When I came to the hospital set up near the battlefield after a skirmish, I marveled at his dedication to save each soldier. I also saw what it did to him when he could not. I don't know how he did it. The screams were…" John sighed. "I hope there are no more wars."

Moses stood on the threshold into the parlor, his battered straw hat in his hand as he nearly crushed it. Tension stiffened him like a statue she had seen in Charleston.

John turned toward him. "What is wrong?"

"There's a problem at the workers' cabins."

"Can it wait until morning?"

"No, sir. Four people are down."

John walked to Rachel on the sofa and passed Louise to her. "I will be back."

"Should you let Nathan know?"

"It might be nothing. I would rather he stay with Sarah in case she needs him. But you might let him know four workers are ill."

"I shall. Bella has a wet nurse for Louise. I shall see if Louise is hungry now." She remembered how hungry Faith was not long after she had given birth to her.

When John left the parlor, Rachel went in search of Bella and found her in the kitchen in the building behind the main house. After the black woman took the baby to give to the wet nurse, Rachel made her way to Sarah's bedchamber to see Nathan.

He sat in a chair near Sarah's bed, his head bowed, his hands clasped. When he heard her come in, he glanced up. A faint smile curled his lips for a brief moment before his expression fell into a neutral one. "'Tis good to see you after all that has happened."

Rachel moved toward him. "How is Sarah doing?"

"Her pulse rate is good. Her breathing even. No more bleeding."

"Then she should be all right?"

"I have been praying for that. Time will tell."

"Praying?"

"Must be your influence." He rose. "How is her daughter?"

"Louise Anne is doing fine. John is enthralled with his newest child."

"I can imagine." A wistfulness edged his words.

He was so good with Ben, Emma, and Faith. Did he regret not having any children? "John wanted me to tell you there were some workers ill. He has gone to see about it. It might be nothing, but he might need you later if Sarah gets better."

"I am not sure there is more that I can do here. Rest is what she needs, but I will wait until John comes back to see if I am needed."

Rachel touched his face. "You look tired. I know this has not been easy for you."

He laid his hand over hers and held it against his cheek. "I told the Lord if He saves her I will do what He wants."

"What if that means being a doctor again?"

"Looking back over the past months, I don't think I have stopped being one."

"What if He wants you to talk with your grandfather again?"

His expression rapidly changed into a scowl, the intensity in his eyes unnerving. "I intend to have a discussion with Grandfather when I leave here. I have questions that he will answer this time."

"What makes you think he will?" The urge to smooth the anger from his face deluged her. She backed away and kept her arms stiff at her sides.

"Because I have the right questions this time." The fury rolled off Nathan as he opened and closed his hands.

"What questions?"

"Was his son my father?"

The question hung in the air between them. The words finally sank into Rachel and their impact stunned her. "What makes you think you are not?"

"Bella told me about when I was born. I was early…too early to survive a birth most likely. And my mother called out another man's name when giving birth to me. Something has happened to change my grandfather's feelings. It makes sense. My mother was with child when she married my father."

"That doesn't mean you are not his son. I have heard of couples who have gotten married with the woman being with child. Do you think your mother fooled your father when she was expecting another man's child?"

"I don't know what to think. But I do know Grandfather has some answers."

The anguish in his voice and expression lured her closer until she stood inches from him. She cupped his face, her gaze bound with his. Slowly he dipped his head toward her and grazed his mouth across hers before kissing her with such fervency that it threatened to over-whelm her senses. His arms folded her to him. His scent engulfed her. The taste of him on her lips tingled down her length. Tom had never kissed her like this, as if she were cherished and precious to him. The sensations bombarding from all sides finally flooded her in an emotional dilemma.

She pulled back but could not take her eyes away from Nathan's. Lost in their blue depths, she wanted to explore more of what he made her feel, and yet fear intruded, cautioning her. Tom wormed his way into her mind, shutting down the new emotions she was experiencing.

The door opened, and John came into the bedchamber. A small

gasp escaped Rachel's parted lips, and she backed away quickly at the same time Nathan did.

John glanced from her to Nathan. "I think it is yellow fever. I need to get Sarah and Louise away from here."

"We shouldn't move Sarah far. It would wear her out even more."

"She can come to the farm." Rachel's nerves settled down, but only slightly with the mention of yellow fever. She had heard about the disease, but it was not a problem where she was from.

"I will need you, Nathan. I know little of how to care for so many. I will send Bella and Moses to help at the farm. If Sarah or Louise gets worse at all, Rachel, you can send for us."

"I will go with Rachel and Sarah then come back. There are some medicines I would like to get."

"I have isolated the workers who have come down ill. I will accompany you to the farm too. I have to see my wife and children safely there."

Rachel's head swirled with all that had happened in less than a day. With yellow fever, the worst was yet to come. What if it spread to her farm?

* * * * *

"How are you feeling this morning?" Rachel asked Sarah when she came into the bedchamber with the first meal of the day.

Sarah propped herself up against the wall. "Better than yesterday. Did Louise nurse all right this time?"

"She's getting better. It is a lot of work and she tires." John had not wanted the wet nurse to come with them in case she had been infected with the disease, living in the workers' quarters.

"I cannot thank you enough for filling in as a wet nurse."

"After all you and your husband have done to help me, it is the least I could do. Louise is asleep while my daughter is trying to roll over. It should not be long before she does. She badly wants to go places."

Sarah laughed. "How is Sean doing?"

"Following Ben around everywhere. They are down at the barn feeding the pigs." Rachel pointed to the mush. "Bella made that. Not me, so it is safe to eat."

"Have you heard anything from Liberty Hall?"

"Not since I told you yesterday afternoon. Three workers have died. More have come down with the fever."

"What about John?"

"Doing his best to keep it contained."

"How? No one knows how it spreads. It strikes then leaves. Close to four thousand died in the epidemic in Philadelphia in 1793. What if this is the beginning?"

"Then we need to pray." Rachel sat on the bed and took Sarah's hand, both bowing their heads. "Please, Lord, heal the sick and stop this fever from spreading. Also watch over Nathan and John."

"Amen."

"If you are up to it, I will walk you into the main room, and you can sit while Bella and Maddy bake the bread."

"And you?" Sarah couldn't contain her smile. A sparkle momentarily lit her eyes.

"I'm doing everyone a favor and staying out of the kitchen. My services are best used in the garden, harvesting the vegetables for our meals. Then later, when Moses is finished with his tasks in the field, he is going to take me to Charleston to get a cow. I have been wanting one so there is fresh milk, cheese, and butter. I am using the reward money to buy one."

"You don't have to go all the way to Charleston. I'm sure Patrick will sell you one. He has a small herd at Pinecrest and can afford to lose one." Sarah slipped her legs over the side of the bed. "You could go to Liberty Hall, but it is too dangerous."

"I'm not sure it is wise to go to Pinecrest. I'm not your grandfather's favorite person."

"Only because he doesn't know you."

"No, I don't think he would be able to see past the fact I am English."

"I have a better idea. Moses could go to Liberty Hall. He has had yellow fever. I have heard people who have had it don't get ill again. I am sure that is why John sent Moses and Bella with us." Sarah inhaled a deep breath and then rose slowly.

Rachel hurried to her side to assist her if she needed it. "You have not had it?"

"No, neither has John or Nathan. I worry about them. It has been four days now. This could go on for weeks."

Weeks without Nathan. The thought bothered Rachel more than she wanted to acknowledge. "If Moses agrees, then that would be wonderful. We can get another update on what is going on at the plantation."

"That was also what I was thinking." Sarah gripped Rachel's arm and made her way into the other room, her pace slow but steady.

"I will get Louise so you can hold her for a while." Rachel helped her to sit in the rocking chair in front of the cold fireplace.

The door stood open, and a warm summer breeze carried the humid air into the house.

"'Tis goin' t' be a hot one today." Bella fetched the big bowl to prepare the bread dough.

"I know. Ben and Emma have already asked me if they can swim in the river. I may let them. It would give me a good reason to take off my stockings and put my feet in the water." Rachel took her bonnet off the wooden peg. "I am off to see if that rabbit has eaten any more of my vegetables."

When Rachel left, she paused in the shade of her house. Although she had tried to sound as if she did not have a worry, it was hard to keep it up. But Sarah did not need that on top of trying to recover from a difficult childbirth. The brief message Rachel received from Nathan yesterday mentioned that John was working too hard. Nathan worried that John's exhaustion from nonstop work would make him sick

What if John succumbed to sickness? Or Nathan? Who would take care of everyone else?

She leaned back against the house. For all the times she had said she could make it on her own, what would she have done without Nathan's help these past three months? She pushed from the wall and headed for the garden with her basket. But she could not rid her mind of the realization that when he left the farm four days ago to return to Liberty Hall, it could be the last time she ever saw him. A pain stabbed her in the heart.

* * * * *

"Moses, Mr. McNeal does not want his wife to know he has come down with the fever. I agree with him. She will want to come nurse him, and I cannot allow that. Understand?" Nathan handed the man the rope to lead the cow that Rachel purchased back to the farm.

"What do I say about you to Miz Rachel?"

"That I am fine."

Moses's eyes widened as if he did not believe Nathan. "I will say nothing of you two."

Nathan patted the man on the back. "Thank you. I cannot have them worrying. I'm determined John will make it. Tell Rachel I will be home when I can."

"Yes sir." Moses began his trek toward the road.

Nathan watched him for a moment before heading back into the house to check on John and take him cold chamomile tea with elixir of vitriol to help with the nausea. His leaden steps slowed even more as he mounted the stairs to the second floor. For days now, he had not slept more than a few hours total. That was the only reason he had referred to the farm as his home. The cabin on his small tract of land was his home, and he needed to return to it before he began to think he could have a future with Rachel.

This outbreak of yellow fever only reconfirmed she needed to go back to England. What if the disease spread to the farm? How could he be both places at once? He had a couple of workers helping him to nurse the ill quarantined in three cabins, but there were not enough hours in a day for him to do it all.

What if he had not been here? What would have happened then? Some of the people were recovering, and he had brought some comfort to others. This was the reason he had become a doctor in the first place.

When he entered John's bedchamber, his brother-in-law lay sleeping. Nathan put the cup of tea on the table next to the bed. He started to leave, but John opened his eyes and stared at him, no recognition in his gaze at first.

"We cannot let Sarah know," John said between hiccups. As they increased, he doubled over, holding his stomach.

Nathan dipped a cloth into a basin of water and wiped John's face and neck. His rag came away with blood on it from his brother-in-law's right ear. "Drink this." He sat next to John and held the cup while his friend struggled to sit up enough to sip the liquid.

"She cannot be here."

Nathan stared into John's eyes, a faint yellowness in them. "I agree, and you need not worry about that. Concentrate on getting well."

Another bout of hiccups attacked John. He collapsed back on the bed, having drunk half the tea mixture laced with laudanum. "I thought I was getting better."

"That happens with yellow fever. You are not to get up until I say so. I want to make sure you are completely well. I have everything under control."

John's eyes fluttered closed. He murmured, "Thank you," then went back to sleep.

Nathan pushed to his feet. Hanging his head, he peered at the floor. He finally trudged to the cot set up in the bedchamber for him and sank down on it. *Everything under control. Anything but that.* He missed Rachel and the children. Five workers had died so far, and twenty were recovering. He had to concentrate on the twenty that were better. If he did not, he would give in to despair.

* * * * *

"I feel so much better. I would like to help in your garden." Sarah sat on the bed and put her boots on.

"I don't know. I don't want you to overdo."

"It has been four weeks. I need to start doing some work so when I go back to Liberty Hall I can do my duties." She sighed. "I want to go back now. Receiving a letter from John is not the same as seeing him."

"At least Moses keeps us informed with what is going on there. I think the worst is over." Rachel missed Nathan. Moses had told her he was holding up under all the work that had to be done. He also confided to her that John had recently recovered from having yellow fever. She had thought of telling Sarah but then realized her friend would charge over to Liberty Hall to see for herself. The action could endanger her, and Rachel would not be responsible for that.

"I don't like being away from home this long."

"It is hard to have loved ones in another place and not know what is going on." Rachel continually thought of her family in England and wondered what was happening there. She missed them. "Later today Moses is driving me into Charleston to get some supplies we need." She would also post the letter she had written to her mother. It was time for her to inform them about Faith and what was going on in her life. Her father might have disowned her, but she was sure her mother had not. Talk of home always brought thoughts of England. She scanned her bedchamber and wondered if she would ever consider this place her real home. "Do you need anything in Charleston?"

"No, I expect to be home soon."

"Take your time coming outside to the garden. I am going to take Faith out with me." Now that her daughter was getting bigger, Moses had fashioned Rachel a carrier for her back so that she could work and have her child with her.

Rachel strolled into the main room toward the cradle where

Faith was. When she neared it, she smiled and said, "Are you ready...?" The rest of the sentence died on her lips as her gaze riveted to a long, slender, orange and reddish-brown snake lying next to Faith, who was still sleeping.

Paralyzed a few feet away, Rachel could not think what to do. The reptile was coiled around itself by Faith's leg. Was it poisonous? She didn't know. The ones she had encountered on the farm struck terror in her, but Nathan, Moses, or Ben had been there to take care of them. The long body hadn't moved since she had appeared. Was it dead?

She took a step closer. It began to uncurl. Now or never. Rachel darted forward and snatched Faith from the cradle then jumped back. She shook so much she was afraid she would drop her baby.

"Sarah, help." Her voice barely worked and only squeaked.

"What's wrong?" Sarah came into the room and stopped next to Rachel.

"A snake in the cradle." Rachel pointed a trembling hand toward it.

Sarah stiffened. "I don't like snakes."

"Neither do I. What do we do?"

"Leave and get someone to take care of it."

"What if it hides somewhere else in here? I don't think I would sleep at all. It was next to Faith. If she had awakened and tried to roll over..." A shudder rippled down Rachel's length. "Can you tell if it is poisonous?"

Sarah inched closer, poised to run, and peeked into the cradle. Some of the tension siphoned from her. "'Tis a corn snake. I have seen them at Liberty Hall. They are great to keep the rats and mice population down."

"Well, it can do that outside. Not in my house. Here." Rachel gave Faith to Sarah then snagged the broom from against the wall.

She crept toward the snake, noticing it was totally uncoiled and its tongue flicked in and out of its mouth. She almost leaped back. This was her house. Her battle. Steeling herself with a deep breath, in one quick motion she flipped the wooden cradle on its side. The snake slithered away from it—toward her. Rachel took the broom and swept the snake outside. She slammed the door then collapsed to the floor, inhaling gulps of air.

I don't belong here. I don't belong here. Those words kept running through her mind.

Trembling, she clutched her arms to her. "It was next to Faith. What if it had been poisonous? What if it had bitten her? What if…" Anger that her baby had been in a dangerous situation mingled with fear that it would happen again. "How can you live here?"

Sarah knelt next to Rachel. "'Tis my home."

"But not mine." She could not still the quaking. These past few weeks she had gotten a taste of what it would be like when Nathan left to go back to his life. She did not know if the farm was the answer for her future. Could she sell it?

* * * * *

Two days later Rachel returned from Charleston with supplies needed and a letter for Nathan. Moses stopped the cart in front of the house, jumped down, and then assisted Rachel to the ground. She carried in the staples she needed in her basket while Moses took the other supplies to the barn.

She opened the door to the house and a blast of heat hit her in the face. Since the snake incident, she had insisted the door remain shut, which made it hot inside. The place was empty. Where had the children, Sarah, Maddy, and Bella gone? She had not seen them outside. Sometimes they would stay under the live oak, the babies taking a nap, especially if a breeze blew. But they were not there, either.

After putting the basket on the table, she started toward the door. It burst open and the children and women poured into the house, with Nathan and John behind them. Her stomach fluttered at the sight of Nathan after four weeks. He had lost weight. His eyes gleamed as they took her in, but behind the light in them she glimpsed the exhaustion.

When he approached her, her heartbeat raced and her mouth went dry. All she wanted to do was hold him. It was so good to see him again. The fact she had missed him so much scared her more than the snake had the other day. Tom had only died six months ago—not nearly enough time to get over his betrayal of her love. She could not afford to love another—not now, when she had set aside her pride in the letter she posted today and begged her mama to let her come home. She had to think of Faith above all else.

"The children have been filling me in on what has been happening here. Ben said something about a corn snake being in the cradle with Faith." Nathan stopped a foot away.

So close Rachel could reach out and touch him—if she wanted. But she couldn't. She needed to start putting up barriers between them. She needed to learn to live without Nathan. "It could have hurt Faith."

"Probably not. 'Tis not poisonous."

"I know that now, but at the time I didn't." Rachel quaked just thinking about the incident again. "Let's talk about something nicer. Are you back for good?"

He nodded. "The last case in a week has recovered from the fever."

"How many died?"

"Seven."

"I see John is much better."

Nathan's eyes grew wide. "You knew?"

"Yes, but I did not tell Sarah. She was not strong enough to go back to the plantation and nurse John to health. Does she know now he was ill?"

"Yes. He told her when he first arrived. She was not pleased that we didn't notify her."

Rachel glanced at her friend, who stood next to John, her frown indicating all was not forgiven yet. "I can see."

"The children had to show me the cow you bought from John. Emma wants to name it. Do you know all the piglets have names?"

"I think living on a farm is not going to agree with Emma. She loves the animals and does not understand some must be killed for food."

"Then move into town."

For the first time Rachel replied to the statement Nathan had said many times before, "Perhaps."

"You are thinking of living in Charleston?"

"We are so close to the swamp. I don't want a repeat of the snake in Faith's cradle again. Next time it could be a poisonous one."

"There are snakes in town too."

"Not like here. I even talked with Mrs. Bridges about it today when I picked up more sewing."

"We need to have a party," Emma announced to the whole group.

"We can't stay," John said, trying to take Sarah's hand. She kept hers folded in front of her. "I am taking Sarah, Sean, and Louise to Charleston. I have neglected my business in town long enough. Moses and Bella can pack up their belongings, and then we are leaving."

Emma's shoulders slumped and a pout formed on her mouth. "No party then?"

"We will have one this evening, and you can help me make a cake," Maddy said to the little girl while Sarah and John retreated into Rachel's bedchamber.

"Oh, I almost forgot. I have something for you." Rachel rummaged in the basket and pulled the letter out then handed it to Nathan.

Nathan's forehead scrunched as he broke the wax seal and started reading the note. A frown deepened the lines on his forehead. He wandered toward the front door and disappeared outside.

Who wrote him? Rachel started to follow him but Faith began wailing.

* * * * *

Nathan sat on the ground with his back against the elm tree. He reread his mother's words for a third time, confirming what he had begun to think after his conversation with Bella at the birth of Louise. "Your father is Edward Worthington. I thought he had died in a skirmish with some Indians along the Canadian border before you were born. He didn't, but by the time he had returned to Boston, he had heard of my marriage to James Stuart and didn't seek me out in South Carolina. Jamie married me knowing I was with child. He loved me and wanted to raise you as his own. All was well until Edward wrote to me. I never loved the man who you thought was your father. I could never forget Edward. Jamie was good to me, and we had a good marriage, but my heart was with someone else. When Jamie died he knew that. He said something to his father on his deathbed in his delirium."

Although Nathan had an idea this was the case, that his father was not James Stuart, knowing it for a fact left a numbness in his chest. He had loved the man he called Papa. He had loved his grandfather. Now he knew the "truth" of why Grandfather turned his back on all those years of love—all because of his hatred of anything English. It should have made it easier to understand. It did not. For thirty-five years Nathan had thought of him as his grandfather, and now he was supposed to forget all those years.

"I was asked to leave Pinecrest. Jamie's father could not tolerate me there once he knew the truth about his son's marriage and your birth. I only agreed if he would include you equally in his will. We made a deal. I would return to England and not have anything to do with my children. He would make sure my children, especially you, were provided for. From your letter, I learn he has broken his word."

Anger surged through Nathan, flowing through his bloodstream to all parts of his body. He bolted to his feet and crushed the letter in his hand. The least his mother could have done was tell him the truth when he had first written her. Then he would not have spent the past five years trying to figure out what he had done wrong to change his grandfather's feelings toward him. Yes, they had fought over Eliza, but they should have been able to mend that rift.

Tossing the letter to the ground, he strode to the barn to saddle his horse. It was time he and his grandfather had the talk they should have had years ago.

* * * * *

Rachel watched Nathan storm inside the barn. *Should I go talk to him? Something is wrong.* She stared at the discarded letter under the elm tree. The breeze rolled it over the dirt toward a puddle of rainwater. She headed out the door to rescue the note. Nathan might want it later.

As she stepped outside, Nathan emerged from the barn, mounted his horse, and set his steed into a gallop down the road. Rachel opened her mouth to call out, but the fierce expression on Nathan's face underscored his fury. At the person who wrote the letter? Or someone else?

Sarah came up behind her. "Where is Nathan going?"

"I don't know. I gave him a letter. He went outside to read it and then left." Rachel gestured to the balled-up paper on the ground. "That is it."

Sarah marched to the letter and snatched it up before it rolled into the puddle. She unfolded the paper and read it. A frown descended over her features, reminding Rachel of how Nathan had looked when he read it.

She hurried to her friend. "Who is it from? What is wrong?"

"'Tis from our mama." Sarah lifted tear-filled eyes. "Telling Nathan that our father is not really his. That his father is Edward Worthington, who recently died in England and has left Nathan a large fortune. It appears that Mama went back to Edward when she was in England."

"Where do you think Nathan is going?"

"To Pinecrest. Grandfather knew about Edward and did not tell Nathan."

That explained so much to Rachel—the anger and anguish she had seen on Nathan's face as he read the letter. His pain reached across the expanse and gripped her. "I need to be there. He will need someone to talk to after seeing his grand—your grandfather."

"With how Grandfather feels about you?"

"I don't care. Nathan has always been here for me. I *need* to do this for him."

"I don't think it is a good idea."

Rachel pivoted away from Sarah and rushed back into the house. "John, may I borrow one of your horses? Using the cart with the ox would take too long. I need to get to Pinecrest."

John peered over Rachel's shoulder at Sarah coming into the house, a question in his eyes.

"I believe Nathan left to have words with Grandfather." Sarah walked to her husband and gave him the letter.

After John read it, he glanced up at Rachel. "I will go with you." Then he turned to Sarah and said, "Will you wait here or do you want Moses to drive you and the children to Charleston? I will come when this is over."

Sarah folded her arms over her chest. "I'm staying. This concerns my family."

"Let's go." Rachel strode out the door and toward the barn.

The images of Mr. Stuart paraded across her mind—all angry, as though he had felt betrayed. Now she knew why. But Nathan had nothing to do with it.

* * * * *

Nathan ignored Patrick as he charged into the house at Pinecrest. His grandfather at this time of day was always in the library. He headed for that room, but when he swung the door open, no one was inside.

"Where is he?" Nathan demanded, curling and uncurling his hands.

"What's going on? Grandfather received a letter and has not said a word since. He is out in Mama's garden, sitting on the bench."

"A letter? From whom?"

"He did not say. He took it with him."

As Nathan strode toward the garden, he ignored his younger brother's pleas to tell him what was going on. He was not even sure himself. But he intended to find out, once and for all. He found his grandfather—he could not think of the man in any other terms. Suddenly, as he closed the space between them, scene after scene flitted through his mind—his grandfather teaching him to ride, to shoot a musket, to fish. The long discussions they had about the Democrats and Federalists trying to run the country, the escalating troubles between America and England.

Nathan slowed his pace. He had learned so much from his grandfather. What must it have been like for him to discover suddenly that Nathan was not really his grandson? That must have turned his world upside down. *As it has mine.*

His grandfather saw him and struggled to his feet, leaning on his cane. "What are you doing here?"

"I received a letter today from Mama." Nathan waved his hand toward the paper clutched by his grandfather. "Did you too?"

MARGARET DALEY

He scowled. "Yes. I am surprised, though, to see you here. She told me she wrote you a letter telling you everything."

Nathan nodded, his throat so tight he was afraid his voice wouldn't work.

"Your real father died recently. She said she did not have to be silent any longer, because he provided for you in his will. He had no heirs, except you. Congratulations. I understand you will be a rich man."

"The money is unimportant to me."

His grandfather's eyebrow rose. "What is important to you? That little Englishwoman you have been helping?"

Fury flooded Nathan. His hands squeezed into fists. He tried to inhale a deep breath but could not seem to get enough air into his lungs. "We are leaving Rachel out of this conversation."

"There is no need for a conversation. I am sure your mother told you all the sordid details. What I don't understand is why my son would agree to marry her when she was with child. I thought I had raised him better than that. Oh, I know he thought he was in love with your mother, but love has nothing to do with marriage. I am sure he figured that out when your mother did not return his love."

Nathan backed away, feeling the blast of hatred emanating from the old man. The childhood memories of their times together had been based on a lie. Now that the truth was out, his grandfather did not have the capability of forgiving and letting go of the past. That would not change. Why did he think it might if only he came to see him?

"I feel sorry for you. Your hatred will eat you up. It takes up too much energy. I came to tell you I have forgiven you for the way you treated me. I should have been told the truth from the beginning.

Both you and Mama did me no favors keeping it between you. For that matter, Papa too." He would not end up like his grandfather, letting the past rule his whole life. He had for the past years, but not any longer.

"He was *not* your father. I am *not* your grandfather."

"In my heart you are, and he will always be my father to me. Family is about ties that go beyond blood, but you cannot see that. For the past five years I have wondered what was wrong with me that you and I could not return to the relationship we once had. Now I know there was not anything wrong with me. Only you. Your life is sad. You are sad. I will pray for you."

Nathan pivoted and strode away, probably never to return to Pinecrest until his grandfather passed away. Not having the energy to explain everything to Patrick, he made his way around to the front of the house where he had left his horse. He would let his brother get the truth from Grandfather. After the emotional upheaval of the past month, all he wanted to do was return to the farm and sleep for days.

When he rounded the side of the house he had grown up in, Nathan saw Rachel and John waiting by his horse. The sight of them threatened to break down the barriers around his heart, but all he had to remember was the coldness his grandfather had exhibited to shore up the wall he had erected to protect himself. He could not go through another five years as he just had.

He blanked any expression on his face and approached the pair. "You rode all the way over here for nothing. We had better leave. It will be getting dark soon."

"Are you all right?" Rachel asked, covering the distance to him.

"Yes, why would I not be? I just found out I'm a rich man."

She winced.

He skirted her and vaulted into his saddle, leaving John to help Rachel mount. Nathan clenched the reins so tightly his hands ached. He did not care. He needed the pain to ward off the grief of finally losing a grandfather he had loved—still loved in spite of what the man felt. Love was not for him. It hurt too much.

After Rachel and John were on their horses, Nathan tapped the sides of his and galloped away from Pinecrest.

* * * * *

For two days Rachel had endured Nathan's silence. After supper each night he had returned to the barn, where he had his bed. The evenings after the children went to sleep were lonely nights for Rachel, sitting by the light trying to sew a gown for Mrs. Bridges. She had enjoyed Nathan's company. Maddy was often with Mr. Baker. She wouldn't be surprised if he asked her to marry him soon. Then what would she do, with both Maddy and Nathan gone?

After nursing and changing Faith's nappy, Rachel swung her around, listening to her child's laughter. She had thought by coming to the farm she could become independent, but that was not what happened. She had become dependent on Nathan for friendship and support, as well as Maddy. She could not cut herself off from the people she cared about—not like Nathan could. He even shut out his sister when he came back to the farm. All he had told Sarah was that it was over between himself and her grandfather, then he had retreated to the barn.

Rachel cuddled Faith to her. "Are you ready to help me outside? It is washing day."

Faith scrunched up her tiny mouth as though she understood what Rachel had said about the laundry and hated it as much as she did.

"I know. Not fun. But it has to be done. Maddy is already outside getting everything set up. It will be cooler out there. Well, perhaps just a little." Heat was building up in the house, and she walked to the door and opened it. After she stepped over the threshold, she propped up a board against the doorframe, a device Moses had made for her to help keep creatures out of the house when she left the door open for a breeze to cool the interior.

Near the well, Maddy had built the fire and set the vat of water on it to boil. The sun beat down on Rachel as she sought some shade to place Faith. She spread a blanket for her to lie on. After settling Faith, she moved toward Maddy.

A lone rider coming from the road claimed her attention. She was not expecting anyone. Nathan was out in the far field. After all that had happened the past couple of months, she grew rigid, gripping the paddle she used to stir the clothes in the hot water.

Then the features of the man came into view. "Richard!"

Maddy paused in putting the linens in the vat. "Richard?" She peered at the rider. "Who is that?"

Rachel dropped the paddle and raced toward the man. "My brother." Excitement erased the months of separation between her and her eldest brother.

He stopped and hopped to the ground, sweeping her up into his embrace and swinging her around. "You are all right. I was afraid of what I would find when I was told in town where you were."

She hugged him tightly and kissed him on the cheek. "Why are you here? How did you get here? When did you come?"

His robust laughter echoed through the clearing. "One question at a time. Let me get a good look at you." He stepped back, clasping her upper arms. "You have changed since I last saw you." His survey took in her face slowly. "You've been out in the sun." He picked up her hands. "They are rough."

"It is called manual labor. It takes a lot to run a farm." She removed her hands from his grasp, realizing she had changed in more than physical ways since she left England. "How did you know where I was? Mama could not have gotten my letter yet. I only posted it recently."

"Not your letter, but she got one from a Mr. Nathan Stuart."

"Nathan wrote Mama?" Nathan never told her that. He must have really wanted her to go home to England, and when she refused, he took matters into his own hands. For the past two days he had ignored her, and now this. It made her realize how much of a burden she had really been for Nathan—an obligation he had to fulfill because he felt responsible for her and Faith.

"Papa too. I am here because Papa sent me."

"He did?" How many times had she dreamed her father would want her to return home, all forgiven? "When did you arrive?"

"Yesterday. I asked around town and found out that Mr. Stuart's family owned Pinecrest. I went there this morning. I thought an older gentleman was going to shoot me until his grandson intervened and told me where you were."

"That's Patrick, Nathan's younger brother. His grandfather hates anyone who is English. That includes me."

Richard glanced toward Maddy, who stood at the vat stirring the clothes and listening to every word. "May we talk inside?"

"Yes." Rachel strolled to the blanket and hoisted Faith into her arms. "This is my daughter. Faith, this is your uncle, Richard."

"It is true Tom died at sea?"

"Yes. Fell overboard, drunk."

Her brother frowned. "That does not surprise me after the stories I have heard concerning Tom Gordon."

"Stories?"

Richard strode toward the house, removing the propped barrier and entering. "Papa had me come looking for you in London, probably right after you left for America. No one knew for sure where you and your husband went. One man told me he won some land in America, but he didn't know where."

"Won?" So her husband's story about buying the property had been a lie too.

"Yes, he had gambling debts, still unpaid in several establishments in London. I'm sure that is why he fled the country right ahead of the debt collectors."

Something else she hadn't known about her husband. How blind she had been to his shortcomings. "When we received Mr. Stuart's letter, we finally knew where to find you."

"Papa sent you looking for me? I thought he was so angry with me he never wanted to see me again."

"That did not last long. You have always been the apple of his eye. His arthritis has been acting up, or he would have come himself. We can leave on a ship day after tomorrow bound for England."

"Day after tomorrow? What do I do about the farm?" Everything was happening too fast. She needed time to think.

"I cannot be gone long. What's keeping you here?"

She started to say "nothing," but the word lodged in her throat. She swallowed over and over but still could not say it aloud.

"What is going on here? Who is this Mr. Stuart to you?"

"I'm her hired hand," Nathan said from the doorway.

"Well, not exactly," Rachel interjected when her brother's frown evolved into a deep scowl. "He has a stake in the farm too. He gets fifty percent of the crops we have."

"We?" Richard looked from Rachel to Nathan then settled his blazing gaze on her.

"I could not have made it without Nathan's help. We are partners in the farm."

Richard rotated toward Nathan. "Will you buy her part? I'm taking my sister back to England."

"Wait! Richard, it has not been decided yet." She loved her big brother, but he was being highhanded as usual—much like her father.

Her brother shook his head. "What has not been decided? You cannot stay here. Your husband is dead. You have an infant to take care of."

Ben and Emma poked their heads through the doorway but stayed outside.

"I have more than Faith. I have Ben and Emma too."

"Ben and Emma? Who are they?"

Rachel gestured to the children to come inside. Heads down, steps labored, they moved into the main room.

Rachel walked to them and put her hand on Ben's shoulder. "This is Ben and his sister, Emma. I have been taking care of them. Their parents are dead, and they don't have any relatives. I am not going anywhere without them."

Richard opened and closed his mouth twice before he pressed it shut. A nerve jerked in his cheek.

He was not happy. Rachel sighed. "Emma, will you watch Faith outside with Maddy?"

The little girl nodded and took the baby from Rachel.

"Ben and Nathan, I need to be alone with my brother to explain to him what has happened the past four months."

* * * * *

Nathan returned to the far field and resumed picking the ears of corn with Ben. But his mind was not on his job. He peered back in the direction of the house, although he could not see it through the pine forest blocking his view.

Rachel needed to go home. He was glad her brother had come to get her. After all, he was the one who had written the family to tell them of her circumstances and the baby she had. So why was he practically yanking whole stalks out of the ground instead of just removing the ears of corn?

The harvest was going to be good. He should concentrate on that. Not the fact Rachel was making arrangements with her brother at this moment to leave. Nathan did not even know who he really was anymore. Having been bombarded with disturbing revelations lately, he was still trying to figure out who he was now. A recluse? A doctor? A planter?

Lord, I need help. What do I do? Rachel doesn't belong here at the farm. She had made an effort with the farm, but it was not for her. He could purchase the farm. It was small by Liberty Hall and Pinecrest's standards, but he did not need much. He could live here by himself, occasionally seeing his sister and brother. If he offered to buy Rachel's land, she could leave as soon as possible. The faster she left, the easier it would be for him. He had to let her go. He had seen the look of joy on her face because her brother was here. She had a way out now. He would not stand in her way.

* * * * *

Later, as suppertime neared, Nathan came into the house a few steps behind Ben.

Ben plopped down at the table. "I'm hungry. We worked all day and got all the corn picked in that field. There's a lot of it."

Rachel took a look at Ben's dirty hands. "Go wash up and get your sister."

Nathan held up his hands. "I washed up before coming in."

"It is a good thing one of you heard what I have been saying."

"Yes, ma'am." Nathan sniffed the air. "What are we having tonight?"

"Rabbit stew."

"I thought your brother would be staying for supper."

"No, he wanted to get back to Charleston and make arrangements for the return trip to England." Rachel grinned. "He looked out the window as I told him about the swamp and the alligator attack. I think that was when he decided he would leave well before dark."

"When is the ship leaving?"

"Day after tomorrow."

"I have decided I want to buy the farm from you. I will pay you top dollar. That way you will have some money when you return to England."

"What if I'm not returning to England?"

He sat in the chair at the head of the table. "Are you not?"

Rachel studied his neutral expression, trying to get a glimpse of what he was thinking. But even his eyes remained blank. "That's what my family wants."

"What do you want to do?"

"I would love to see my family." She paused, taking in a deep inhalation to proceed.

"Then it is settled. I will buy the farm," he said, before she could continue. "What are you going to do about Ben and Emma?"

"They will come with me."

"How does your brother feel about that?"

She had not asked Richard because she thought she needed more time to decide. She shook her head. Obviously now she did not need more time. Nathan had sent for her family and wanted her gone. "He does not know."

"If you decide to leave them here, I will take them in. They are used to the farm as their home."

Rachel tossed down the dishtowel she held to take the kettle off the fire. "You will not take them from me." She whirled around and ran to her bedchamber, slamming the door and collapsing back against it.

Sliding down to the floor, she buried her face in her hands and cried. She should be happy she was returning to England, to her family, forgiven and welcomed, but she was not. She wanted more. She knew that if she insisted on taking Ben and Emma, her brother would agree. That was not what was bothering her.

* * * * *

Nathan stared at the closed door and shook his head. What did the woman want? He was going to pay her a good price for the farm. She was returning home—the favored daughter again. No doubt her brother would agree to take the two other children. Although Nathan would hate not seeing them every day, they would probably be better off in the midst of a family rather than with just him. Rachel was a good mother, and they looked to her to fulfill that role.

He stood and crossed to the cradle, watching Faith sleeping. He would miss her too. Her smile. The twinkle in her eyes. She was going to turn men's heads when she got older. Like her mother.

Maddy leaned against the doorframe with her arms folded over her chest. "Me and the children will remain outside until you fix this."

"Fix what?"

"You and Rachel. Do you have to be hit over your thick skull to realize you are in love with her and should ask her to marry you? If George can get the courage to ask me, you can ask Rachel."

"No, you are wrong."

Her eyebrows shot up. "I am? Be honest with yourself. Do you want to end up like your grandfather—embittered and alone in your old age?"

"She told her brother she was leaving."

"No, she didn't. She told him she had to think about what she wanted."

"She did?"

Maddy closed the space between them and knocked on his head. "Thick. Is it hollow too?"

Nathan blinked then roared with laughter.

* * * * *

How dare he laugh when she was breaking in two? Rachel shoved herself to her feet and reached for the handle to open the door.

It flung wide, nearly knocking her on her bottom. She flapped her arms to steady herself. It did not work. She went down with a crash.

"Rachel, are you all right? Where are you hurt?" Nathan knelt next to her, his hands running up and down her arms.

She wrenched away. "I am fine. Have you not heard of knocking before coming into a room—a bedchamber?"

Nathan burst out laughing again and sat back on the floor next to her.

She punched him in the arm. "What is so funny? That I am lying on the floor hurt?" *That my heart is breaking over you.*

He sobered. "Are you hurt?"

"Yes."

His gaze swept down her length. "Where?"

She patted her chest as she rose. "Here."

"There?" Standing, he pointed at her torso. "How did you hurt yourself there?"

"I didn't hurt myself. You did."

"What did I do? I know I should have knocked, but I was tired of wasting any more time."

"What in the world are you talking about?"

He grabbed her arms and pulled her around to face him squarely. "I love you, Rachel Gordon, and I don't want you to leave for England. I want you to stay here and be my wife. There. I have said what I have been trying to deny for weeks."

"Do you feel better?"

"Not yet." He dragged her against him and kissed her long and hard. "Now I do. So what do you say? Will you stay and marry me?"

Rachel bit her bottom lip. Did he really mean it? If she said yes, was she making the same mistake as she had with Tom?

"Scared?"

She nodded.

"Here is a woman who tried to fight off an alligator and got rid of a snake from her house. How can you be afraid to love me?"

"I love you. That's not the problem."

"Then what is?"

"I thought I loved Tom. I was wrong. We married so fast. I cannot make that mistake again."

"Then you and I will be engaged for as long as you want, and when you are ready to wed me, we will get married. How is that?"

She smiled, a warmth welling up from deep inside and suffusing her whole body. From this day forward she was his. She flung her arms around his neck and gave him a kiss that sealed their bargain.

Epilogue

May 1818

"I thought I would find you out here on such a beautiful morning." Nathan approached Rachel in the garden behind their house in Charleston.

She cut off another rose and carefully laid it in the basket for a bouquet for the dining room table. The scent of her flowers peppered the air as she turned toward her husband and smiled. "You know me so well."

"That and Faith told me when I came home. She and Emma are playing in the parlor."

"Playing?"

"They are having a tea party 'like Mama does.' You know Emma."

"What is her reason to have a party today?" Emma would have a party every day if she could.

"'Tis Jamie's six-month birthday."

"Is Jamie in the parlor too?"

Nathan removed the basket from Rachel's hand and put it on the stone bench nearby, then he took Rachel into his embrace. "No, our son is up in the nursery sleeping. Emma was quite put out that he would not stay awake for the whole tea party."

"Dinner will be in an hour. I have a feeling our daughters will not eat a thing."

"Ben will make up for them. I have never seen a boy grow so fast. He is going to be my height in another year."

Rachel snuggled up against Nathan. "What are you doing home early?"

"I was at Mrs. Collins' house down the street and thought I would stop by here to check on my beautiful wife."

"How is Mrs. Collins doing?"

"Better. Her fever is gone and her cough has nearly stopped. I think she will be able to attend Sarah's ball next week. At least she is planning on it. She kept asking me about Liberty Hall."

Rachel wound her arms behind his neck and urged his head toward her. "That's nice. I remember the last time the ball was at Liberty Hall two years ago."

He brushed his lips across hers. "A lot has happened since then."

"Yes, Maddy and George are married and expecting their first child. I hope she will be able to come to the ball. The farm is not too far for her to travel." On the Butlers' wedding day, Rachel had given Dalton Farm to Maddy and George. "Do you think Patrick will get your grandfather to come?"

"Anything is possible." Nathan's mouth settled over hers in a deep kiss.

The warm sensations his possession created in Rachel spread throughout her whole body. In his arms she always felt cherished and loved as though she had come home.

About the Author

MARGARET DALEY is an award-winning, multi-published author in the romance genre. One of her romantic suspense books, *Hearts on the Line*, won the American Christian Fiction Writers' Book of the Year Contest. Recently she has won the Golden Quill Contest, FHL's Inspirational Readers' Choice Contest, Winter Rose Contest, Holt Medallion, and the Barclay Gold Contest. She writes inspirational romance, both contemporary and historical, and romantic suspense books. *From This Day Forward* is her seventy-fifth book.